THE HIT

THE HIT

a novel by JERE HOAR

CONTEXT BOOKS, NEW YORK

www.contextbooks.com

Jacket design: Charles Kreloff
Interior design: Johanna Roebas

Context Books
368 Broadway
Suite 314
New York, NY 10013

Library of Congress Cataloging-in-Publication Data

Hoar, Jere R.
The hit / Jere Hoar.
p. cm.
ISBN 1-893956-34-2 (hardcover : alk. paper)
1. Vietnamese Conflict, 1961–1975—Veterans—Fiction.
2. Triangles (Interpersonal relations)—Fiction. 3. Psychiatric
hospital patients—Fiction. 4. Murder for hire—Fiction.
5. Revenge—Fiction.
I. Title.
PS3558.O33565 H58 2003
813'.54—dc21
2002011874

9 8 7 6 5 4 3 2

Manufactured in the United States of America

FOR BARRY

Prologue

My psychiatrist has grizzled hair and wears the puzzled expression of an intelligent dog. Cheap, drug-store glasses ride his nose. He sits on a shiny metal stool in the corner of my room.

"Well, Luke, what's been happening since we talked last?" he asks. "How are your notebooks coming along?"

The notebooks are therapy. For two years, Doc has had me write my story using colored pencils—pastels when I am unsure, darker colors for certainties.

I shake my head.

The most recent notebooks are safe under my shirt. I clutch ten colored pencils. Some have pastel leads and some dark leads, but none is dark enough.

"I'd like very much to see what you've written," he says.

If I show him the notebooks I can sit on the porch and I don't have to wear restraints, although Mike watches me all the time. Mike is stronger than I am, but he's my friend.

I shake my head.

Doc flips pages fixed in an aluminum binder. For most of the veterans here, when a psychiatrist flips through a chart he's trying to find out who they are. Then he looks for a diagnosis. A diagnosis is an iron maiden. We both know my diagnosis—post-traumatic stress syndrome.

From time to time all of us delayed-stress syndromes get hot, shake, and can't breathe. We may jelly under little pressures and endure big ones. There is no predicting. A tune breaks us, or a screech of tires, or a hot smell. Once we were soldiers, then, on a day like any other, the earth cracked beneath our feet. Out came the wail of our dead. Demons bounded out, shook themselves, and came home.

You tell him what happened if you can push words off a thick, lazy tongue you bite . . . if it matters. During a panic attack, the man keeps you tranquil. He's the largest legal user of Valium in America: a boxcar-load last year.

Delayed-stress syndromes on Valium don't cause much trouble. Five Valium tablets will knock out an elephant, he says. He holds the world's record for Valium prescriptions for a single individual, he says.

At the bottom of a Valium pool you are suspended in a green layer just above mud. Your heavy limbs float, dragging behind. You do not require oxygen. Most people who fish your pond only splash the surface. The psychiatrist drifts down inquiries. You may ignore them, and usually do. They are not brightly colored or interesting. It takes too much energy to get angry about a disturbance. Intensity is not possible. Focus is difficult.

You can function. That is manageable. You float at the bottom of the slow, green tide. Someday you will begin to drift up, layer by layer, as they reduce the yellow tablets. If they care . . . if you care.

I care. A shark lazes across the surface of my pond, casting a shadow. He's a shark with a human name.

My story should be written in blood.

THE HIT

Notebook 1

1.

Kinnerly backed her car too fast. The tires spun.

"Easy. Your nerves are showing," I said.

She glanced in the rearview mirror. "Are you watching to see if we're being followed?"

"Yeah."

"Are we?"

"No."

Her shoulders relaxed. She drove ten minutes, then turned down Clay Road. It is uninhabited now that the Cheraw brothers went broke in the sunflower business. Sunflower oil was to be their salvation after popcorn failed. Popcorn followed soybeans. Soybeans followed cotton . . . cotton since 1840. Now the old fields grow bitterweed and sedge grass, but the Cheraw brothers hang on to the land. Their parents must have whispered to them in the cradle, *Never sell the land!*

At night, from the outside, the once fine barn seems solid, but when you're inside moonlight glows through the spaces where boards are missing. Stars twinkle through the rusty tin roof.

"Drive to the left of the barn about six feet, then around to the back," I said. She followed my instructions. The Ford's bumper folded weeds and they swished against the undercarriage.

"That's it. Now swing wide and pull into the alleyway."

She cut the engine. "It's dark as a tomb tonight." Her voice was small.

"Cloud cover. You'll get used to the dark in a minute." I took her hand and pulled it. "Come here. I want to stroke you like a cat."

"But you're a dangerous man."

"All the nicer for you."

She came to me on her knees, wrapped her arms around my neck, and bent my head back for a kiss. "How's that, big boy?" she said in a Mae West voice.

My hands slid under her fur coat and wool skirt. All she was wearing under there was a garter belt and stockings.

"What are you doing, Sir?"

I pushed back her coat with my face, and nuzzled her blouse. She cradled my head in her arms.

"This was a hell of a week," I said.

"I know, I know," she murmured.

"I can't get along without you."

"I know."

"This one is going to be quick," I said.

"Poor baby. Does he want it so bad?"

"Absolutely. Right now."

She reached down between us. "I know. It's OK. Don't wait for me . . . don't wait."

After about five minutes of sex and ten minutes of talk we drove off the Cherow farm. Shadowy fence posts and the flickering gleam of barbed wire held us to the narrow, sunken channel of the road. Rocks flicked up to tap the car's chassis. The wind whistled. Clouds curled to the east, and the air was charged with static electricity.

She drove with the headlights off. The dash lights cast an eerie glow. Once she misjudged a washout, and the car bottomed.

"Slow down and watch the road."

She didn't slow down. She hunched over the wheel and leaned closer to the windshield, crone-shaped, nothing like herself.

At the exit from Cherow Road, I said, "Left, toward Thaxton."

She flipped on the headlights and gunned the engine, showering gravel with the tires. Give her an order and Kinnerly won't argue—she'll not hear it. Only when we were safely away from that place of failed dreams did she rest her shoe on the accelerator and settle against the car seat.

Usually I'm a happy man after sex, but something was wrong between us this night. I was glad she couldn't see my face.

"What's the matter with you? You're so far away I feel like I don't even know you tonight."

"I'm right here."

She was silent awhile, then said calmly, "Why don't you get out of my life, Luke?"

"I can't."

"Leave me alone."

"I can't leave you alone."

"You can until you're horny. I was getting over you, learning not to think of you but half of every hour. Then you called." The car veered.

"Careful!"

She steadied the wheel, rode the road edge to a level place, and pulled to safety. "You want your free bachelor life and me on the side. Well, no thanks. The end of that story is we get caught, Tom divorces me for adultery, and I don't have a cent."

"We can still leave town. There's that option."

"And live on your disability check? We'd hate each other in six months."

"Give it time. I'll come up with something."

She braked the Ford and parked behind my Jeep. We'd left it on a seldom-used gravel road.

"You already have a plan. That's the way your mind works, three moves ahead of everybody . . . what I'll do, what he'll do, what you'll do. But now that your appetite is satisfied, there's no hurry."

We sat in the dark. It wasn't safe. None of this was. I sucked in air. Once this thing started there could be no turning back. It was one long plunge into an icy river with treacherous currents.

"All right. I hear you. When is he going out of town?"

"Tuesday. He's showing a film of his bear hunt to the Sportsman's Club in Pontotoc. "

"Tuesday, then. That's the date."

The car motor chugged vapor into the crisp night air. The parking lights glowed ahead and behind. We were sitting in one place too long. Anyone passing would have to slow. Her tag numbers would be visible in the headlights. Maybe they'd recognize our vehicles, or us.

She grabbed my arm. "I can get a woman to seduce him . . . pay her, make it a set-up and get pictures. Then I can divorce him and get enough alimony to keep us."

"We can't have a third party in a deal like this. No third party."

"There has to be another way."

"We've been through all that."

She let go of my arm. Different expressions worked across her face. I saw a flicker of indecision, then a moment of softness at some memory. Next, she stared through the windshield into the dark with a blank gaze that saw nothing, while pictures and thoughts I couldn't penetrate played through her mind. From the way she was acting you'd have thought killing her husband was a new idea, all mine.

"What time will he leave for the meeting?" I said.

"Seven, about seven."

"It's dark enough then. It'll do."

She gripped my arm again. "Will it hurt him? I don't want it to hurt him. Promise me he won't suffer."

What she wanted was a lie. This time I gave her one. "He won't suffer. Your part is to see that he goes by the lake house on the way to Pontotoc. He's got to pick up the sunglasses you left there."

"My sunglasses? I wouldn't leave my sunglasses at the lake house. He'll suspect something if I say that."

"Listen! You left your glasses. He's got to drive down Woodlie Road. Make an issue of it. Say . . . I don't know what you say! Just see that he drives down Woodlie Road. Give him a note so he can't later say he forgot. Tuck it into his right coat pocket. Got that? I can take it off of him afterward."

"Don't say that. Don't say 'afterward.'"

"Get an alibi. Be with friends. Play bridge or go to a movie with other people."

"No, Luke. This is too fast. We haven't thought it through."

"I have. Catching him away from home was one scenario."

She tugged my jacket collar. "Kiss me."

"Not now. Someone might drive by."

"Kiss me. You've got to kiss me *now*."

I pressed her lips with mine. Hers felt fevered, and her sweet breath had soured.

"All right, Luke," she murmured. "Whatever you say."

So we left it at that. It wasn't what I wanted, not by a long shot. If we got caught I stood a good chance of getting the electric chair. She stood a good chance of getting off because Mississippi juries rarely convict upper-class women of murder. But when we talked, that's the way it came out. This whole thing with her husband was what *I* wanted.

For a few seconds she had me believing it.

2.

At 11:00 P.M. Monday I unhinged the doors of the Jeep, stored them in the shed, and packed disposable plastic gear, rope, bow, two arrows podded with succinylcholine chloride, a tarp, and a Q-Beam light.

I was very cautious with the succinyl. In Mississippi, deer hunters pack it into a pod that wraps the arrow shaft behind a broadhead. When the arrow enters flesh, the pod peels back and a few grains of white powder fall into the wound. A hit animal quits breathing. So does a hunter if he sticks himself.

The stuff is legal. The idea is that it saves for the freezer deer that would otherwise run off and die with arrows sticking in them.

I got this batch from a college boy I met in the woods in

Marshall County. He had knocked the fletching off of one arrow and buckled the broadhead on another. I had extras. We didn't swap names, just hunting gear.

If you buy from a pharmacist there is a record. I don't like records.

It was about midnight when my lights probed the entrance of the National Forest, and the tires crunched over a gravel road lined with big pines. I figured that by midnight the poor people, whose truck seats serve as motel beds, would have moved out. Wise youngsters don't park on lonely roads far from lights these days. Married women who risk it shrink from headlights, and turn their faces into the necks of lovers. Used condoms litter popular parking places like snake skins at denning caves.

A slow drive along main and secondary roads made it clear that no one was romancing that night.

I lifted the 100,000/200,000-candlepower floodlight out of its yellow cardboard box, plugged it into the cigarette lighter receptacle, and searched the road borders. Moths beat blindly in the long cone of light. The solid shapes of trees emerged as bark, limbs, twigs, and needles. Down the road, six hot whorls of light flashed back. I thumbed the switch to 200,000 candles. Three does stood transfixed. Their jaws moved sideways. Their ears flicked and spread horizontally.

I'd installed a clamp on the door frame for the searchlight handle. My cheek snuggled against the cocked crossbow and the largest doe's gray chest came up to fill the open V of the sight. I squeezed the trigger. Cable twanged. The bow jumped. Something smacked like a hit softball. The doe vanished from the tunnel of light. Dust motes swirled in the empty beam. An owl asked *who-wit-who?* I heard harsh breathing, but it was mine.

I pulled the Jeep to the side of the road, cut the headlights, and jumped out carrying a plastic bag and a rope, my eyes fixed on the spot where the doe had vanished. She lay nineteen steps from where she had been shot. Her large, tender eyes filmed as I watched. I put one foot on her ribs and pulled the bolt. It slipped through my fingers. On the next try the poison sack cleared flesh. Then the bolt head slid free.

She was not pretty dead. Ears splayed as if she had been bludgeoned. Long, hollow hairs bristled on her shoulders. The slim legs, the horsey aristocratic face, the sloping butt, and the droopy little tail that had been twitching moments earlier were bothersome now. They were very feminine. A sorry feeling comes over a man when he kills a doe.

I dropped the wrapper containing the stuff I needed on the grass. Coveralls first. I slipped them on while looking at the stars. It was a soft night. A layer of cool air crept between me and my shirt. I pushed between the fingers of each glove until they fit, then looped the doe's feet together with the length of rope.

She lost a little hide and hair on the drag to the Jeep. Once she wedged between two small trees. It didn't matter. I heaved her onto the spread plastic tarp, and folded the tarp so she wouldn't leak. Then I got out of there.

The gloves went into the first roadside dumpster I passed. The coveralls went into the next. I dropped the rope over the side of the Tallahatchie River bridge and watched it coil away in slow water.

There wasn't any trouble. There were no witnesses.

My German shorthair, Adel, barked once when I reached my cabin. I unloaded the doe and hung her in the shed. By 2:05 I was in bed. At 2:10 I remembered the crossbow and searchlight, and hopped out barefooted to get them. Back in bed, I swallowed a 7.5-mg sleeping tablet shaped like a coffin. Sleep came heavy and chemical. When the Big Ben hammered its bell I jerked awake and saw dawn. It was 5:46 A.M.

I drank three mugs of milky, sugared coffee in the silent

house. Outside, trees spread black foliage against a gray sky. Cold drifted under my robe. I sat and watched the sun slice through the dark. Then light poured across the landscape and birds began their harsh melodious cries.

At 7:30 A.M. Tuesday I dialed Al Huff, my accountant. He would be moving slowly around his quiet house on Jefferson Avenue— scratching whiskers, yawning, spitting phlegm—getting ready for the day's business of selling his honor. Al's into perjury. He uses a professional license to swear to false documents.

His hair would be slick with Vitalis. He'd be wearing yesterday's shirt, badly re-pressed, and with a sweaty smell. He'd be squinting around his first stogie . . . thinking, thinking. Al is tough on charities this year. He's against charity. The profile of his clients is that they don't give. They entertain professionally instead. Al's goal is to avoid an audit.

My call would be an interruption to some great caper he'd be fantasizing about. He'd stand by the phone in run-over shoes, the heels of which he'd leveled with plastic taps. He'd jump his eyebrows high on his forehead and drum his fingers as he talked.

The cheap phone trilled. The receiver clicked, and a wheezy breath later Al said, "Al Huff here." This could be the deal he'd waited for . . . a master fraud.

My voice was apologetic. "Al, I'm sorry to bother you at home but I've got a problem with my tax return. Yeah, Janet gave me an appointment for January 7, but—sure, I understand. Just one question, Al. What's the mileage allowance for going to get my tetanus shot, and to see Dr. Kaiser when I had the flu? Twenty-three cents? Not worth *bothering* with? Listen, Al. Some guys can afford to kiss off five or ten bucks. Some guys can do that, but I— OK. You have a nice day, too."

An hour later I called another accountant, a woman. Billie looked overweight in clothes. In a swimsuit she looked great. She was thirty-six, and thought she was heavy, so she was eager to please.

"Hi, Billie. This is Luke," I said. "It *has* been a long time. Listen, Billie, Al Huff has been doing my taxes, but the way he talked today when I asked a simple question—the guy has problems."

She murmured sympathetically.

"I wondered if you could help me. What about today?"

"Everybody wants me today," she said.

"Well, answer one question for me, please. Should I depreciate my McCullough chain saw as equipment or group it in supplies?"

"Supplies," she said.

"Let me make a note: 'expenses rather than capital investment.' Why doesn't Al tell me the good stuff?"

She said she knew other good stuff. My voice dropped. "How about you and me getting together for a drink after work? You have to stop work sometime."

She hummed and thought, and said that would be nice.

"When?" I said. "Will about seven suit?"

"Seven would be fine," she said.

"Would you ring me before you leave your office? You don't mind, do you? I get engrossed when I work on taxes."

She didn't mind. Was cooler, though. A little affronted that I might not remember.

"Thanks. The number is 239-9645. Write it down because I'm not in the directory yet."

I said goodbye, poured another mug of coffee, and thought. Then I got a timer out of a kitchen drawer, a wrench, tape, a piece of bright copper pipe, two pipe couples, a pen, and yellow pad. On the legal pad I wrote and rewrote a script.

PHONE RINGS. DOG BEGINS TO BARK. . . . *Hello, Billie.* (Off phone) *Quiet! Quiet!* (impatient laugh) *I've got a problem here.* (Dog barks) *A pipe burst in the kitchen. Water is spraying everywhere. The damn dog thinks somebody is in the woods and won't shut up. I banged my hand with the wrench.* (Dog barks on and on) *Everything is . . .* (Off phone) *Shut up!* (On phone) *Sorry about tonight, Billie. I'll call you tomorrow.* (Hang up as dog continues barking).

For this to work, timing was everything. And naturalness. There couldn't be time for her to speak. My voice had to sound harried and apologetic and definite. She could not call back.

I practiced reading the script. My voice shook at first, but when I had read the script six times the quaver was gone. I called Adel to the telephone and put him at attention. "Speak, Adel!" I said, and pushed "record" and "start" buttons on the machine. Adel barked on and on. He didn't stop when I came to "Quiet!" in the script because he was trained to obey commands only if his name was called.

When the tape was done I shushed the dog, put the recorder on "check," and listened. Adel was a method actor. I was awful. Over and over we went through the performance. Adel barked like fury, with his ears bouncing. He liked the game. I thought about taking a drink to relax me, but alcohol seldom does that. By the fifth try boredom and familiarity did it.

I set the timer to cut on at 6:45 and off at 7:30, plugged the recorder into the timer, and plugged the timer into the wall socket. It was a risk, but my guess was that if Billie called back it would be after a couple of drinks. I wouldn't be answering the phone then. I'd be busy "repairing the pipe."

I cut off the water to the hot pipe in the kitchen and replaced a length of galvanized with shiny copper and two new couplings. Water sprayed on the wall and floor. I wiped it up, threw the rag under the sink to sour, then carried the galvanized pipe to the Jeep in order to throw it into the creek.

Someone would call me at home that night. I would be coping with a barking dog and a burst pipe. Billie would remember the date and the time because she'd been stood up. She'd remember she had called when she was ready to leave for a drink. I expected a bonus on the time. She'd want to make me wait. She'd call *after* seven.

Without shaving, and with mussed hair, I drove to Bailey's store, filled the tank and sloshed some gas on the concrete. Mrs. Bailey peered through a screened window. Our hands met on a shelf below the screen. I handed her a twenty and didn't wait for change.

She called me back for it and said, "I've got the Troost you wanted. Want me to collect for it?"

"Forgot my change, did I? Sure, I guess so. I've got a leak in the kitchen and, besides, Adel isn't acting right." I laughed. "I guess I'm a little addled."

"Adel?" Mrs. Bailey's voice climbed. "He isn't sick, is he?"

"He barks toward the woods and won't stop. I hate to leave the cabin when he's like that."

Mrs. Bailey nodded. Her chins swayed. "Probably somebody is in those woods. Somebody up to no good. People will steal you blind." She leaned toward me. "The dog knows." Mrs. Bailey's gaze fixed on a black carpenter ant on the shelf. She smashed it with the heel of her hand and brushed away the carcass. "You've got to watch what you've got if you want to keep it." She swung her head to survey the narrow-aisled, one room store crowded with a bread rack, freezer, drink box, and counter. She turned back to me and said, "We can't be too careful, with all the badness in the world."

"No, we can't. I'm glad I don't live in the city. The woods are safer." I started to leave, then put on the foolish smile of a chronic bumbler. "Mrs. Bailey, I didn't mean to give you that twenty-dollar bill. I need the cash. Could you charge the gas and tobacco?"

Very slowly she opened the cigar box and handed me the bill. Very slowly she took up a ledger, a Bic pen, and turned blue-lined pages until she came to my name. She recorded $10.52 for gas, eighty cents for Troost, and the date.

She would remember I told her about the burst pipe because she had to give back a twenty-dollar bill. The date would be in her ledger if I needed support for what I'd told Billie.

"You let me know how Adel gets on," Mrs. Bailey called as I left.

When I entered the cabin, Adel scampered to the telephone, cocked his head, and barked. Then he played tug-of-war with my arm.

"Adel, leave it!" I ordered.

I slumped in the chair with the newspaper in hand and scanned the television section. My alibi was going to be that I had watched television after replacing a burst pipe, had taken care of the dog, and had worked on tax returns.

From the TV listings I selected a John Wayne movie I'd seen twice before, and a broadcast of Masterpiece Theater's "Upstairs Downstairs" I'd watched earlier in the week on another channel. I didn't read the program descriptions because I didn't want my recollection of the action to fit too closely with what was published in the newspaper.

There was one more thing to do. I opened the filing cabinet and took out a jumble of tax papers I'd put away in manila folders. Each folder had a cover sheet listing dates and amounts. On one page I dated a new entry *November 3*. It wasn't proof of anything—just a puff of smoke for the illusion.

That was it. All bases covered. I felt so good I napped without alcohol or Tranzene until it was time for the mission. I awoke and silenced Big Ben before its bell jangled . . . a good omen.

3.

Tom Morris was due at about 7:00 P.M. After he took the turn from Highway 6 onto Woodlie Road, I'd get him just over the first hill.

My Jeep puttered into Woodlie Road. I parked it in a grove of screening trees, then propped the doe's body upright in the road with two-by-twos painted gravel-yellow. A couple of her legs poked out in awkward positions, her head canted, and a tongue dirty with trash hung out of her mouth. None of this would matter. The target vehicle would be moving fast. The driver would be thinking about his speech and buzzing with frustration because he was stopping to retrieve sunglasses his wife had left at their getaway cabin. Probably he would have had a drink or two. He wouldn't realize the deer was dead. He'd see what he expected to see in the National Forest, a deer crossing a road.

I crouched in cover thirty yards beyond the trap, and went to my belly in weeds. A dusty scent arose. Stuff crackled around me with every movement. I poked the bow through the grass. All I needed from the arrow was a little puncture. It didn't have to drill him.

The lights of a car approached on the highway. One beam fingered the sky. The other must have bored ahead. I could only see the high one. It wouldn't be the Porsche. When any car climbed the hill my breath came fast and my legs felt weak. My heart thudded against the ground. It felt as if the earth itself beat.

Maybe he wouldn't come. I hoped he wouldn't. All I had to do to change my future was pick up the two-by-twos, throw the doe to the side of the road, and drive home, but I couldn't do it. If events followed their natural course I was going to kill a man who wasn't wearing a uniform or carrying a gun. A powerful little place in my brain, fortified against reason, said I had to do it to protect Kinnerly, that she was worth it . . . that this was the only way. It said, *This isn't about money.*

Fifteen minutes crept by. I stood up and yawned, stretching as high as I could reach. The glowing dial of my watch said it was over. He wasn't coming. I was very glad.

Then a car slowed on the highway, speeded up, and slowed again. It screeched onto Woodlie Road. I dropped to my belly and nocked an arrow. My heart pounded so hard blood pulsed against my ear drums.

The car roared in fast. It would knock hell out of my deer. It might skid beyond the ambush. The driver might see the trap and reach for a gun. A thousand things could go wrong. A cold, rational part of my mind said, *You can still back away. You can slip into the field and run. There is nothing incriminating here, just a deer body propped up in the road . . . a weird joke.*

I slid backward.

The car whistled by, spinning gravel. Brakes howled. Dust flew from locked tires. The car slewed left, flashing its lights across foliage, illuminating details of leaves and limbs. It turned sideways and slid into the deer. The deer bounced away. One supporting timber sailed through the light beam. The Porsche's front wheels churned in a ditch. They reversed and churned again. The motor raced and the back wheels spun. Then the motor quit. I nocked the arrow and waited. It would be an easy shot by the overhead light of the car. The driver's-side door opened. I heard a voice, a jingly tune. On the car radio Burt Bacharach was singing "Raindrops Keep Falling on My Head."

I lifted the bow. The interior light did not come on.

The target got out and walked unsteadily to the front fender. He bent and said, "Damn it to hell!" Then he stomped his foot like a frustrated little kid. That froze me, it was so human. With that gesture, he wasn't a target anymore. Tom Morris was a man, a civilian, and unarmed.

I was no William Calley, Jr. It was over. I was getting out.

Only twenty-five yards separated us. One broken twig and he'd detect me. I slid back six inches.

He walked to the deer, bent, and came up with a two by two. He looked huge standing against the glow of highway lights, turning the board in his hand as if thinking things through. I slid back four inches, another six . . . then a stick popped. It wasn't loud. It wasn't as loud as Bacharach's little voice inside the Porsche.

Morris dropped the board and turned on me. Suddenly, in his hand I saw a stainless steel revolver. It glinted as he aimed it. *Sonofabitch! Where'd that come from?* He meant to kill me. Instinctively I released the arrow.

He screamed and kept on screaming, leaning to one side. The high-pitched keening went on and on while Bacharach played piano. I grabbed my K-bar and crouched, hoping I wouldn't have to use it. Abruptly Morris sat down and coughed. A soft, bubbly waft of air came from his mouth as he toppled to the side. It was not a human sound.

I went to him and turned his body with my foot. The arrow stood in his thigh. It had been a hell of a bad shot. I sheathed the knife and pulled and twisted the arrow. It came out with the head and poison container still attached. Luck! You need *luck*. I had it this night.

I got on my knees, held my flashlight six inches off the ground, and crawled the beam, shielding it with my hand. The bones in my fingers showed through red-looking flesh where they wrapped the flashlight head.

Where was the gun?

My left hand bumped metal, and the bumped thing rolled away. My light swept the ground and centered it . . . I'd made a mistake. A big, bad mistake. Morris had pointed a Brinkman penlight at me, only a penlight, small-barreled and chrome-plated.

All my body heat burned like a coal in the center of my chest. My hands and feet were icy. I wanted that music to stop. *Keep your head*, I told myself. *It's over. You can't call death back.* I got some distance, built a wall, as I had done in other years, in other places, in a better cause.

I laid the bow on the car, wrapped my arms around his chest, and dragged him. Dirt soiled his coat, so I draped him over the car hood and brushed him down.

Then I pulled the body under its arms, opened the door of the car with one hand, turned off the radio, and shoved him inside. A half-crushed Coke can lay on the floor. A briefcase and a film box lay on the seat. I took out my handkerchief, cleaned the radio switch and the backs of his shoes, dusted his trousers, got in beside him and restarted the motor. Then I thought, *If I move the car they'll see from the tracks it's been moved. Dead men don't back up.*

I cut the motor and got out, shaking like a cherry on his first mission. *Damn it! I'm touching the door!* I jumped away, took out my handkerchief again, and wiped the prints. The state doesn't have a crime lab, but sometimes a sheriff sends prints to the FBI. Our coroners aren't medical doctors or even technicians. Mississippi doesn't have a forensic pathology lab. I told myself little mistakes didn't matter.

They do. The plan was slipping.

The body lay twisted, turned toward the middle of the car. My flashlight fingered through the Porsche front seat, skipping Tom Morris's face and hands. I didn't want to see them. That's where I most keenly sense humanity in the dead. The light flashed from feet to chest, flickered over the corpse's head, returned, and stopped.

His face and head were—I centered the beam on Morris's face—there was no mistake, his face was black, a dusky black. I couldn't believe it. It was *black!*

Calm down, I thought. *If a man's face turns dark after death that means something. What? It means a broken neck, that's what.* I felt his neck. It wasn't broken. That didn't make sense. The flashlight played over Tom's face again, casting shadows from the nose and chin. What else could cause it? *The poison?* The poison must have had a side effect I didn't know about.

Tom Morris wore musk perfume and his bowels and bladder had let go, but I had to get in the car with his body and break its neck.

I opened the door, grasped the hard shoulder under the tweed jacket, and pulled the body upright. As I slid onto the edge of the seat the body leaned against me. I turned the chin away and wrapped the back of the head and front of the neck in a Japanese strangle hold.

The fingers of my right hand plowed through stiff, sprayed hair and cupped his skull. My left hand gripped the inside of my right elbow. I jerked my right hand down to break Morris's neck against my left forearm. It didn't break. The neck was supposed to break. *Damn it! It's supposed to break!* I tugged the body into position to increase leverage. The corpse's arms arose like a drowning man's. Its chin tucked into the humble position of prayer. Vomit rose hot in my throat.

I snugged Morris's head and neck from behind. My cheek lay against the harsh wool of his jacket. My breath sucked in, locked, my resolution firmed, and I snapped the neck as I had been trained to do. The little *pop* it made was more felt than heard.

I rearranged the corpse's posture, backed out, and released the door. The clunk it made was too noisy for that quiet place. *Who might have heard?* Nothing moved in the forest but wind.

Get rid of the prints, I told myself and wiped the door handle. Then I thought in panic, *That's wrong! That's wrong! Why would one door handle be polished?*

I heard a motor and looked toward Highway 6. Headlights flicked toward the sky. A vehicle had turned onto Woodlie Road and it was coming fast. I turned to run for safety, but stopped. I couldn't make it. My Jeep was parked in the brush. Its tag was a dead giveaway to my identity.

A Ford pickup truck climbed the hill and came over the crest, throwing dust and pinning me in its headlights.

Tom Morris sat in a Porsche twelve feet away, his face black and his mouth twisted in a rictus, the laugh of the dead.

4.

If there was one person in the truck and it was a man, I'd have to kill him. I didn't want to, but I'd have to. Then I thought, *What in hell will I do if it's a woman?*

The high-bright beam of the truck lights blinded me. I waved my arms and squinted. "Hey! There's been an accident here. It's bad."

I trotted toward the truck, keeping my gaze down to recover my sight. "Thank God you came," I yelled.

The face inside was craggy. The shoulders hulked below a Western hat. I thought about stepping on the chrome running board and chopping across his goozle when he opened the window, but the bumper was too narrow to anchor my swing.

"Luke, what in hell's going on here?" a high familiar voice

said. It belonged to Angus McKay, the right-hand man of the man I had ambushed and killed.

"Angus! Thank God it's you."

"Let's leave God out of this piece of business." The door clicked and the overhead light in the cab flashed. Through the window I saw Angus's right hand shift to his hip. When he stepped out to face me the strap on his .357 magnum was flipped and his hand hovered above it. A four-cell flashlight blazed in my eyes.

"Turn that light off."

"Soon's you answer a few questions, pod'ner."

I nodded over my shoulder. "That man needs help."

"Not likely. Not with him alone on Woodlie Road with you. He's probably had all the he'p he can handle." The light beam dropped a fraction, relieving my eyes. "Is it old Tom?"

I considered the chances. I was wearing my K-bar. It would do if I was quick enough and lucky. But there would be no way to make the second death look like an accident.

"Yeah, it's Tom. He looks dead."

"He's *dead?*" The voice climbed to falsetto.

"Dead as he ever will be."

The flashlight beam focused on my eyes again. Angus's right shoulder shifted. He'd read my mind. "Don't try it, pod'ner. Don't even think about it. I'd blow you to hell with pleasure."

I raised my hands.

"You don't have to do that. Just stay clear and back off. Walk to that car, and don't try anything."

I did as he said.

"Lean over the grill. Hands on the hood, wide apart."

I did it.

Angus walked to the car door. A band of light cut through the interior and settled on Tom Morris's face. "Sweet Jesus! He's turned black!"

"Only thing I can figure is his neck snapped in the wreck."

The beam flickered through the car. Angus reached inside and shook the seat. "He ran into that deer?"

"Looks like it."

"Does, eh? Well, it don't to me. The deer yonder has been dead so long it's stiff. This corpse is soft and fresh. And something else. A stick of wood yonder looks camouflaged."

The flashlight centered the two-by-two Tom had held when the arrow hit. The board must have fallen under him. It showed blood.

Angus pushed back his hat. "Another thing. Usually people don't die from hitting a deer, not in a car like this." He reached in and shook the seat. "If I was you, I'd break the anchor bolts or the cable, or whatever holds the seat in place."

When he reached into the car I saw a momentary opening, a slackening of attention. Before I could jump him he whipped out the pistol and crouched with it leveled at my chest. The hole in it looked the diameter of a garden hose.

"Listen, stupid. This particular killing don't concern me. What I'm going to do is git in my truck. Then I'll back out and drive to town. When I git there I'll write all this out, have it notarized as a statement, and put it in a safe deposit box. Until I die, you won't have a thing to worry about from me. Now, take those hands down and put them on the car hood."

I turned and placed my hands on the car hood. He kicked my feet from behind. I moved them back.

"A word of advice, pod'ner. Don't even *think* of drawing a knife when a man is holding a gun on you. Especially me. I'm a combat pistol cham'peen."

I stood stretched out like a common criminal, and felt humble. Angus lumbered to his truck, opened the door, and slid inside. The outline of his hat brim showed through the window opening. "In case you're thinking of taking me out tonight by ambush, like you did old Tom, well, don't. I'm spending this night in jail. Me and the jailer plays spades. Sometimes we gamble on who gets the best-looking woman in lockup." He chuckled. "It makes for an interestin' evening."

The truck lights flashed on. The motor caught and the truck backed. I followed at a distance. From the top of Woodlie Hill I saw it turn onto the highway toward town.

Then I did what the man said do.

I washed blood off the board with water from the ditch, and disposed of it with the others. I got my prints off the hood of the car and broke the seat anchor. That was a hell of a job. Then I picked up my bow and arrows and went home.

After I had a beer I checked the telephone answering service. One recorded message had been delivered, and only one.

But all of the cleverness and all of the planning was shot to hell. I was in the hands of Angus McKay.

Notebook 2

5.

My downfall had begun six weeks earlier, with a telephone call from a stranger.

I was buying groceries in Bailey's store when the pay phone on the wall tingled. The proprietor dropped off her stool behind the counter, waddled to the phone box, and said, "Ha-*low?*," then turned to me, disappointed. "It's for you, Luke."

My head ached from the beating I'd taken the night before in a Memphis bar. The ring finger of my right hand was as thick as a Polish sausage. As I reached for the receiver that finger stood unsociably apart from the others.

"Luke?" somebody said on the phone.

"Yeah?" I hesitated because the voice at the other end of the wire rang a tiny bell in my mind. I didn't heed it. "Yeah? Who's asking?"

The wire hummed. "I've got a job for you, Iceman."

The bell went off louder. The bell in the back of my skull that warns me of trouble. The bell I ignore. "Doing what?"

He laughed, and the laugh was nasty to let me know he knew I worked at subsistence-level jobs—pulpwood cutting when the roads were dry, commercial fishing when the water was right, deer poaching when I was hungry. Maybe he knew that I fought in bars when the memories got too heavy.

"It's outdoor work in an area where you're the expert," he said, and snickered. I didn't like it. Grown men show respect in the South. They don't snicker. It's not a healthful attitude.

"—Your kind of thing, Iceman. I want a man moved."

"Who do you think you're talking to?" My mind was cool now, diving deep, searching for a name to go with the voice.

"You listen, Iceman. Tomorrow you'll get an envelope, general delivery. It'll contain money. Not much. Just enough to let you know I'm on the level. If you want to, take the cash and forget this conversation. If you're interested, there's five thousand easy money in this for you. Just build a trash fire in back of your place any day at 2:00 P.M. and we'll contact you."

I glanced at old Mrs. Bailey across the display room of the store, lowered my voice, and cupped my hand around the receiver. "I don't do that for money."

Silence hung in the wire. Then the guy said, "Hell, Luke, I must've got things wrong. Didn't LBJ pay you? You mean you killed nineteen confirmed for motherhood and apple pie? You mean you didn't *like* doing it?"

I couldn't think of anything to say. Never had a more probing analysis been made of my character since an Army doctor wrote in evaluation that I can peel civilized restraint like a snake sheds skin.

There are costs to society when it bloods its young men . . . when it teaches them it's all right to kill certain human beings. At first, war to me was hunting raised to a higher power. I liked stalking, the rush of danger, and using my woods skills. Hell, I was a kid. By the third tour I was sick of it.

The guy on the phone said, "Call the fire tower so they won't worry about smoke. We don't want anyone snooping around your place, do we?"

"You want me to build a signal fire? Right beside the National Forest? You've seen too many Westerns, buddy."

But he knew me, all right. Knew about the cabin and ten acres snug on the edge of the National Forest. Knew about the waiting and the hunger that had built up. "Go to hell," I said.

He hung up.

I eased the phone into its cradle and stood very still, trying to think calm thoughts. Scratched in the metal were three lines, painted over, but still legible. The first said, "God is dead," signed "Nietzsche." A little to the left was, "Nietzsche is dead," signed "God." Below, it said, "Call Mary, 349-1211—a wonderful sorority screw."

You get a better class of graffiti near a college town.

The store owner perched on a stool twenty feet away, watching *General Hospital* on a twelve-inch screen. Her thick ankles dangled old-lady shoes four inches off the floor. She didn't glance up. I slid back the frosted door of the freezer and took out a loaf of wheat bread stiff as a corpse. From the dairy display I chose a wedge of cheddar cheese and two cups of banana yogurt. The tobacco shelf offered only Red Fox, Garrett Snuff, Prince Albert in the red can, Half and Half in green and white, and Borkum Riff. I picked up two packs of the Borkum Riff.

"I've ordered Troost for you," Mrs. Bailey called without turning her head. Her voice turned coy. "You give any more thought to selling me that place of yours in the woods? My gran'daddy owned that piece of land one time."

"Thanks." I slid the stuff onto the counter. "No, I haven't."

She climbed down from the stool. "That'll be four twenty-five, and twenty-nine cents tax. Four fifty-four." She didn't use a calculator. "You ever want to sell it, be sure to let me know first."

The five I handed her left my wallet thin. Abraham Lincoln. In God We Trust, it said.

She held out change but her fingers curled over the coins. I wanted my forty-six cents.

"Was it important?" The bright eyes behind blue-framed glasses probed mine. "I thought it might be bad news when the man tied up the line so long and you seemed mad." She laughed and sputtered. "Don't think I'm nosy!"

"No, not bad news. Don't know why he couldn't have waited. My rounds are so regular anyone can find me."

She showed her even, white dentures. "We're all creatures of habit. My day wouldn't be right without *General Hospital.*"

Yeah, but not me, lady. Not me. I didn't last three tours in Vietnam by being predictable. Not by having mama-sans know what pipe tobacco I want before I ask for it. Not by the wrong guy knowing what days of the week and at what hour I buy groceries, what path I take and when. If that were true, I'd have got a punji stake up my ass long, long ago.

I nodded goodbye to Mrs. Bailey, and opened the white wooden door of the little store and the baggy screen door imprinted with faded orange letters that spelled NEHI. It was unseasonably cold for November.

I turtled my neck into my shoulders, anticipating the run to the Jeep. The doors, pulled by old coiled springs, swished shut behind me, muting the voices from the old woman's television set.

There was nothing to do but go.

I ran to the Jeep with icy rain pelting my face, collecting on my lashes, and sticking my shirt to my skin. Flinging open the

Jeep door, I tossed the purchases to the far seat, got inside, and closed myself in.

There wasn't another Jeep like mine in town. Battered and spot-primed, it reminded me of a certain patrol vehicle in Saigon. Anyone who knew me knew that Jeep. Knew where it was, I was . . . knew it because I wanted them to know.

It had taken discipline to drive to and from the cabin at predictable times, by predictable routes; to exchange one set of survival instincts for their opposite.

I thought it had worked. I thought I had slid into the scenery. Now, some son of a bitch was onto me.

6.

I cranked the four-banger motor, eased the bare metal clutch pedal while it tapped against my boot sole, and moved into traffic, taking the bypass around town. Thick black clouds rolled in. Thunder rumbled. Huge icy drops muffle-thudded on the Jeep's rag top and splattered against the windscreen.

The short wipers *wick-whacked, wick-whacked* outside, and I wiped beads of moisture from inside the glass with my hand. Vehicles passed me, their occupants indistinct behind swishing wipers. I waved. I always wave.

Traffic thinned east of town. Five miles out, where big loblolly pine trees line the highway, a narrow dirt road forks left. I turned in, then stopped to take a look. Since I had last traveled it, the road had been cut and churned by the tracks of a half-dozen vehicles.

Deep in the forest a civil defense horn bawled like a love-sick elk.

Someone was lost.

I got out to twist the wheel hubs. Sleet pounded my back and ran a cold wet finger down my collar as I hopped from tire to tire. Once the hubs were set to four-wheel drive, I kicked mud clots off my boots and crawled back in. Dirty water rippled across the Jeep's floorboard.

I'd meant to shoot a hole in the floorboard to make a drain.

I rubbed my hands together and listened to the lonesome bawl of the horn, pitying the poor S.O.B. lost in this weather. Then I turned the key, the tires spat clay, and the Jeep slewed from side to side, chewing the road as I headed for home.

About a mile deep in the forest, four vehicles sat on the verge: the civil defense wagon, a U.S. Forestry truck, a pickup marked *Volunteer Fire Department,* and a green truck used by state game wardens. Three men wearing coveralls and caps stood with their collars up and their backs hunched, looking miserable.

I stopped and spoke through a window crack to a forester. He bent to peer into the Jeep, keeping his hands jammed in soggy pockets. His blue eyes looked smudged behind his glasses. "Hey, buddy!" he said. "You live up the road here, don't you?" I said I did. "Tom Morris's boy got his self lost. I don't guess you've come across tracks, or anything he might have thrown away, have you?"

I said I hadn't, but if I did I'd let him know.

He said the boy wore Maine hunting shoes—leather-topped, rubber-bottomed boots that make distinctive chain-link tracks. But once he'd reached the pines, they couldn't track farther because of needle cast. The forester studied the clouds. "I hope we don't get a hard freeze, because—" He left the sentence unfinished and shook his head.

"I hope so, too," I called, and drove on.

Angus McKay sat behind the fogged windows of the last

parked vehicle. He blew the civil defense horn, *Ooo-ga!*—ten seconds, pause—*Ooo-ga!* The idea was that the kid would hear it and home in, but he hadn't.

I could find that kid. I knew I could. I felt the responsibility a highly-developed ability imposes on a man. I fought it. *It's not your problem!* I told myself.

It would be foolish to bring my skills as tracker and outlaw hunter to the attention of game wardens. *There are other woodsmen who can handle this,* I told myself. Still, I was uneasy. It was going to be a miserable night.

I gave Angus a wave as I passed the van. He cold-eyed me through a window tracked by melting gobs of sleet.

7.

A half-mile beyond where the Morris boy had disappeared, where Angus McKay sat on his butt in a warm, dry truck, wailing that lonesome call, I pulled off the road, turned the ignition key, and listened to the motor chug, wheeze, and die. The sleet had melted here. No tracks but mine had torn the mud. My cabin and its brushy perimeter had the right feeling. Empty.

When old-timers built a cabin on the frontier the first thing they did was girdle trees. A frontiersman hates trees. In the South we've got that attitude still in us. Let a subdivision go up and the builder pushes down trees worth thousands of dollars in cooling and esthetics. Then he plants sprigs—potential trees. The editor of our local newspaper editorializes about the need to whack oaks a hundred years old in order to display a "canopy of lights" at

THE HIT

Christmas. She wants to cut a lush magnolia so tourists can better see the county courthouse.

My cabin doesn't displace trees, it blends into them. It's one huge room, a loft, and lean-to. A stone chimney pokes through the cedar roof. I dug and hauled each of those stones. Brush grows to the log walls. Pines sing in fair weather, and in wet they sigh and drip. Sunlight through the pines is light and diffuse, like flour after sifting. The few people who have seen the cabin think it's lonely. I think it's just right. It has certain conveniences, necessities you might say, for a man not at ease in the world.

It was difficult to train my dog Adel not to bark when he heard the Jeep engine. He understood he wasn't to bark at other cars or trucks, but must have thought it was all right to greet me. After awhile he adjusted. He barked when I told him to. Other times, he lay in the dark cabin like a copperhead snake under a fallen log. If someone had entered without my being there Adel wouldn't have warned. If the intruder were unarmed, Adel would have body-blocked him and sat on his chest, watching the blood pulse in the guy's throat in an interested way. If the intruder had fought, carnage would have resulted.

I circled the cabin. No tracks in the mud but mine. The little shred of brown paper I had left between door and frame, six inches from the floor, still poked out. The twin locks clicked as the keys turned, and I stepped inside. Adel wiggled across the floor like a puppy, sat at attention and offered his paw.

"Adel, you are a deceiver," I said.

His stub tail fanned and he shivered. His eye whites gleamed and his fangs glittered. When I touched his skull he sprang as high as my waist. A sound like a race car engine started deep in his chest. I grabbed his skull and shook hard. He snatched at my wrist with compound cutters, and sat happily with my veins and arteries pulsing between his teeth. He buzzed ominously while I pried at his tushes.

40

"OK," I said, "you've had your fun. Adel, leave it!" And then the son of a bitch gave me back my arm.

He looked at the door, and he and I walked there. He pushed through the screen and went to the woods to empty.

Adel is a German shorthaired pointer of the old type, man-sharp, eighty-five pounds of muscle and bone, solid liver-colored, and programmed for certain refinements Germans do not require even of utility Siegers. A silent trailer, he drifts like mist through the forest. He ignores distracting scents until he locates the maker of the trail. He will point it if alive, and if dead return and lead me to the kill. This is convenient for collecting deer when you use my method of hunting.

Adel silently alerts me to wardens or to other hunters in the forest. He has been trained as an attack dog by one of California's best. In town, he looks soulful, wags his tail, and hangs out his tongue. He licks little kids on the hands while "smiling" in the grimace dogs have. The son of a bitch enjoys acting.

There's a small radio in my kitchen for local news and weather, but no television set. Books are the first thing you see inside my cabin, most of them worn, with tattered jackets, but some crisp-paged and new-smelling. Library discard sales, garage sales, and storage bin sales offer treasures for nickels and dimes.

Books turn bullets, insulate walls, impress women, and protect against radiation. That's in addition to providing company, solace, information, and entertainment.

I carried a *Pocket Book of Verse* through Vietnam, and had it recovered twice to protect it from the wet. My yellowed twenty-fifth edition, dated 1945, has a label on the back that says, "Send this book to a boy in the armed forces anywhere in the U.S., only four cents." I hope someone did, and I hope the poems helped an old soldier as much as they did me.

Every wall of my hooch is covered chest-high by shelving. Books by Faulkner and Hemingway jam shoulders with Hardy and Dickens and Gold Medal writers. I've got Trollope because in Barchester's treacheries I best get away from present-day treacheries. I don't know why that medicine works for me and not another. It's homeopathetic, maybe.

The dark stuff is shelved in easy reach of my lamp and rocker . . . James N. Cain, Charles Williams, Hammett, Chandler, and Chaze. Those guys don't feed me lies of glory. John Wayne and all that charger bullshit got many a good boy killed.

The stranger who enters my cabin sees only one door, but I'm not such a fool as that. Plywood backing under the kitchen sink opens on hinges. A crawl space there goes to the lean-to. In the loft a piece of roof folds up, making an escape hatch. Under the threadbare oriental rug in front of the fireplace is a trap door, and under that, a four-foot hidey-hole leading to a tunnel made of drain pipe.

I'm encouraging the brush beside the paths to grow.

Some people would say that sane men do not need rat holes. So be it. My shrink at the VA hospital said to humor myself.

By the time Adel returned from dumping and checking the perimeter, I had shucked my wet fatigue jacket and boots, toweled off, dressed in crisp khakis, poked the hickory fire into sputtering, and settled into a butt-sprung chair with a glass of J.W. Dant's ten-year-old bourbon. Adel flopped just beyond reach of sparks sizzling like miniature comets, muzzle on paws, looking aggrieved. He likes friendly oak fires that don't spit.

An hour passed and it stopped raining. For a long time the rescue horn had moaned *Ooo-ga, Ooo-ga*, sounding as far-off as a ship at sea. Then Adel pricked his ears, tensed, and swung his muzzle toward the door, giving me the silent alert. I listened but didn't hear anything but the dripping eaves. Then a flurry of light knocks rattled against the two-inch oak.

8.

When I opened the door there she was. There was a time when a mere glimpse of her would set my heart on edge.

There's always one woman in your life that's wrong for you, who's going to get you into trouble. You'd be better off never having met her, but she's the one you think about and want and can't get out of your mind—not ever.

"Hello, Luke," she said. The voice huskier now.

"Hello, Kinnerly."

I asked her in. She wiped off her shoes and entered. We hadn't met face-to-face since I'd joined the army.

Her hands came together in a gesture of peace. She didn't know what to say to me or how to begin, and I didn't help.

"I knew you were in town, but I didn't know if you wanted to see me."

In fawn trousers and ratcatcher coat she looked slender and firm. Her lips curled to expose a pink and vulnerable edge. As a girl she had worn a wash of sunburn in summer that brightened her eyes. I supposed she still laid out because her skin was as golden as the lining of a honey locust pod. One of her blue eyes, the left, contained a tan fleck. I remembered a little mole hid on her neck below the collar edge.

I'd been telling myself that coming back here two years after separating from service had nothing to do with the unresolved thing between us. Eight years had passed since we'd said good-bye. Now she was a rich married woman, living the life she'd always wanted. I was too old for fantasies.

"Why didn't you call me, or speak to me on the street? Did I hurt you that much?" she asked.

A little alertness was all it took to avoid her . . . a look down grocery store aisles before blundering into them, a turn of my head in order to not "see" her at a distance, a dodge into store entrances to prevent head-on encounters.

I smiled and lied. "Of course not"—then added an undeniable truth—"we don't travel in the same circles."

The four strata in Bridge County were the rich, the poor but nice, the not nice, and trash. She lived in the first stratum and I in the bar-hopping, fist-fighting third.

Once that wouldn't have mattered to either of us.

When we were students at Ole Miss I worked my way through. Dropped out twice, always scraped for tuition money, and didn't graduate until I was twenty-four. She was a Miss-Everything who wore cashmere sweaters, camel hair coats, and alligator heels her Delta-farmer daddy couldn't afford but bought anyway. Still, something clicked between us. From the time we met outside an English class taught by A. Wigfall Green until she "came to her senses" when I graduated and volunteered for Vietnam, we were best friends and lovers.

"Luke, you must know why I've come," she said, lifting her hands again in that gesture of peace. Twin bands flashed on the third finger, left hand. "My son is lost and we desperately need your help."

"Your son? I didn't know—"

"My stepson, Tommy."

There was that warning bell again. It had rung when I saw her standing in my doorway. Now it dinged like crazy.

A woman who desperately needs help doesn't compose sentences. She doesn't say, "We desperately need your help." She says something like, "Help me, please. For God's sake, help me!"

"We?"

"My husband and I. Do you know Tom?"

"We've spoken," I said, then added, "I never trust a guy with a ten-dollar haircut."

Everybody knew Tom Morris. He owned three buildings on the square, a thousand acres of land, eighteen or twenty rental properties, a neoclassical house, and—most important to me— a sporting art collection that included a Wootton, a Fernley, a Stubbs, and a Sartorius.

There was plenty to dislike about him other than what he spent on haircuts.

Morris was a strutting little man who used the weight of his wallet to keep other men down because bigger boys had tyrannized his childhood. He worked the shady edges of property law where the rich have rights and the poor get humped. Tax titles and foreclosed deeds of trust were his meat and potatoes.

That's the way I saw him.

Kinnerly ignored my rudeness. "Will you help us?" she said.

I had daydreamed she would one day be forced to ask for my help. Now I'd outgrown the need and was ashamed of the desire. Besides, connecting my name with the Morrises would be stupid, since I intended to relieve her husband of his art collection.

"Get a bloodhound and handler from the prison. They can find him," I said. "I can't do it. I'm sorry."

"Luke, please! There isn't time. The weather—" She touched my hand, and a rush of wanting her stirred in me.

You may not believe a woman's face and words. God knows I don't. They learn to control them. But you've got to believe the way they move and stand.

"All right, take it easy," I said. Then I felt bad, the way I do every time I ignore my hunches.

It was the damn newspaper story that brought her to me— a legend-making ink splash about a local soldier and the good medals he'd won in a bad war. For a little while I was a gung-ho immortal. What the story didn't say was that by the third tour I was riding nerves as slick as a junker's tires.

She looked about to faint. I got a chair under her and poured a stiff scotch. She took a swallow of it and put the glass down, first wiping the bottom with her hand. There was quality under the imperfect finish of the old Sheraton table beside her.

"I was afraid you'd say no."

"There are a lot of guys who can do this as well as I can. Better, maybe. They may not need me." I hoped the search party had enough pride to keep me out of it.

"You have a reputation for being unsociable. They thought you wouldn't help. Angus McKay said you'd driven by and hadn't offered. They said there was no need asking, but I had to. Will you go after him tonight, Luke?"

"The dog can trail, but I can't see. I'll go at first dawn."

"Will Tommy be all right in this weather?"

"Sure," I said, giving her what she needed.

"Thank you, Luke."

"No need for thanks." I led her to the door. "Have Angus

bring me a walkie-talkie tonight. When I find the boy, if I need help I'll radio coordinates."

She turned, looking up.

"And one more thing. I don't want anyone else in the forest. No amateurs tramping around messing up the trail. No choppers overhead disturbing the dog. And no publicity."

"I can't promise that. My husband will want to do everything possible. And I can't control the press."

"Screw him. Screw the reporters. You keep them away."

She looked steadily into my eyes. "Whatever you say, Luke."

That's when I knew she was as tough as the day she dumped me and took up with an assistant professor with a convertible and two tickets to Spain.

A half-dozen professionals had searched that forest, but they were going to clear out. Her husband would give up command. No one would like it. They'd say it was foolish. They'd try to reason with her. In the end they'd go. She'd make them go because she'd found a man who could get a job done.

The night was colder but clearing. I slouched against the doorjamb as she walked away, looking her over, letting her know I was watching.

She was a hell-of-a-looking woman.

9.

Remember the guy in the O. Henry short story "Alias, Jimmy Valentine"?

Gentleman Jimmy was the best safe-cracker in the business. He'd come to town to rob a bank and he'd done the job. After Jimmy slipped away, a kid locked himself in the vault where the money had been.

In hours there wouldn't be enough air to breathe. The vault was time-locked. There was no way for the banker to open it before the boy died.

So, Gentleman Jimmy sat down his satchel of money in front of the cops, and coolly cracked the vault again.

What caused Jimmy's downfall? Compassion? Not just that. Think about pride.

It wasn't enough to take their money and get away with it. Jimmy wanted to show them how easily he could do it.

Nobody in my senior high-school class liked that explanation, but I know Jimmy Valentine. I've been trying to keep that part of me under control all of my life.

This time I didn't have a satchel of money to lose. I hadn't scored, and didn't know when that score would come. The Morris art collection was the only job I'd seriously considered, but I knew I was ready. I had established an identity as a solitary man the war had ruined. A visible man, but not too visible. A man who might cut his losses and leave town with no one thinking much about it.

Connecting my name with the name of the man I intended to rob was dumb. Running the foresters and civil defense experts out of the woods so I could show off to a woman was stupid.

It was my Jimmy Valentine coming out.

Angus McKay arrived at my house about 10:00 P.M. with the walkie-talkie and a typographic map. A squatty guy with deep-set pig eyes, Angus had the hard, fat body that is just about unstoppable in a fight. He pretended to be harmless. His voice squeaked off-key, and he laughed easily. Adel didn't like him at all. He sat at attention watching Angus's hands.

"Damn, Luke. I know I ain't much of a woodsman 'pared to you, but how 'bout letting me and the other fellows he'p find this kid?"

I didn't answer.

"Be reasonable, man. It's more than a job to me." Angus shifted his big butt in my best chair and parked his forearms on his knees. Mud from his cleated boots littered my floor. From the wrists hung a pair of hands I'd seen ripping old-style steel beer cans into ragged pieces of metal. "That boy's daddy is just—just—distraught, and his momma's plumb gone crazy."

"You work for Morris, don't you Angus?"

"Yeah."

"Well, you ain't going to bring the boy in."

Angus lifted brown, corded forearms and folded them across his chest. They looked like the hawsers that moor ships. He knew when I said *ain't* I meant what I said.

Adel's ears flattened.

Silence stretched. Angus's fingers drummed battle songs on his biceps. Bagpipes must have skirled in his head.

The moment passed. He got to his feet. "Damn you, Luke. I'll remember this."

"You do that, Angus," I said.

10.

On a four-pound aluminum frame I packed a down sleeping bag, a ground cloth, a shelter half, first-aid supplies, flares and a flare gun, dehydrated meat and soup, two pounds of dog chow, punk for fire-starting, a cruising axe, and a folding shovel.

When I opened the wardrobe and lifted out thermal underwear, bush pants, a wool shirt and foot gear, Adel cocked his ears. When the twenty-foot webbed tracking lead and heavy belt shackled to it thumped on the floor, his tail stub fanned.

I packed the ruck and gave it a shake to see if it rattled, just as I would have in Indian country. It didn't rattle.

The dog and I left the house and cast below the boy's abandoned pickup, staying well back from the road. The searchers had pulled out. Whippoorwills called. The woods rustled with life.

Adel sat at "stay" while I searched the truck for something

that had belonged to the boy. On the floor lay a flap-sprung Winchester cartridge box—150-grain Silvertips, deer round. A dirty handkerchief stuck out of the glove compartment.

Well away from the muddle of scents around the boy's truck I gave Adel the handkerchief to sniff and told him, "Track." We cut a quarter mile arc before picking up a strong trail. Adel dropped his head and tugged. I hooked the web to the belt and held tight to a jerking, plunging, eighty-five-pound, All-Pro dog, while limbs slashed my face, and cold water leaked over my boot tops, and rain dripped endlessly from the evergreens. I threaded my one hundred and eighty pounds through one-foot spaces that accommodated Adel, bumped down ditch banks on my butt, and time after time untangled the web from saplings he'd circled.

I'll say this for the Morris boy. He wasn't a road hunter.

He'd become disoriented and had circled six miles in the forest. His trail ended at the edge of a gully, which he must have stepped into in the dark. We peered over the top and saw him in slush and mud at the bottom, where he'd fallen. His thirty-thirty carbine was strapped to a broken leg with pieces of his belt.

I stripped the gear off Adel and left him at "stay."

The boy opened his eyes and watched me slide down the bank to him. Didn't say a word. I swabbed mud off his face, eased back the clothing and checked his vitals. His skin was clammy and cold and maybe he shouldn't be moved, but he sure wasn't going to warm up in slush.

After asking him to wiggle his fingers and toes, and turn his head left and right, I offered water from my canteen. He gulped until I pulled it away. Then I gave him a shot of morphine.

"Where in hell you been?" he asked, no smile on his white face. He meant it.

Sweet kid, I thought.

I scraped together a pile of dry leaves from under the wet ones, sat, and smoked my pipe while the morphine worked.

When the kid's muscles relaxed, I rolled my sweater and parka into a firm tube, eased the pad it formed between his legs from crotch to heel, and lashed both legs together with rope from my pack. I got him out of the gully as gently as I could, but bone showed under the skin of his calf and the injury was horribly painful. He cursed plenty.

Wrapped in a space blanket, he watched as I built a tiny teepee from the inner bark of a cedar, lit the teepee at its base with my Zippo, and blew the fire to life. Twigs were its first food. Later it snapped and popped and threw up yellow flames as I pushed in shaved sticks.

Then I poured a dry mix into my cooking pot, splashed in water from my canteen, stirred twice, and set the pot on a rectangle of stones I'd placed around the fire. After a few minutes the soup bubbled.

The scent got to him. He swallowed three times, casting glances over that well-bred nose.

Not a bad-looking kid, but he wore too much of his dad's expression: a downturn of the lips and a barrier like the Berlin Wall behind his eyes. At fifteen, he was already asking lesser beings to justify their space on earth. I couldn't remember what his mother looked like—the wife before Kinnerly—but she hadn't imprinted the kid at all. He was a Morris, and we weren't going to hit it off.

I passed him the pot with the detachable handle and watched his hand shake as he spooned in the hot stuff. Then he went to work on dehydrated meat, sucking and chewing.

After snaking the antenna out of the walkie-talkie, I hailed Angus.

"Hot damn!" he yelled. "You got him?"

"Listen, Angus, and listen good. Write this down." I gave him map coordinates. "The kid's got a compound fracture, left tibia, so bring a litter and bearers. The flare gun and walkie-talkie will be here for him to use in case you get lost."

"Wait now. Say again, son? Do I understand you're leaving? You're leaving that kid?"

"You got it."

There was a crackling silence.

"Over and out."

Tom, Jr., watched, lips quirking.

I put the walkie-talkie and flare and my canteen beside him, and shouldered the rucksack. "They'll be here in an hour. Stay in touch with the radio."

"What about your gear?"

"Leave it at Bailey's store."

He nodded. "My father will appreciate this."

"Tell your father he's welcome."

"He will want to pay for your trouble."

I let the silence grow, shifted the rucksack, then turned with a soft voice. "You know the dump you took before you broke your leg, kid? And the two Snicker wrappers you threw away?"

Deep inside him there was a flinch. He didn't like being reminded he was an animal, and not woods-broke.

"Don't worry about it. I buried your shit."

Then I left him.

I went home, put my gear away, and Adel and I took a nap.

The dream came again . . .

Searching for the boy brought it on, maybe, or packing the rucksack and checking for a rattle, or working through woods on a mission. I had this dream, or it had me. I almost realized it was a dream, but couldn't surface from it. No matter how I struggled I was imprisoned in its slow unfolding.

In the dream I was leading a killer team. The other team members were formless unless the dream required the presence of a hand, a face, or a voice. Triple canopy hung above us, enveloping us in gloom. Drops of water worked their way down, soaking everything. My M16 wore a foil wrapper on the muzzle. Phosphorescent pools of light glowed on the jungle floor around my boots as they sank into five inches of wet sponge. There was hardly a sound. If a hundred men had marched there, their combined tread would have been one sodden thump. I was lost but didn't want anyone to know. The topo map was useless. All of the "feel" of land, the way it lay, my sense of direction, and my compass were gone. I expected to cut my trail any minute and have to confess that I didn't know where the hell I was, or where the extraction point was. That worried me intensely. I couldn't hear anything approaching. I couldn't detect the enemy if he was upon me.

And he was.

A gook popped up ahead with an AK47. We froze, staring at each other. I lifted my M16. Unaccountably, it wouldn't obey. I jerked it up but it still didn't move. My arms were missing. There was nothing but air space between my floating hands and torso. I ordered my will to take over and fire the rifle. It obeyed, although the effort required for the command to leap armless space was enormous. After one shot the M16 jammed. I fell to the jungle floor, yelling to the big man walking slack, *"Shoot! Shoot!"* He wouldn't shoot. He said in a judgmental voice, "This is not a free-fire zone." Then the gook shot that guy very precisely. One round between the running lights. He was dead but didn't seem to know it. I thought, *Serves you right.* I shot the gook without any problem. Emptied a magazine. The brass of twenty rounds flipped in the air before the first one hit the soggy earth.

The enemy was down on his chest and stomach. I examined the wounds blown through his back, and turned the body over. I jumped away repelled. The face was—I couldn't look again because the face was mine. It looked like mine. I screamed *Medic!* and woke up screaming *Medic!*, sitting up in bed, gasping for breath.

11.

The night after I rescued the kid she came to my cabin. At the patter of her knock I opened the door. She was always very style-conscious and color-coordinated. This night she wore a tightly-belted skirt, a yellow blouse, Cole Haan loafers, an Hermès scarf, and her signature scent, Chanel No. 5.

"Tom couldn't come. He was called out of town again on business, but he wanted me to tell you how very much he appreciates—how much we both appreciate—what you did," she said. "If there is ever anything we can do for you, you have only to ask."

"Your husband is a busy man. He's out of town a lot," I said.

The air in the room got as heavy as the stuff we often have to breathe in Mississippi summers, dirty with pollen and dust, or thick with humidity—saturated with verbena, cotton poison, and tractor fumes. I sucked it in to get a little oxygen. We stared into each other's eyes.

"But it doesn't matter that he didn't come, does it?" she said. "No."

"—because you did it for me."

Kinnerly had been a golden girl pursued by athletes and campus politicians when I was a poor boy from the wrong side of the gin. I tried to persuade her that the cotton-candy life her daddy, Chi-O friends, and beaus with Delta lisps wrapped her in—that Old-South stuff—wasn't real. She wouldn't hear it.

The night we broke up "Blue Velvet" and "Our Day Will Come" drifted from her car radio, but what she said to me was unmistakably real: "Don't call me, don't write me, don't sit on my doorstep, and don't send me yellow roses. We'll never be together again."

We were together . . .

I wanted to reach for her, but couldn't swallow my spit. I wanted her out of my cabin. I wanted her to stay. That bell in my head was going off four-alarm.

She drew a shaky breath. "Maybe this was a mistake."

Her face was fifteen inches away when I pulled her to me. She looked startled, the way some Southern women do. A moment's resistance held us fractionally apart. Then her arms circled and her lips opened.

"In class and out I always liked you best," she murmured when we took a breath. "You were the tough one, the iconoclast."

"And you always knew exactly what you wanted."

"Oh, Luke! I was only a girl. The war . . . I was so confused. I'm still confused about it. You were obsessed with me, and that scared me. You weren't like other boys."

I cupped her waist in my hands while considering the best way to get her onto her back. She needed a screwing she wouldn't forget. Once I'd wanted Kinnerly's love. Now I wanted *ruv*. In Guam, where native women couldn't pronounce *l*'s, *ruv* was a G.I. word for sex. *Love* was reserved for girls we carried pictures of and might someday marry. She'd forfeited that option.

My hands moved to her hips. Her red nails followed them. She leaned back and the devil-fleck showed in her eye. I went for her, like a bass on a bright new spinner, and she hooked me good. I didn't want that. I wanted it the other way, her crazy for me, but I was the one to pull back.

Kinnerly slipped out of my arms and looked at her watch. "Tommy and the cook are expecting me for dinner. I can't stay a minute longer. I'll call you as soon as I can."

"I'll give you my number, but be careful."

"I'll write then."

"Nothing personal. It's too risky. Type an innocent message. Don't sign it. Mail it from a downtown box to general delivery."

We whispered like people in a minefield setting charges, as if the slightest mistake could be the end of us.

She touched my face. "I want to be with you, but I have to sort out my feelings. Try to understand."

I should have sorted my feelings, too. Sorted the hot one in my groin from the cool one in my brain. Kinnerly was married. She was trouble.

All I'd wanted before was Tom Morris's art collection. Now I wanted his wife. Wanted her bad.

12.

Cecil Lundy peered up at me from the stack of mail he was poking into general delivery slots.

"'Morning, Cecil," I said.

"Luke," he acknowledged.

We were alone in the front section of the post office.

Cecil slowly reached for a stack of general delivery mail to let me know I wasn't rushing him, thumbed through the letters, and dealt them. He picked up a second stack.

"May I have my mail, Cecil?"

"That time of month, ain't it, Luke?" he said sourly as he reached into my slot and flipped a stack of bills with glassine windows, mailing pieces, and a free circulation newspaper in front of me.

OK, so the telephone call from that guy had been a joke.

"One more." Cecil took a white envelope from the last stack and thumped it onto the counter. I looked at it. Maybe I stared. Maybe I drooled at the thought of a little money. That could account for the stupid thing Cecil did.

Cecil's puffy lips curled into an insolent smile. "It's a real one, Luke," he said. "Even a blind sow finds an acorn once in a while."

"Say what?"

"I said, even a blind sow—"

"—Say again?"

"You got a piece of mail that's not a bill."

"Say again?" I cupped a hand behind one ear.

"You got a real letter today."

"Say again?"

The old Underwood typewriter in the postmaster's office ceased tapping. A guy in the back moving gray mail sacks turned his face my way. Cecil looked confused and concerned: "You got a letter."

I took my hand from behind my ear. My gaze leveled on him. "What the fuck did you say the first time?"

He stepped back from the counter. If I had reached across, grabbed his throat, and punched my thumbs in below his Adam's apple, Cecil would have peed his pants.

Now we both knew it.

I crossed the shining tiles, left the post office, and walked across the street, squinting in the brilliant, cold light. I opened the Jeep door, settled on the bucket seat, and closed the door behind me.

I bounced the thick envelope in my hand, then ripped open the flap to expose a wad of bills. Fifteen twenties. Three hundred lovely American dollars. All for nothing. I had no intention of killing for money.

I poked the bills between the lips of my wallet. They made a nice bulge. If you're so rich you wouldn't chase a dollar bill blowing on the street, you wouldn't understand my feeling. I'd been thinking about money ever since I got out of the army, and about the men who should have served a turn with us. A lot of nineteen year olds died who were drafted to make up for guys who could afford college, or who ran to Canada. All of us who served our country lost years in which we could have become established.

Daddy used to say only a fool or a child believes in a just world. "The world is a crapshoot, and the dice are loaded."

Maybe so, but I meant to cut the weight out of the cubes.

I couldn't whip all of the protesters and draft-dodgers who spat on us, literally or figuratively. There were too many. But I could hurt a few where they lived, where they loved, where their souls were—in their wallets.

After months of getting ready, I was sure which slacker I would relieve of his loot. That he was *Jody*—which is what we called a guy who messed with women we left behind—was lagniappe.

I first saw Tom Morris's collection of sporting paintings and bronzes when he lent it to the Bridgeport Museum. To let it be known that you owned art was considered safe in our town. Awareness of art stopped at Pollock, Wyeth and Picasso. The town thieves were men of low vision—lawn mower lifters, Handy Store stickup artists, and chop-shop operators.

Middle- and upper-class women decorated their homes with cheap reproductions framed in prestige wood. They didn't care what was inside the frames so long as it was inoffensive and matched their color schemes. But the Stubbs in Morris's

collection—brood mares in one of those misty English fields—
damn near stopped my breath. Veining stood in the mares' slim
legs. You could feel heat of the afternoon in their dilated, sienna
nostrils.

The bay had turned her head and skinned back her ears,
threatening a fly. The big-bellied chestnut in the foreground
would foal soon, judging from the droop of her tailhead and the
firmness of her bag.

I remembered from a course in my art history minor that
Stubbs had stunk up his studio and neighborhood when dissect-
ing horses. Englishmen had held their noses and walked on the
other side of the road. But Stubbs knew bones and muscles. That
painting was worth $400,000 at auction—maybe $60,000, sold
discreetly.

I had eased around the Bridgeport gallery, trying to look
calm, but feeling an intensity I never feel any other time except
about art, fighting, and women.

An Edward Troy portrait of a stallion from the best period,
when he wandered around Alabama, caught my eye.

In a gold frame in a corner, rocking-horse Thoroughbreds
with undersized jockeys in red and yellow silks passed the mile-
post at Epson Downs. I mentally ticked off one Sartorius.

The squarish Wootton showed a Turk in a blue robe and tur-
ban lounging under a palm tree, holding the lead of a crop-eared
Arabian stallion.

In the delicate little Howett watercolor a sporting parson
and a pair of parti-colored cockers flushed two woodcock into a
winter sky. There was a Moreland of an ale-drinking yeoman
sprawled on a bench in a tavern, his greyhound curled at his feet.

A chipped plaster frame circled an oval canvas depicting a
coach and skewbalds mired in a snowbank. A coachman in buff
greatcoat with mother-of-pearl buttons lashed his whip at four
horses. The signature was Pollard's curious, joined initials.

The lot was worth a million, easy, and it could all be transported in a Honda or a motorcycle sidecar.

Not a guard stood in that room, unless you counted old Miss Levell bending over her desk. It wasn't likely that even Morris had kept up with the collection's value since the Japanese and Arabs had entered the market.

I had the expertise to select what was valuable, the skill to lift it, and the know-how to sell it. With no arrests except for bar fighting, I was an unlikely suspect.

When you pull a bank job, the Feds are after you. Sometimes the money explodes and green paint marks you.

When you deal dope, somebody gets killed.

When you steal art, it's easy and no one gets hurt. Usually, no one gets caught. It's the safest major crime.

Make that *usually* the safest major crime. Somebody in town had seen through my hapless, harmless, ruined-veteran act. He figured me as a bottom-feeder. He thought I'd kill for money.

13.

As I turned the rest of my mail face-up, a small envelope with a typed address fell out. The paper held the scent of her hands.

I ripped it open like a kid. The first line of the note read like a sweet inscription in an old high-school yearbook. The last changed to terse phrases and dramatic capitals: "MUST SEE YOU! FOREST ROAD. TWELVE NOON TODAY."

I smiled, imagining her hunting and pecking all-caps.

Forest Road leads to the picnic grounds, and beyond them, to Black Willow Lake. Mature pine trees surround the lake. The pines are an ecological desert, feeding nothing but an occasional squirrel or woodpecker. No hunters would be skulking there. It was too cold for picnicking, and enough wind blew to kick up whitecaps and keep the fishermen at home.

I drove from the post office to Forest Road and entered from the north. Washouts hollow the service roads. Chains stretch across some of them. I wheeled around the chains in four-wheel drive and found a place to wait.

Two crows cawed overhead, telling any living creature with ears to hear and eyes to see where I was. Sparrows rattled among leaves, making more noise than a deer herd. Fifteen minutes later her red Ford passed by me as I sat deep in brush on one of those chain-blocked side roads. No one followed her. After smoking half a pipe, I did.

The Ford sat on the shoulder of the road beside a picnic table. I passed it without a glance. As I hit the first curve her motor started.

She was smart enough not to tailgate. After circling the lake I pulled off and got out of the Jeep. Two roads led away and a forest of loblolly pines sheltered the position. An approaching car would be visible through their trunks.

This was going to be as safe as making love in the middle of a cotton field.

My hands shook the way they do about women and fighting. I punched tobacco into the pipe, spilling shreds of it on my trousers, and scratched a kitchen match. Acrid fumes, about 90 percent sulfur, ran over my tongue.

She pulled in ten feet away. I knocked out my pipe on my boot, stepped on the glowing dottle, opened the door of the Ford, and slid onto the white leather seat.

She was put together with care, every subtle tone of her clothing and makeup harmonious.

"You got my note. I was afraid you wouldn't. I don't know when you check the mail," she said. "There are so many things I don't know. But I'd have been here tomorrow if you hadn't come today, and the day after."

"What if I hadn't come then?"

"I'd have come to your cabin."

"Is Tom in town?"

"Yes."

"That wouldn't have been smart."

"None of this is." She leaned toward me and closed her eyes. Her lips mashed under mine until I felt her teeth. Her breasts pushed heavy and firm under the silk. She sighed a little when I drew back, and her mouth followed mine. "Yes . . . yes."

Her buttons came open and her nipples pricked under my fingers. She pushed me away to get space to swing up her legs, saying words I couldn't make out. I opened the car door behind me to make more room. In my head that warning bell dinged.

I jerked out her silk blouse, uncoupled the tiny front hook of the lacy brassiere, and released her breasts. She cupped the left one, aiming it right at me, and slid her free hand around my neck, prickling the little hairs there. Her lips moved on my ear and I tingled to the rub of words and her warm breath. My hands slid under her skirt. Her panties were too tight to get under. The cloth ripped.

It didn't matter what the cost. It didn't matter who got hurt. I was gone way deep inside myself where caution didn't exist.

Notebook 3

14.

We lay entangled on the narrow seat, holding each other, as we came back to the lap of water and the flutter of wind in the trees. The steering wheel poked my side. I swung myself up and shut the passenger-side door. She offered her hand and I pulled her up.

She tugged down her skirt, looked into the rearview mirror, and brushed back her hair. Her eyes shone too brightly.

"Did I hurt you? I didn't mean to."

"No . . . yes, a little."

"What, then?"

"Oh—" She wiped her eyes. "Nothing. Everything." She came to me and tucked her face against my neck.

"Tell me."

I stroked her hair. There's an old-fashioned feeling I get when

I've made love to a woman. She's special. I want to take care of her. I want to make things right.

"I've been thinking about you ever since you came back, hoping you'd notice me, hoping you'd let me talk to you," she said. "It was wrong of me to deny what we felt before the war. I've regretted it a hundred times. Now that we've made love I don't know—"

"Don't know what?"

"—what I'm supposed to do about it."

I felt edgy. *Do about it?* What did she mean, "do about it?"

"It's too late for us, isn't it, Luke?"

Why, hell, yes, I wanted to say. You're married, and that makes it a different deal. But I didn't answer.

"I can't think about anything else since I first saw you," she said. "When I'm alone I daydream about your mouth and your hands. I want—I don't know what I want. I want us to have another chance. And Tom senses something's going on."

"How could he?"

"I can't stand his touch." Slowly she drew away, wiped her tears, and took out a lipstick. Putting on lipstick is strictly business.

When she turned this time I noticed her blemish. That's what she called the little brown fleck in her right eye. It hadn't seemed a blemish when I was tomcatting back fences and she was a cream Persian who'd slipped her bell. It didn't now.

She dropped the lipstick tube into her purse. "How are we going to manage this? Tom is out of town a lot, but he's jealous of his possessions. His men spy on me."

I must have smiled.

"They *do* watch me. He'll say, 'What were you doing in Tupelo yesterday?' Or, 'Did you buy that blue dress you were looking at Wednesday?' God. It just undoes me."

"So get a divorce."

It was a casual remark. What the hell did I care if she was divorced, so long as she was available?

Her mouth twisted in an expression that wasn't pretty. "I *can't* get a divorce. I don't have grounds. He'll never let me go. I'm something that belongs to him, like his Purdey shotgun, his paintings, and his Porsche. I'm one of his things."

I got out my briar pipe, stuffed it with tobacco, and scratched a match. Smoke coiled between us. "If you move in with me and we have an open affair, then he'll divorce *you*." I laughed, making it a joke, but she grabbed my arm.

"Do you mean it? We can be together? Do you have enough money?"

On the lake the wind still pushed hard little whitecaps toward an eroding shore. The sun sank in a fantastic lavender sky that would have seemed unbelievable in a painting.

You think you know women, but you never really do. Women are two or three different things. One is the bird feathering her nest. She can't stop being that, whatever else she is. Maybe I had held a secret hope that things would be different between us this time. Maybe I had hoped a man didn't have to have power and money. But Kinnerly hadn't changed. She was still insecure. And I was still a damn fool about her.

"What's the matter? You're withdrawing. I feel it," she said.

"No."

"You're withdrawing. Don't lie. Was it because I asked about money? Do you think having a lot of money is important to me? If I wanted money I'd stay with Tom forever. You'll never have the kind of money he has!"

I thought awhile, sucking on the pipe. "Here's the ideal thing, Kinnerly. You stick with security, and when your husband is out of town we'll fuck."

"Don't talk like that!"

"Yeah. It's crazy."

"Don't talk like that."

"OK."

"Don't do it anymore."

"Sure." I hid in pipe smoke and stared out the windshield at the whitecaps meringuing the lake. Far away, a quail whistled *bob white*. Wind inverted the last few leaves on the maple trees. They looked like malformed yellow valentines.

She slid away and put her hands on the wheel. "I have to go now."

"OK." I got out and shut the door.

She ground the starter, looked up with a small, brave smile, then drove away.

So Kinnerly cast the lure like an amateur and I spat it out, right? She was lovely but dangerous, and her baggage was heavy, so I would fold the cards and never see her again. Right?

The next night I'd sit by the fire, listening for the patter of her knock. The door would be unlocked, her Scotch poured, and Adel would be warned.

15.

She came into the cabin without saying anything and sat on the rug, drawing up her knees, her back to me. I handed a J&B in a pewter mug to her over her shoulder.

She wore a wide belt, buff slacks, and a turquoise blouse with silver buttons. The label of the blouse stuck out of the collar. I smiled at the endearing little mistake; she was meticulous about her clothes.

"My drink," she said, and turned.

"I remember."

"Why did you say that to me? You made me sound trashy. Whatever else I may be, I'm not trashy."

"You want it all, Kinnerly—a rich husband and romance on the side. That's fine and dandy. I like being at public stud."

"You bastard! You *bastard!* I love my husband."

"No, you don't."

"You don't know anything about women. Not one thing! A woman can love one man and be attracted to another. He's dependable and gives me security. You're exciting. You make me a little afraid, and that's . . . something else."

"Security is worthwhile, but don't tell me you love your slicked-up Snopes."

"I do."

"You think you do. Come away with me. Come away with me for one weekend and I'll prove you don't."

She shook her head. Her pretty scowl changed to a crooked smile. "You're crazy."

"Come for a weekend . . . one weekend."

"How could I get away with it? I can't."

"Sure you can. You're a smart girl."

That smile lit her face again. "You make me feel I can do anything."

She told a lie that seemed plausible to her stepson and husband. Don't ask me what. I didn't care.

We drove separately to a cheap motel in middle Tennessee. Outside, a sign said "Citizen Operated." The owner's naturalization papers hung in his office, flanked by two American flags. Nine aliens slipped through the halls, some carrying buckets. The scent of pungent cooking floated everywhere.

Bargain paint scaled on the ceiling of our room. The matted olive rugs needed a deep cleaning, the blind hung crooked, and the heat control didn't work. Heat belched out of the vents all night, making the room unbearably hot. But the mattress felt moderately firm, the harsh polyester sheet only burned my knees and forearms, not hers, and the hot water was at least warm. The important thing was we were together for thirty-six hours without interruption.

The one time we left the motel to go into town we passed an upscale haberdashery that was fighting chain store competition with beveled glass doors, suave clerks, and top brands. She stopped to stare at the mannequins in a display window. "There! I've looked for one all of my life," she said.

"A good man? They're hard to find," I said.

She *tsk-tsked* and shook her head and said my jokes were hopeless.

The mannequin nearest the glass wore a blue jacket, white pinpoint shirt, and red striped tie. His jacket was Hart, Shaffner & Marx's most conservative style. The other mannequin sported a lime blazer and neckerchief that would have gotten a real man laughed at. A fan of ties spread across the pigskin saddle his hand rested upon.

"That tie." She pointed to a solid. "It says old money."

I lifted my brows.

"Remember Clark Gable in the movie about the advertising game? He spent his last thirty-five dollars for a 'sincere tie, the color of old money,' to wear to a job interview."

"I don't remember old money on any color chart."

"The movie was black and white but I can tell you one thing." She tapped a front tooth with a fingernail. "It had to be navy or maroon."

"Did Gable get the job, as if I couldn't guess?"

"Sidney Greenstreet, who played the mogul, did this nasty thing. He spit—spat?—on the boardroom table. All the candidates for the job but Gable looked shocked. Gable sat there grinning, wearing a new white shirt and an old-money tie."

"Good story, but I don't—"

"—I'm buying you a present."

"I don't wear ties."

"Don't waste time arguing," she whispered. "I want to hurry you home to bed."

Inside the store, she selected a tie and stood on tiptoes to loop it around my neck and adjust the drape. I don't think words like *adorable* often, but I was gone on this woman.

She ordered me to button my collar. "There!" She patted the tie as if our money problem were solved. Then she paid the clerk, grabbed my hand, pulled me out of the store.

Later at the motel when we had come back from wherever it is we take each other in sex, we lay together with our fingers meshed.

"Tell me about your first girl," Kinnerly said.

"There's nothing to tell."

She poked my side. "Tell me! I want to know."

"Well, her name was Sara Jenkins."

"—and?"

"I was playing high-school baseball, and lots of girls hung around the team."

"I'll bet."

"I went steady with Sara, but when the team played games away I dated other girls. The funny thing was, Sara found out but she didn't date other boys."

"Men and their double standards!"

"There was a double standard, I guess, but the way we looked at it, if a woman wasn't loyal she was nothing."

"What about men?"

I smiled. "That was different."

We weren't touching anymore. She'd pulled away.

"What's the matter?"

"Thanks for being honest about what you think of me," she said.

I propped up on my elbow. "What in hell are you talking about?"

"I'm here with you, so I'm—how did you put it?—nothing."

"Wait a minute!"

The last thing I wanted was her getting pissed off during one of the best weekends of my life. "I was talking about high school. Sara waited for me because if she hadn't, that would have been it. Those were the rules then. That's the way things were."

"Well, they aren't the rules now."

We dropped the subject. Like lovers everywhere we thought differences didn't matter, or we could change each other.

Kinnerly slid back to me and put her head on my shoulder.

I like whiskey but can pass the bottle. I like hard work and fighting but can laze in the shade and rest my fists. VA shrinks have a hard time persuading me to take mind-altering drugs. They say I don't have an addictive personality.

Making love to the woman I had fantasized about as long as I'd been a man and having her come to me with the same desire . . . laughing with her, telling stories . . . being together for thirty-six hours when she wasn't hurried or worried, bonded us in ways I didn't fully realize at the time.

Could I have given her up? Sure, I would have said. But cold biological fact is this: When a scientist taps a platinum wire into the pleasure center of a rat's brain, tickles it with a charge, and shows the rat how to receive that charge upon demand, he will pleasure himself without ceasing until he dies.

16.

I stirred the next morning, reached for Kinnerly, and realized I was in my own bed at home.

I'm seldom lonely, but I was that day. Images of her played and replayed in my mind.

I got out a putty knife and scraped dry chunks of caulk from around a cracked window pane, but wandered away leaving putty flaking the sill. I laid out dull kitchen knives and a white Arkansas stone on the kitchen table, whetted one, then walked to the window to stare out at nothing.

A broom leaned against the living room wall. A plastic dustpan of dirt and lint sat forgotten beside it.

A tie the color of old money lay across a chair.

A lacy bra was in my laundry. It smelled like perfume and her. Smelling it, I could almost pull the touch of her skin through the barrier between memory and the moment I was in. She'd offered her breasts. The taste of desire welled in her mouth. Her thighs opened to my touch. She'd made lovemaking a ceremony of giving. Fancy words like "ceremony of giving" don't come easy to me. I couldn't have said them aloud, but that's the way this woman had me thinking. The compulsion I'd felt for her before the war had returned, and something more.

Except for mental pictures from our weekend, my memory bank was seared. I had been out of my thinking, calculating mind.

As a way of getting out of my mind, lovemaking beats the hell out of fighting strangers in bars.

After our thirty-six hours together Kinnerly came to my house whenever Tom was away—part of each week—giving me the look, walking in that feminine way, touching a button on her blouse.

Pleasure is not natural to me. It came as an unexpected gift. I looked at it like a found coin, shining in my hand, not quite believing my good luck.

A psychologist might say I loved an insecure woman because I doubted I was worth loving. Like seeks like. I wanted a dependent one because it tapped into my infantile need for loyalty.

To that I say *bullshit*.

I don't know exactly why this woman and no other was right for me.

Maybe I loved her for her small Nordic nose that marred the perfect proportions of her features, maybe for the curves in her inner thighs we called "my place." Maybe I loved her for her crooked smile, her brassy laughter and the way she reached to touch when we wordlessly shared a thought. Or maybe I loved her for some half-fraudulent memories of perfect happiness during our college days.

It was hell when I didn't see her for twenty-four hours.

She told me not to telephone her, and I stayed away from pay-phones, but if she missed a day coming to the cabin I imagined things. In my fantasies she came to me wearing only a raincoat, or I went to her house and took her on a tabletop, or we met to talk and found that all of our problems had vanished.

Once four days of silence passed. I smoked a pack of Turkish pipe tobacco a day. My tongue and the inside of my mouth tasted foul. My fingers reddened from chewed hangnails. I lied to Mrs. Bailey at the store—said I had to go to the doctor and my Jeep wouldn't run—so I could borrow her Ford for surveillance.

That night I circled Kinnerly's house. Only two upstairs rooms were lit. One was the boy's bedroom. She was still sleeping with her husband, had to be. I sat in the dark and felt my heart pound.

The fifth morning we had been apart, Adel cocked his ears, pressed his nose to the glass, and *woofed*.

Her car sped into view, throwing gravel. She parked, jumped out, and ran to the cabin. We murmured words against each other's mouth and face and hair as we stripped each other and got on the floor. Her skin was cold under my hands and her hair was cold under my nose, and her breath was warm on my throat. Black socks were still on my feet. A pink garter belt dangled around her waist, and the straps of an unhooked bra hung from her tender, strap-dented shoulders.

Abruptly, the dog's cold nose poked my back. I kicked and yelled, "Get away!" He circled us, smiling in the way of a dog, delighted at the game. He sniffed us and licked our feet. Kinnerly laughed. "There went the mood," she said. "Let me up. I'm squashed."

Later, she explained that Angus McKay had been in her house every day, installing plumbing. Tom had asked her to stay at home because Angus couldn't be trusted. She didn't believe a word of it. Angus was Tom's spy.

I got out of bed, located the "sincere tie" in my closet, and brought it to her. "This is a symbol," I said.

"Of what?"

"I'm getting a steady job."

"Are you?" Her smile was radiant. "And we'll be together?"

She hadn't said the M-word, so I said, "It's a promise."

"What kind of a job?"

I shook the tie. "Not so fast. I just came around to the idea. Putting on a halter is a big change for a man."

"I'm not making you, am I?"

"You're not making me."

She clasped her knees and smiled like a happy little girl. "What do you think you'll do?"

"I don't know, but it will be unskilled labor."

"Be serious, Luke. You have an education. I know you aren't rich. But what do men in your family do? Are you teachers, clergymen, managers?"

"Sharecroppers, at first. Neither of my grandfathers farmed his own land, but my daddy did. He earned a Silver Star and a Purple Heart in World War II. And when he came home to Mississippi he used the G.I. Bill to buy a hundred sixty hill acres. As a child, my spine never touched a chair back in his presence. I spoke only when spoken to, and what I said was, 'Yes, sir, Daddy, sir.'"

"Luke, that's awful. You must have hated him." She looked away to hide quick tears.

"It wasn't awful at all. I admired him. Daddy did the hard thing. He put the war behind him and raised his child. I think about him every day. It was my mother who abandoned us."

It had been a long speech for me. With a tense little smile, she reached to touch. "Luke, you don't intend to farm, do you?"

"Not a chance."

She looked relieved. "My daddy farmed eight hundred acres in the Delta."

"That's a hell of a lot different from a hill farm."

"Most of ours was rented. Sure, we had a big house, but Daddy wore overalls, drove a tractor, and got his hands dirty. Every year he borrowed money. When he made a good cotton crop he bought a big new car and the nicest dresses in Memphis for Mother and me. And when the weevils were bad, or it didn't rain, he took out a second mortgage and bought dresses from New York for us, and an imported car. Not top-of-the-line, but imported." She paused. "Do you know how it made me feel, living from crop to crop?"

"Tell me."

"I had a—I guess you'd call it—Cinderella nightmare over and over. It's the only dream I can remember."

I took her hand. "Tell me about it."

"To make a dance floor for the Rosedale Christmas Cotillion the people there used to pull the benches out of the courthouse. Actually, it wasn't still done when I was a teenager, but it happened in my dream. My date's tux was mud-splashed that night because he had gotten his car stuck on the way to the dance, and had pushed while I drove. I was worried about my dress getting muddy, too. We danced awhile, then over his shoulder I saw the floor where we had danced only seconds before cracking in a jagged line. You've seen ice break behind a dog when it wanders too far out? It looked like that. My date was drunk and didn't seem to be aware, so I whirled away alone, smiling as if nothing was wrong. I should have been terrified but I wasn't. A dance floor cracking wasn't the end of the world. All I had to do was keep moving and pretend it was solid." She smiled wanly. "My daddy had been dancing on thin ice for years, you know."

I smiled, too.

"Did I ever mention Maggie Dorchester, the social arbiter of our group? Maggie cupped her hand, the one with the big diamond, and whispered, '*Pssst*, Kinnerly! Your skirt is muddy and the sole of your shoe flaps. Did you know?' I stopped to look, and that was a big mistake. When I stopped the floor cracked in a rush toward me. Everything went silent. No band, no music. Wood under my feet burst and I fell in slow motion without a sound. Then, like a radio switched on, Solid Gold boomed 'Walk Right In' and feet pounded the dance floor above me. My friends talked and laughed again. Nobody noticed I was gone."

I wanted her to keep talking. "What about your muddy Prince Charming?"

"Oh, Bo called my name once or twice but I didn't answer. I couldn't because I was ashamed of the way I looked with my hair dangling and my dress dirty. After awhile he stumbled away and cut Maggie's partner."

"How did you know that—that he cut?"

"Maybe I could see through the floor. It was OK, really. Bo couldn't have helped me down there in the dark. He couldn't even see me."

"Don't tell that to a shrink or he'll have you catalogued in ten seconds."

She smiled a hard smile and snapped her fingers. "It can go that fast, just like Daddy said. When you were in Vietnam the banks foreclosed. We lost the house, land, tractors, cars . . . everything."

17.

The employment agency shared a dirty brick building with a bail bondsman. The green-and-white plastic awning extending over the sidewalk was pigeon-spotted, the film smudging the windows so dense renters didn't need blinds.

Holleyhead, my agent, was a tall man with sandy hair. Wrinkles had been pressed into his shirt by a fast, not-quite-hot iron. His slick gray suit copied its lines from better brands, and his smile was straight out of *How to Win Friends and Influence People*.

We exchanged Southern greetings—which meant shaking hands, smiling, inquiring about each other's health, swapping opinions about football, and remarking about the weather. Then he cleared his throat and tapped my resume with his forefinger, signaling that business was commencing.

"This is very impressive. Mind if I call you Luke?" I said I didn't. "Well, it's very impressive, Luke, very impressive. I envy you, really do. I tried to get in the war. A bad back kept me out." He shook his head, regretting the bad back that had probably saved his life. "Let's see what we've got here. It says, 'B.A., honors, University of Mississippi. Taylor Medal in English. Enlisted as private, U.S. Army. Airborne, Ranger. Purple Heart, Bronze Star, Silver Star with oak leaf cluster. Honorably separated from the service. No dependents. Thirty-two years old.'"

A frown puckered between his eyebrows.

"Looking for something?" I asked.

"A page seems to be missing."

"No, it's all there."

"What have you done since you got back from Vietnam?"

"I wandered around a couple of years. Since I've been in Bridgeport I've cut pulpwood, fished, and hunted."

"Great life—at least the fishing is." He put down the resume. "What salary are you expecting, Luke?"

"All I can get."

"Don't blame you. Don't blame you one bit. Don't we all? But a specific figure would be—" The pen poised in the air, circling.

"Six hundred."

"Six hundred a month?"

"A week."

"A week." He bent to write in the figure, looked up, and asked, "You wouldn't consider anything that pays a little less, would you?"

My old-money tie was about to choke me. I shook my head.

He inked figures onto a form. "You say you're not particular about the area of work. The hardest job for us to find is 'anything.'"

"It doesn't matter, just so it's decent."

"Refreshing, very refreshing." He stood and offered a firm handshake. "I'll mail your resume, make some calls, and let you know."

I had a job in two days, but thought I'd better break the news to Kinnerly in person.

18.

There was nothing ambivalent about Kinnerly's femininity. Her face was sweet and innocent, her body lush and soft, but her sexual magnetism went beyond that. She projected unguarded sensuality . . . a dependent femaleness . . . the expectation that she would gratefully receive protection from a man. It was the Marilyn Monroe flaw.

Men who admired real women, and not lean, androgynous, boy substitutes would always look at her, and want her. I accepted that.

Adel and I stood waiting at the door as she stepped out of her car.

She wore green pumps and a dark-green wool coat. Her strawberry-blond hair lifted in the wind. She caught it with one hand and turned up her face to the distant sun.

A woman with any touch of red in her hair can drive me a little crazy.

When she came inside I hugged her and settled her on a couch I'd picked up from the Salvation Army. She watched with a smile while I told her I had a job and built it up a little, saying I'd be made a supervisor soon. The smile faded when I mentioned going to parties and guarding things.

"Guarding things? I don't understand, Luke."

"That's the job, guarding things."

"Do you mean you'd be a security guard? You don't mean that, do you?"

"On most jobs I'd wear a suit and an old-money tie. I'd circulate like a guest."

She smoothed her skirt. "I can't stand to see you work as a security guard."

"That sounds pretty snobby, doesn't it?"

"You're a war hero. You're not a stubble-faced man in a Day Detective uniform watching a shirt factory gate. It's not right."

"I wouldn't wear a uniform often. It doesn't matter, anyway."

"Something would die in me knowing I'd made you do that."

"I'm doing it on my own."

"You're doing it for me."

"Nobody makes me do anything. You remember that. As for a job, one is as good as another."

"What do they pay? It can't be much."

"Four hundred a week. It's more than they usually pay."

"My God."

"I can save half."

"You'll have, what? Nineteen thousand in a year? No, less than that. You haven't thought about federal and state taxes, have you? Or Social Security? Or medical insurance? You haven't figured those in."

I said I hadn't.

"You have to think about things like taxes."

"Right."

"And Social Security deductions."

"You've mentioned that one."

"And health insurance. Do you have health insurance?"

I shrugged. "No, but I'm healthy."

She glanced at a watch studded with small diamonds. "Tom will be home for lunch in an hour." She stood, straightened her skirt, and brushed my cheek with her lips. I reached for her but her hands came between us. "I'd love to stay, darling, but there isn't time."

"Sorry you can't have lunch with me. It's a sweet potato casserole with lots of brown sugar, pecans, and marshmallows."

"Sounds wonderful." At the door she stopped and said, "Maybe we'd better think this through, Luke."

"Think what through?"

"You, me, us—this whole affair." She ran to her car.

19.

I didn't take it seriously. She was getting a case of nerves. A woman whose stock in trade is her looks thinks once the hard lines come, and the boobs sag, life is over. In examining my prospects she was following an axiom of war: *Time spent in reconnaissance is seldom wasted.* But it made me sore just the same.

I worked double shifts and didn't hate the blue uniform or dislike the men I worked with. Three, including my supervisor, had military experience. The others were typical Southerners, thick-jowled from fried food, beer, and the regional disdain of exercise. Whether they were tough, or only empty suits, didn't matter. They were symbols, wearing badges and uniforms.

My first major assignment was to provide protection for a party in River Estates, an enclave of the nouveau riche. I liked the caller's husky voice, but didn't think her concern for her guests' jewelry was realistic. She didn't need three men.

"Well, Mrs. Craddock, to be frank, this is not Atlanta. People don't pop through a window and rob twenty people sitting down to dinner," I told her.

"Would you like me to call another firm?" she asked.

"No, ma'am. We'll be there," I said.

Her Southern revival mansion stood on three acres that wore the bright, mean green of winter rye or Astroturf. I was admitted by a maid in dark stockings, a short navy uniform, a frilly cap, and lace-edged apron.

A designer working on a tight budget had decorated the house. The oriental rug was from central Europe, probably Romania. The highboy and hunt board were reproductions with a distressed finish. The paintings were copies by starving artists.

The woman of the house was a real woman. As she crossed the room to greet me, swaying her small hips under a green sequined dress, she reached up to touch her dark hair. "Mr. Carr, I presume?"

"I'm he," I said, "and it looks perfect. Your hair does."

Ladies of the house are not used to security officers who say "I'm he." She smiled and turned a quarter turn to give better exposure to the coiffure. "This is a dress rehearsal for the party. Hair, nails, everything. I'm glad you approve, Mr. Carr."

Mrs. Craddock led me through the house, showing the entrances and exits, which she called "egresses," and gave me an eyeful of her shimmer. She was younger than I had thought, or she had had a successful face lift. I asked if there had been robberies in the neighborhood, and for a list of her guests and former and present employees. The usual stuff. We looked at the parking area, and I told her where I'd post men. She called them the "security force."

"Most of the guests are local, but a few will be motoring in," she said.

Motoring in summed her. Born Baptist, now Episcopalian, I would bet. Ex-poor girl whose parents had scrimped to send her to college. She probably never saw them anymore. Ex-cheerleader or majorette who'd studied the crop of law school and pre-med students the way her old daddy had studied mule colts. She'd gone after one smart enough to make law journal and who had the balls for trial work. Or, she'd majored in med-technology in order to show off to doctors her sinuous way of moving in a uniform.

The tour ended in the little rose garden. I was making notes when I said, without looking up, "Were you ever a cheerleader, Mrs. Craddock?"

"Why do you ask?"

"You have that ruined whisky voice."

"Wasn't that a rather personal remark?"

"It was, ma'am." I grinned, showing a lot of teeth.

"I thought it was. What you hear is vocal cords ruined by cheering, not whisky. I'll call in the final arrangements. What is the telephone number?"

I handed her an office card. On the front was printed the office number. On the back I printed my home number.

Emily Craddock didn't call. I was glad because I didn't want to get mixed up with her. Disappointed, too. She had started a lech.

The way I see it, when a man wants a woman, she may be a bimbo, somebody's wife, or the college girl next door. It's balls talking, not brain. It's only wanting. He doesn't *have* to act on it.

The security job came off without a problem. By which I mean there was no need for security. We were decorations, like the huge bouquets of glads in tall vases and the dark-skinned, white-jacketed waiters carrying trays of canapes and drinks. If there had been a need for security my two marshmallows in blue would have melted.

A couple of things, maybe, I should mention.

Mrs. Craddock was a widow. Seems her husband had died after completing summation in a wrongful-death case. He won a judgment for two million, although dead, and his contract with the client was for 50 percent.

Another thing. A guy who had "motored in" from the Delta stuck his hat in my hand as he went by. He had his arms wide, crying "Em-ily, my dear!" and made the mistake of not looking at my expression.

I caught him by the shoulder and returned his hat.

Then a gray-haired woman in lavender tottered over to ask me to walk her Yorkie so it could "poo-poo." "I know you won't mind," she said. "You have a kind face." She held out a dollar in a hand wearing a diamond the size of a hazelnut.

I declined the tip and walked her dog. Then I walked out the front door.

Emily Craddock called four hours later.

"Mr. Carr, this is Emily Craddock. Can you come over?"

"Why?"

"I want to apologize for my guests."

"Consider it done."

"I'd like to be allowed to do it in person."

"Why?"

"Mr. Carr?"

"Yes."

She had that husky whisky voice. "Wear the uniform, please. The blue jacket. And a very white, crisp shirt. Knot the knot of your tie tightly. Make it long and thin. And don't knock."

I walked the floor in the sleeping loft for awhile, then called Kinnerly. She picked up her receiver. "Are you *crazy?*" she said. "Do you want Tom to answer? Never call unless I give you a time."

OK, baby. I cradled the receiver. Then I selected a crisp white shirt, knotted my tie tightly, and put on the uniform.

Mrs. Craddock, as she wanted to be called in fantasy, wore a garter belt, panties, and skin-colored stockings. The scene she'd arranged in front of her dresser mirror you could imagine on a naughty Victorian playing card, labeled, "A Lady Surprised By Her Gardener." From the bedroom doorway I could see her pretty, dimpled legs, small breasts, nice skin. Dark hair fluffed on her shoulders.

She gasped and lifted a hand. "Carr, how *dare* you come in here? Get out! Get out!"

I walked across the room and lifted her from the dresser stool. She writhed in my arms while watching us in the mirror, whispering "Carr, *no*," without any wish to be obeyed. Then she fastened her dark painted mouth on mine.

Hers wasn't the only fantasy we acted that night. I had to pretend she was Kinnerly.

20.

Emily called at eleven on Saturday, a purr in her voice. She asked me to come over. I said no. She called again Sunday. I said no.

"So that's it, lover? You've had me and you're through?"

"Don't play the victim, Emily."

"Ooo-kay!" She slammed down the receiver and I thought *that's that.* Adel and I went to Bailey's store for Campbell's tomato soup (which I spice with strong curry powder and chopped green onions), a half-dozen York apples, a loaf of wheat, two Texas sweet onions, a package of Troost, and the *Commercial Appeal.*

At the cantaloupe bin I sniffed the butts of out-of-season cantaloupe like a dog who hopes to find a friend. Mrs. Bailey watched me through blue-framed glasses. Her tennis shoes swung rapidly just above the floor as she said, "He called again . . . that man."

I put the melon down to Adel's level. "What about this one, bud?" The dog ignored it.

"I never forget a voice," Mrs. Bailey declared. "It was the same one, all right. I asked him for a name and number. 'Who's calling?' I said right sharply, but he wouldn't say."

"Probably it was some guy with pulpwood to sell who doesn't know I have a telephone. It's unlisted. Sorry he troubled you."

It didn't trouble *me*. The guy had said take the three hundred and, if I wanted, walk away. I'd done it. If he insisted on anything more from me, he wasn't going to like what he got.

Adel waited by the counter, wiggling his tail, while Mrs. Bailey sacked groceries in a cloth bag for him to carry. She said to me, "Have you give any thought to selling me that cabin?"

"No, ma'am." She sighed and shook her head, but her expression changed to happy as she offered the bag to Adel. "You're *such* a smart dog," she cooed.

It's a bit of a nuisance to keep cloth bags in the Jeep, but I do it because it tickles me to see Adel prance out of stores with such pride.

The next working day my supervisor asked for my badge. A customer had complained that a gold Shaeffer fountain pen and an antique watch had been lifted by someone while I was in charge of security. "Nothing personal," my supervisor said, "but this gal is mad. She has a lot of influence."

I asked who'd complained, as if I didn't know. He said he couldn't say. I thought about making him say, but he was a nice guy doing a job he didn't like. I told him to mail my check, thumped the badge on his desk, and walked out.

———

When Kinnerly and I next talked by telephone she said she was sorry. They were fools to fire me. I was too good for the job. But perhaps what happened was for the best.

She said we needed to talk about something very important. She wanted us to meet on neutral territory, at a Methodist Church nine miles out of town.

Notebook 4

21.

The white spire of the little frame church was topped by a rusty cross of welded iron. Each pane in the church's lower window sashes was painted blue, green, or red in imitation of stained glass.

The grass had been mowed close at the end of summer. There had been no time for it to recover. Now it was a thin brown carpet, worn through in spots.

I drove around back over gravel, with the sanctuary on my right, the cemetery to my left.

Five or six old graves were bordered by colored medicine bottles stuck into the ground. The hollow of a new grave framed by brass posts, red plush ropes, and piled yellow clay awaited an occupant. Two plinths pointed toward the sky. Other gravestones humped like broken men. Some were dirty and neglected. Some had fallen on their faces. All around, imperishable plastic flowers decorated the field of human rot.

Kinnerly had parked behind the church building, hidden from the road. I stopped the Jeep beside her Ford and she opened a door for us. Adel and I got in. Our breath made frosty clouds. Adel generated a fair amount of heat, turning from window to window. I wiped the beaded windshield while looking at the graveyard and thinking of my dead.

She said, "We can't go on this way, Luke."

"I know what you want. We can go to the chair for what you want."

"I don't know what you mean."

"The hell you don't."

"Don't start anything. I don't want to fight you. All I know is we can't go on this way. We have to discuss options."

"That figures."

"What figures?"

"You've got a romantic idea about death, that it solves problems. Theoretically, it's an interesting idea. No Hitler—no murder of the Jews, no World War II. No Stalin—no purge of the Kulaks. Not many historians agree with you, but it's an interesting idea."

"I don't know what you're talking about."

"Sure you know. You want your husband dead."

"I do not!"

"Yes, you do. You write scripts and cast movies in your mind. Everything works out in them. You're Lana Turner and I'm John Garfield. I kill your husband offstage, sanitarily and painlessly. We get amnesia, and live happily ever after. Well, it doesn't work like that."

"Don't be ridiculous, Luke. I want a divorce. Any other way is unthinkable."

"Sure it's thinkable. You've thought it, and I've thought it."

I was testy because she wasn't leveling with me. Adel reached up quickly and slurped my chin. I hate to be licked. He knows that. "Adel, back!" I ordered. He dived in a liver-colored blur over the seat top and landed with a thump. We sat in silence awhile.

"I'm sorry. That was uncalled for," I said. "If you want a divorce, get one."

"Listen to me, Luke. I can't! I *can't* get a divorce! Get that through your head. Incompatibility is not grounds for divorce in Mississippi. Cruelty is, but it means real cruelty, legal cruelty. It doesn't mean that a man's wife is unhappy, and they don't get along, and she doesn't want him to touch her, ever again."

"See a better lawyer."

"I have."

She had seen a lawyer in Tupelo, and he had given her an illuminating short course on Mississippi divorce. The state does not want divorce to be easy or convenient, he said. When neither party is at fault, divorces in Mississippi are usually obtained through collusion. The man allows the woman to charge cruelty or adultery, and he doesn't contest it.

The lawyer told Kinnerly if she sued for divorce on one of the allowable grounds, and Tom contested her suit, she had to prove her case.

"What would that require?" I asked.

"I need to have evidence of his wrongdoing I can bring into court. I don't have it. But Tom can sue me for divorce and win if he finds out about us. He wouldn't have to pay alimony, and it gets worse. In Mississippi adultery is a crime. Tom could have us arrested. He and a deputy could march in on us when we're together. It's been done."

She looked awed by the possibility.

"I wouldn't advise that. I really wouldn't."

"Tom could sue you for alienation of affection."

"He'd have to announce he'd been cuckolded. And I don't have a dime. I'm judgment-proof."

I could see from her expression I'd said the wrong thing, or taken the wrong attitude.

"I'm trapped like an animal, and you won't help me!" she yelled, then wiped her nose with the back of her hand. Her eyes were red-rimmed and determined. "You take care of me, Luke Carr, or let me go!"

By the time we parted that day she had done everything but hand me a hunting license.

Sometimes you go by instinct. A smell in the air, a chill that prickles hairs on your arm, an inexplicable need to take a deep breath. Something big is coming. That's for sure, but maybe it doesn't have your name on it yet.

Say you're bivouacked in a safe zone. You roll out of the bag one morning and two or three of the guys with tours under their belts get quarrelsome, slam gear around, then haul ass. They act as if they don't know anybody in the company, and don't want to. The cherries banter and clown like friendly puppies. "What in *hell* is eating those guys?" one says, pointing a thumb over his shoulder in the direction of the departed.

An incoming round screams in. One round. From nowhere. And the new guys, the ones who haven't developed instinct, never will.

22.

The next morning the ice on the Jeep's window was a quarter-inch thick. The motor whined but wouldn't turn over. I said to hell with the old wreck, loaded a rucksack, and Adel and I walked to the highway. We hitched a ride on a lumber truck.

The driver was turning west after a Tennessee delivery. I helped him offload four-by-eights at a building site in Germantown. The village was a Memphis suburb of the horsey set where priorities were announced by barns larger than houses. That was changing. Yellow bulldozers chugged through pecan groves, shoving over ancient trees to clear the way for subdivisions with prestige addresses. I said my thanks to the driver above the roar of tractor motors. He was a tall, thin guy with a crooked smile who didn't seem to feel cold—wore a thin shirt with the sleeves rolled.

"Sure, no trouble. That's a real nice dog you got there." He rubbed Adel's ears. "You should be able to hitch a ride to 240, no trouble."

I shouldered my gear and looked around. There was a white barn in a grove of pines across the road. Sunlight glittered on the sheet-metal roof. In the outside training ring a rider worked a black Walking Horse mare. The mare's shoes cut pocks of soil and tossed them behind. The rider's posture was the ungainly slouch of a professional.

Three men leaned on the rail to watch. Adel cocked his head.

"OK, boy," I said, "let's take a look." We crossed the road and joined the men.

The mare strutted by with her back hoofprints overlapping the front ones by thirty inches. The man nearest me turned his back to her, and stole glances as if she were a woman he couldn't have who was driving him crazy.

Somebody yelled *Let'um walk on!* the way a ringmaster does at a show. The filly jumped two gears and passed us with eyes glaring, foam flying from the red rubber bit guards, sweat slinging from her belly. The trainer slouched in the saddle with his hat brim low, nodding indolently, aware of the effect she created.

You could sit her back while holding a brimming glass of water, and not spill a drop. "Wahoo!" the youngest man there yelled, pushing a fist into the air. The trainer released the reins. The mare skidded to a stop. He stepped from the saddle in one smooth motion and cocked his head. "What'cha think, boys?" he crowed. They called out appreciation. The filly drooped her head and shook herself. "Chauncy!" the trainer yelled, and a gray-haired black man came from the barn to lead her away.

When the little crowd drifted off I asked the trainer for a job. He gave me one mucking stalls and feeding at $3.35 an hour. I could sleep in the barn, but he eyed Adel suspiciously. "That dog bite?"

"He'll bite thieves."

"Hell!" My new boss chuckled. "I'm gonna get dog-bit."

The barn seemed a good place because of the horses' aroma, their solidity and grace. Ten stalls were occupied by high-headed show horses, and one by a magnificent breeding stallion. White wraps bound the show horses' jowls to keep them thin. Their tails cocked in high plumes, pulled up by tail sets.

Walt Whitman said he could "go and live among large animals because they are placid and self contained, they do not lie awake in the dark and weep for their sins, they do not make you sick discussing their duty to God. Not one is dissatisfied, or crazed with the mania for things." To which I said *amen*, and settled in.

The trainer told me to call him Mousey, "not Mr. Mousey, not Mickey Mousey—just Mousey." He showed me the office with a regal sweep of his arm. It was a cluttered square behind a bug-spotted screen, furnished with three folding chairs and an oak desk flayed of veneer. Faded ribbons—red, yellow, pink, white, and blue—dangled from dirty strings across the ceiling. Polished saddles rested on racks. Leather bridles with bright patent headbands and long-shanked bits hung behind each saddle rack. Green cardboard boxes of leg wraps, baby pads, and other gear stacked the shelves. The mellow scent of leather, the astringent one of liniment, and the sweetness of horse manure mingled in the air.

Mousey showed me the feed area where I was to get grain and hay for each animal. Fifty-gallon metal drums spray-painted with owners' names stood in a row. The ground was scattered with rat droppings.

A wash rack, cross-tie, box stalls with Dutch doors, and an alleyway wide enough to work a horse in bad weather took up the rest of the space in the one-story building.

Adel's job was to guard the premises from human trespassers. He killed rats as a volunteer. I was glad he'd had lepto and rabies shots. As soon as my back turned he was watching a rat hole. Each day there were fresh bodies. Once Chauncy stepped on one I hadn't buried. The thing rolled under his boot, and he screamed.

When the dog wasn't flinging rats into the air after breaking their backs, he sat with the stallion. In the company of Adel, Night Train stopped showing the whites of his eyes and neighing challenges to the geldings. He hung his great head over the half stall door to watch Adel go about his rounds. Night Train's mane hadn't been clipped. It parted over his face and shaded his eyes, giving him the look of an elegant bully.

I polished leather, mucked stalls, and exercised horses. Order was created out of disorder. Cleanliness, while not white-glove cleanliness, was outstanding. Human trespassers did not enter. Rats went underground or retreated between the double walls, where they squeaked weak defiance. If I do say so, the dog and I achieved in our responsibilities a kind of perfection.

My employer kept watching me as I mucked stalls and soaped leather. One day as I chained the stallion's head in order to clean his stall, Mousey came to lounge in the doorway.

Adel didn't like Mousey, maybe didn't trust him. He left a rat hole unattended and sat between me and the little man, smiling pleasantly. Mousey had no idea he was under surveillance. I never saw an animal trainer who read animals less well.

"Why are you doing this?" Mousey asked.

"I like horses, especially him." I nodded toward the black stud, who showed the whites of his eyes and bugled, signaling that he didn't give a damn about me if I wasn't bringing him a mare.

"You don't have to do three-dollar-an-hour work. Chauncy here"—Mousey tipped his skull backward toward the black man in the alleyway who was grooming a bay filly in a cross-tie—

"Chauncy can't do no better. Chauncy can't read. This job is gone-to-heaven good to Chauncy. Ain't that right, Chauncy?" he crowed over his shoulder. "Ain't it?"

Chauncy said it was.

"The cops after you, Luke?"

"No."

"You like nigra work?"

I threw a forkful of wet horse manure in the general direction of a plastic bucket. Somehow it hit Mousey's boots. Mousey hopped away, and the thought of firing me played across his face.

"I like horses," I said as I carefully deposited the next forkful in the bucket.

"I don't like horses," Mousey said. "Horses are dumb. They're stoo-pid! You got to train both sides of their brain separate. What I like is competition." He leaned back in fake lizard boots. His laugh was a stutterer's *he he he.*

"You work mighty small arenas, Mousey," I drawled.

"Say *what?*" Mousey threw tantrums like the only male child of a widowed mother.

"If you like competition, why not go for the big challenge? Why not try to win the Walking Horse Celebration?"

When Mousey had a point to make, words failed him. His eyes rolled up, revealing veined whites. Then they rolled down. You could almost hear eyeballs click into their sockets. He said, "Who's the one here shoveling shit?"

I leaned on the fork handle and laughed. The stallion crowded the hay rack, danced, bowed his neck, and flared his nostrils. I couldn't stop laughing.

Mousey *he he he*'d. Chauncy chuckled.

I reached into the air to mark a large, invisible *one* for Mousey's score.

———

Mousey, Chauncy, and I "made some shows," as horse people say. Mousey strutted and crowed when he won and threw tantrums, well away from the judge, when he lost. The animals were fine to be around, but the petty crookedness of the humans in the horse business gnawed at me. Worse was the cruelty that resulted from turning horses into gross exaggerations of what they were meant to be.

A reaction to pain from blister caused them to gait higher in front than was natural, and squat lower in back. Tail muscles were cut, rendering the tails useless for swatting flies, but proud looking. Lead weights were inserted under shoe pads to make horses sore-footed so they would snatch their hooves from the ground and appear to be walking on air. Pads were stacked under horseshoes until horses sometimes bowed tendons.

Feed was stolen from owners' barrels. Judges were pressured to exchange favors. Good horses were held out of shows they could win so an inferior performer, whose owners paid more in training fees, would get a ribbon.

I began to feel unhappy, so I asked for my pay.

Chauncy rubbed Adel's head a long time the day we left, and fed him half of a lunch sandwich. Adel ate from Chauncy's fingers, chomping mustard, tomato, lettuce and all.

Anything must taste better than rats.

"I bet this dog could run rabbits," Chauncy said. "He could even do that! He ever has him any pups, remember Chauncy."

After saying good-bye to Chauncy and Mousey, Adel and I walked to the road. Looking back over my shoulder, I saw the same scene at the stable I had first seen . . . sunlight bouncing off a tin roof, a handful of owners and spectators standing around the ring, and Mousey riding a fine black mare.

We waited about thirty minutes before an old man driving a

rattly blue pickup wobbled onto the verge. He stepped out of the cab, soft-eyed and fumbling, his head cocked in the way of someone listening to the irregular bump of his heart.

I changed a tire for him and he offered us a ride. I didn't ask where because it didn't matter. He was going to Bridgeport.

It's got my name on it, I thought.

I was remembering an old John O'Hara story about fate. In it, a servant in Baghdad rushes to his master and begs for protection because in the marketplace he encountered Death. The master gives in to the servant's pleading, buys him a train ticket, and sends him to Samaria, where the servant wishes to hide. After packing off the servant the master goes to the marketplace, sees Death there, and angrily confronts him. "Why did you frighten my servant so?" the master demands.

"Sir," Death replies, "I did not mean to frighten him. It was just that I was surprised to see him here, for I have an appointment with him tomorrow in Samaria."

We three crowded into the cab. Adel blew bad, happy breath into our faces. The truck jounced out of Germantown on collapsing springs and turned down US 55. The old man gave his attention to driving, sliding his liver-spotted hands on the wheel, peering nearsightedly through a dirty windshield. I gently pulled Adel's ears and tickled his chin as we traveled home.

The driver let us out at the turn to my cabin. I said my thanks, dug into my pocket, and gave him the lucky silver dollar I had carried in Vietnam.

23.

The morning after I got home Kinnerly hammered on my door. She pounded so hard Adel was confused and barked a sharp warning, though he knew who she was through two inches of oak.

She stalked in wearing polished loafers, blue pleated trousers, a cashmere sweater and gold earrings. Her hands fanned on her hips. I didn't touch her.

"I've been going crazy. I've called or driven by here every day. What happened to you?"

I shrugged.

"I'm entitled to an explanation."

"I figured it was over."

"Like that? I don't believe you. You talk to me! It was the job . . . "

112

I almost laughed. The job? The job she hadn't mentioned when we talked last? The job I had been fired from weeks ago?

"The job didn't work out," I said.

"Of course it didn't. It couldn't."

"I nearly hit a guest who handed me his hat. A woman asked me to walk her dog and offered a tip."

"My, my. You *did* try." She came to me, took my face between her hands, and kissed me on the lips. It didn't help.

She took a deep breath. "I told you I love Tom, and I do in my way. When a woman has a rich husband, she convinces herself she still loves her man even if she can't stand to watch him eat. Giving up a man who takes care of you goes against common sense."

"I don't want to hear about nest building."

"It's the truth."

"The truth is greatly overrated. You want truth? I was with another woman."

She put soft, cool fingers over my mouth. "You mustn't tell everything. I've done some things I shouldn't have, too."

She was close. I hadn't had a woman in five weeks. I could smell that old Chanel No. 5 on her warm skin, anticipate lips opening under mine. "I got frustrated about us being apart and about losing the job."

"It was my fault. I'm supposed to take care of you." She ran her hand down my chest. "Just so you didn't love her. If it was only sex I can make myself not think about it. You didn't love her, did you?" She pulled my zipper.

"No."

"Swear?"

"I swear and hope to die."

"Don't say that. Don't hope to die. Don't do that."

"I won't." The zipper was down.

"Did you kiss her?"

"Yeah, I guess so. Probably." I was thinking about Kinnerly's hand.

"Bastard." The word cracked between us. "I don't want you to die, though. We all will, I know. Time's like one of those old-time train sleeper cars. Night and day, whether we're asleep or awake, the car keeps going. Know what I mean?"

I nodded.

"I want to spend a lifetime with you, and when we're old I want us to be old together. You in your rocking chair and me—"

"Like hell."

"—me in mine. But promise one thing."

"What?" I would have promised anything.

"Promise me you'll never have sex with a woman you could fall for. Go to a call girl if we're not together and you have to. A nice clean one that won't give us a disease. Use a condom, and don't tell me, even if I ask."

"You're crazy."

"Not crazy. I know men and I'm practical."

Our lovemaking was tender and sharing. You wouldn't have thought we were the same people who had ripped off each other's clothes and grappled on floors and tables and car seats, struggling for satiety like tumbling sharks.

I've always been a fool about women. If one cooks for me, warms my bed, and is loyal, I spread my ragged jacket over the rain puddles in her path, and throw my battered body between her and any wild calamities she steers toward.

But that night I wanted more from Kinnerly than sex or love. I wanted to believe in her.

24.

Talk makes the unacceptable thinkable. What is thinkable becomes understandable. The understandable merges into the tolerable. The tolerable becomes acceptable. That's how civilized people rationalize murder.

The next time Tom was out of town and Kinnerly came to my cabin, she pulled up her cardigan and blouse to show purple finger marks across her breasts, bite marks on her neck and arms, and stripes on her back. I eyed the bruises. My voice got soft. "He did that to you?"

She knew what would trip my hammer.

"No, Luke. I don't want him dead, even after this. I'm not good with words. I'm glad I said the wrong thing to you in the cemetery, because without that happening I might have said it someday to some other man who wouldn't understand that I hate violence, and would do something terrible to help me because I'm so desperate."

Her fingers didn't tap, or her foot jiggle. She didn't lift a hand to her mouth to hold in a lie, or stare into my eyes to prove her honesty. Macro and micro we called the big and little signals of deception. I'd been an interrogator in Vietnam for as long as I could stand to watch my ARVAN counterparts engage in persuasion.

"Did you start a fight with him?"

"No, he beat me and raped me. He needs that sometimes and . . . other things."

"Then what?"

"He left on a business trip, said goodbye as if nothing happened."

"What *other things?*"

Her face was hard as Michigan ice. Not a tear, not a whimper now. She wasn't going to tell me.

"I said no, I said I was sick, but he forced me. I called the lawyer in Tupelo and he said he was mighty sorry to say it, but a man can't be convicted of raping his wife in the great state of Mississippi."

"*What?*"

"It's not rape if two people are married. He said marriage joins them as one. 'What kind of law is that?' I asked him. 'The common law, madam,' he said. 'We're a common-law state, and neither the legislature nor the courts have seen fit to address this matter.'"

"That doesn't sound right."

Her fists clenched at her sides. "He told me police laugh and joke behind women's backs when they say their husbands raped them. Then he said go to the police anyway and say Tom beat me. They will come to the house on a domestic disturbance charge and talk to him. He told me to file a charge of battery, and get photographs of my bruises. The photographs will help prove cruelty. I screamed at the lawyer. '*Help* prove cruelty?'" She stomped her foot. "'*Help* prove it?'"

"I hear you."

"You said you would take care of me."

My head ballooned. I could feel the arteries pulsing inside my skull. She cried then, her words blurring against my chest, her tears wetting my shirt.

"I don't want to come to you from Tom. I don't want his smell on me. I'm your woman. I can't stand any more of this."

I released myself from her arms, walked to the kitchen, poured two cups of coffee and dolloped in sugar and milk. "OK, baby. I'll take care of it."

She stopped crying and watched while I stirred the coffee. "What are you going to do?"

I swilled my coffee and poured another cup. "I said I'll take care of it."

We didn't meet each other's eyes. She walked to the table, picked up her cup, and sipped.

"You haven't gone to the police, have you, or called?"

"No."

"You didn't threaten Tom, did you, when you talked to the lawyer?"

"No."

"Lawyer-client confidentiality will take care of him, but you'll need an alibi."

"I don't understand."

She understood all right. She understood plenty.

"I said I'll take care of you, and I will."

"I didn't mean—" She looked right into my eyes. Her pupils were so dilated I could have fallen into them.

"I've thought it. You've thought it. We've walked around it for weeks."

"We can run away."

"On the money I've saved? On the change you can find around the house? Not likely. You're an expensive lady."

"You think I wouldn't live with you wherever you go?"

She needed a lie but I wasn't giving her one. "You set your pattern a long time ago, Kinnerly. And the choice was for the guy with dough, and a pair of plane tickets to Spain. That's OK. I'm going to have that."

"That's despicable!"

"But true." The words were rough. If she was going to turn on me, I needed to know it.

"We still won't have any money."

"Yes, we will, from Tom's paintings and bronzes. I was going to rip them off anyway."

She frowned, taking in that idea, and not liking it. "You were going to steal our paintings?"

"Tom's paintings. I thought of them as Tom's. I'd planned it before you came to my cabin the first time."

She thought about that. "Are they worth a lot?"

"More than anybody here knows." I didn't tell her a million, maybe two million, on the open market.

"But isn't there another way? You could steal the paintings and bronzes and I could leave him later and join you in South America. Costa Rica, maybe. That's a democracy. It's safe, isn't it?"

"It's in Central America, not South. And there's a war all around there."

"But couldn't we do that?"

She was married to the guy. She had to protest a little to save her self-respect, but I could tell from those eyes what she wanted, so I laid it out in spades why he couldn't be left alive.

"If I had ripped off the art before you and I got involved no one would have figured I did it. Not you, not Tom, not the police. I could have drifted away. If the insurance detectives got wise, so what? A single man in a foreign country is hard to track. Especially me. If two of us are running that changes everything. Tom won't let the case go stale. He'll hire detectives and use political influence to extradite us. He'll come after me because I took his property. He'll come after you because he bought and paid for you, and you give him what he needs, and he thinks nobody else can."

She made a face. "And you hold that against me."

"I don't hold anything against you, but I hold plenty against him."

"I could leave the door or a window in the gallery unlocked, cut off the alarm, get him drunk, make love to him so he'd sleep. That would give us hours to escape. I could hire a prostitute who doesn't look like a prostitute to seduce him, and have a detective make pictures. Please! Isn't there another way, Luke?"

I'd hate to have been Socrates with her arguing my case before the dikastery. Her voice didn't carry one ounce of sincerity or conviction.

"Listen. I'm going to explain this once. We have to sell some art. If Tom's around to miss the stuff as it's taken, I'll get caught."

"So there's no other way."

"There's no other way."

"And you're going to do it."

"We're going to do it."

I didn't tell her she'd never be the same.

I never knew anyone killing changed more than it did Jimmy Leyburn, a quiet, college-educated kid from Arkansas who had been in PsyOps, spoke Vietnamese, and all that. He must have

THE HIT

fucked up something awful to have been reassigned to combat. Leyburn moped around, acting like a pussy, so everybody treated him like one. Before he shot off his big toe or somebody fragged him for being a coward, the sergeant ordered FNG down a VC tunnel. The squad gathered to watch. Sarge must have read my purpose as I stepped out to volunteer for the detail, because he waved me off.

"Drop down there," he told Leyburn, "and see if Charlie is home." He handed Leyburn a bundle of PsyOps leaflets written in Vietnamese. "Pass these out." Leyburn stripped to the waist, his face wrinkled like a prune. Tears were in his eyes as he slid into the hole, gripping a .45 in one hand and a K-Bar in the other. Sarge called down, "Hey, new meat! Sheath the K-Bar. You need one hand to crawl with. And put your ear plugs in."

Tunnel rats have no time to think. If an image moves, they fire the gun or use the knife. A kind of recklessness takes over. There are enemies down there, sure, but there is an exit, too. There is a clear goal if they can get there. The walls squeeze in. The direction they crawl is straight, eliminating anyone in the way. The experience is wonderful for clarifying a world view.

Leyburn came out of that tunnel a different man.

25.

The six questions investigators ask about death are who, what, when, why, where, and how.

Usually in murder the whys are passion or money, and the whos are relatives or friends. If these make a match, they ask what—and come up with a six-letter answer, murder.

One way to avoid that tag is to make a killing look like an accident.

During floods, snowstorms, and tornadoes the authorities expect deaths. Cars are swept off roads, buildings collapse, people freeze, or drown, or die of exhaust fumes, have heart attacks, disappear. During hunting season hunters are shot. There are driving accidents. Usually there's no autopsy.

In Mississippi the office of county coroner is combined with the office of ranger—the guy whose job it is to impound loose livestock on the highways. The state doesn't have a forensic pathologist. Not many coroner-rangers suspect murder if there aren't bullet-ridden bodies or some butchery.

I'd come up with a natural-looking how. Kinnerly could help with the when. I was an unlikely who. Three for our side. But something worried me.

One guy in town thought I would kill for money. I had to know who he was.

I put Adel in the cabin, told him to be quiet, and built a fire of oak slabs, activating the contact-me signal given in the stranger's telephone call. When it licked blue and orange flames, I dumped on a sack of damp garbage and watched smoke boil up.

In about fifteen minutes two men from the Forest Service wheeled up in a green truck pulling a little Cat on a lowboy.

The fat guy of the two stepped out, and hitched wrinkled britches. His hard hat glinted. His face had seen action. He said to the other man in the truck, "Wait here!" To me he yelled across fifty yards of brush, "What in hell do you think you're doing?"

I kicked a chunk onto the fire. "Burning trash." I let my mouth hang open. It wasn't hard to look stupid.

The thin one in the cab looked through the open door, slid down on his spine, and tugged his cap brim. "Belon, just tell the man the woods are dry and let's go," he said. "It's no big deal."

"Hell it ain't. It would have been a big deal if he'd started a woods fire." Hardhat came rolling toward me. "Mister, we've been chasing fires all over this county. Five today," he held up five sooty fingers, "then you go burn your god'am trash without tele-phoning the tower."

The guy way back in the cab yelled in sing-song, "This is not good public re-la-tions."

I looked at Hardhat and my voice got soft. "Sorry about that."

"Yeah? You're sorry. Ain't that peachy." He hitched the belt on his big belly. "*Some* folks got no consideration. If I wasn't on duty, I'd kick the crap out of them."

"You don't want to mess with me," I said softly.

He thought about that and looked me over. His face was deeply solemn while the process took place.

"Hey!" the guy in the truck yelled. "Let's go."

"You don't," I said again. "I was sending a message to someone else."

Hardhat widened his stance, spread his hands on his hips, and leaned in my face. He hadn't brushed his teeth. "You think you're some kind of a tough guy, soldier boy? Do your talking to me."

"Tell your boss if he wants to talk to me, I'm here."

"Listen, bozo. You talk to me!"

Red spots came into my field of vision and I got dizzy. I said for the benefit the boy in the truck, "I don't want any trouble." Then I whispered: "I've had too much fun screwing this guy's sister to be mad at him."

Hardhat's eyes bugged like a happy bar fighter's.

"I'll put this out," I said for the guy in the truck as I kicked the fire apart. "I don't want any trouble."

Hardhat was on the way, rolling. Big and tough as a Mack truck.

"Hey," the guy in the cab yelled, scrambling to open the driver-side door. "Hey! Belon, are you crazy?"

Hardhat's left chopped at my chin.

"Take it easy!" I said, again more for the other guy than Hardhat.

Hardhat's right hammered toward my collarbone. I wasn't there. My left fist shot between his lower ribs, making gristle spread. Wind whooshed from his lungs. The steel pot clattered on the ground. The man would have folded but he couldn't. My right hand clamped his wrist and spun him. My left hand hooked his greasy neck. I wrenched back his neck and jacked up his wrist. Muscles jelled. I told myself to let him go, but a kind of red haze fell before my eyes. "Shit," he grunted. The joint bound. It felt good. "Jesus," he whined. "Jesus God." I held him a minute, letting him sweat.

I almost yanked it. I almost broke the bone. I wanted to.

The kid jumped out of the truck and ran to us. He scrubbed his hands down his pants front. His face twisted so that you knew exactly what he had looked like as a baby when he was about to cry.

I shoved Hardhat against the log wall. He sagged there with his right arm high behind his back. His color faded to putty. "You're a crazy man," he said.

I laughed, but it came out a bark. "Yeah."

"Let's get out of here." The kid grabbed Hardhat by the shoulder. Hardhat yelped.

"You brought it on yourself. You had to pick a fight with this guy."

They stumbled to the truck. Dirt spun from the tire lugs as they wheeled out.

I stood watching, my hands on my hips, concentrating on breathing slowly and deeply. Damn it, I'd lost it again. That was piss-poor behavior for a guy once called Iceman. I sat on a log and thought cool thoughts.

There is a place I go, deep inside. I can get there just by thinking. I don't know where it is, but it's somewhere out West. Montana, maybe. I'm wrapped tight in a buffalo robe. Through a breathing hole I see the slopes of mountains. Pine or spruce trees stab into the snow. Crows skate across a gray, metallic sky. Tree trunks and branches are like indigo pen marks. Everything is gray

or black except for one moving spot. Sometimes the brightness—
the unbelievable hotness—is a cardinal that dips across a snowbank
and lights on a crusted limb. Sometimes it's the red Mackinaw of
a rider. His horse braces its forelegs and hunkers behind, breaking crust with every deep step. Crows circle overhead.

My breathing slows. It's very safe here. Very calm. Air under
my hood warms. My breath drifts outside the hood like a fog. I
don't hear the screams anymore, the screams of Vietnamese in a
room stained with blood and urine, and stinking of my fear. The
clicking I hear is only a bird's beak battering an icy branch, or a
stirrup iron in stiff leather, or ice crackling on sheathed limbs
moved by wind. It's not the sound of a pistol with one loaded
cylinder jammed against my head, snapping. . . .

A second truck arrived thirty minutes later. The driver had
wide shoulders and no hips, just enough blond hair to cover his
skull, and the practiced smile of a bureaucrat. He walked loose
and easy after stepping out of a green step-side pickup with the
emblem of the Forest Service on it.

I sprawled on a stump, waiting.

Notebook 5

26.

The man stopped ten feet away and pushed back his cap. "Mr. Carr, any particular reason why you didn't call the tower today before burning trash?" He chuckled. "I'm not asking why you nearly broke one of my men's arms. There could be reasons for that."

"I didn't call the tower because somebody told me to. Somebody who wants to do business with me thinks I take orders. He sent an underling to deal with me. I don't take orders. I'm an independent contractor."

"You disabled a man to say that?"

"I'm not proud of it. In fact, I'm very disappointed in myself. At the time it didn't mean a thing."

"It's against the law to burn outdoors without notifying us."

"A regulation?"

"The county supervisors have declared this a no-burn period."

"I'm good about things like stopping for railroad crossings and stop signs, keeping the Jeep inspected, and observing the speed limit."

"But you weren't good about it today."

"Not today."

"And that was for a reason?"

"Yeah."

He kicked a chunk of charcoal and stuck his hands in his side pockets. He looked at the sky and pursed his lips. His eyes were a peculiar green. "I hear you're in the stump removal business."

"I've removed a few under government contract." My grin wolfed at him. "I worked for the government, just like you do."

"I'm a bureaucrat, a guy with a desk job. You were a specialist. The tree I want stumped is the biggest in the woods. The fall of the damn thing could smash me."

"A big tree can kill anybody if it falls wrong. You've got to plan how to fell it, and where you're going to be when it cants, and out of reach of the branches when they try to drag you down." My voice whispered soft and sweet as a kindergarten teacher's. "That's why tree removal is well-paid."

"I'd pay five thousand for a clean job."

"Ten."

"I don't have that kind of money."

"There are guys in this town who will do a job for a gallon of rosie or a nickel grudge."

Rosie is cheap wine, and guys who kill for it are winos and Dr. Tish drinkers.

He walked two paces and turned, working up a case of indignation against me for asking ten thousand dollars for doing his killing. "Do you care who it is?"

"Yeah. I won't do children, nuns, old ladies, cripples, or friends of mine. Nobody that would drag in the F.B.I., like postmen, army officers, national park rangers, judges, or blacks. No preachers, because I'm superstitious. And nobody with a big accidental death benefit. Insurance detectives never give up."

He was looking at me as if I were a nasty puddle he had to cross. I was feeling somewhat like that about him, too.

"Six thousand. I could go six," he said.

"Ten. And the next time you dicker with me the price will be twelve."

The pretense folded. He wanted someone dead—reliably dead—and no trail to himself. Cost didn't matter.

I said, "Let me know three weeks in advance for a local job— six weeks for out of town."

"Then you need to know now."

"Who is it?"

"Tom Morris."

I kept smiling.

"Now that I know the hit, who're you?"

"Jeff Ballard."

"OK, Jeff Ballard. Why do you want Tom Morris dead, and does anybody know you do? I have to know that because if you get caught, I get caught."

"Fifteen years ago he cheated me out of our farm."

I knew the Old Ballard place. That's what people still called the sprawl of fescue and coastal Bermuda grasses, big white barn, and two-story white house sheltered by old oaks. It was the kind of place that made a man a planter rather than a farmer.

"Have you threatened him?"

"I've been smiling in his face for years." He smiled a broad, friendly smile.

"What else?"

"He had an affair with my wife. She divorced me over it."

I watched him for signs of deception. The hands and feet speak the truest language. He was telling the truth, or at least part of it.

"I'll let you know in a couple of days," I said. "The answer will be *yes* or *no* on a single sheet of notepaper."

If it was *yes* I said he was to deliver the money in old bills and I would let him know the date and time to cover with an alibi. If *no* he was never to come near me again.

27.

I cut wood the rest of the day. When I showered and slid between flannel sheets I should have slept. But thoughts chased around in my mind the way naked people chase around the friezes on Greek urns.

In the dream I was chasing Kinnerly, and she chased me. We were naked on this frieze, going around and around.

I had a hooked nose, a running band around long, curly hair, good flat muscles, and a little Greek cock at half ready.

Kinnerly's butt flexed just out of reach. Her long foreleg stretched like a horse's in jumping a fence. She half turned, showing her breasts in profile. Her hair bushed like a curly mop. The potter had painted us off-white, with blue eyes, against a yellow background.

Ahead of her—or maybe behind me—a man ran spraddle-legged, with his arms wrapped around a jar of gold coins. He wore a senatorial beard like a disguise.

I fretted and turned in bed until consciousness came. In the dream who was chasing whom, and for what? Why did the man, whose face blurred like an image on an old coin, look senatorial, when I merely looked bare-assed?

I didn't like the way he was coming up on my blind side.

I sucked on the idea of somebody on my blind side the way you worry a tooth that seeps a bad taste. Then I called Harry Reinberg, a friend who works in insurance investigations. Commercial Credit pays him piece work, so much for each investigation he completes and writes up. He works fast.

Harry is a big, slope-shouldered guy with no hair on top, hard eyes, and a tight smile. We were in the army together. Harry is loyal.

"Sure," he said, yawning over the telephone. Harry covers five counties in north Mississippi, and always yawns when I call. "I'll check this guy out."

He asked why I didn't give him a call when I was in Memphis. He said we ought to get together. So we yakkety-yakked about how we were going to do that, and about who we'd seen from the old unit. When the things had been said that had to be said, we hung up.

Two days later I drove to a pay phone to call Harry. Don't know why I didn't use the home phone for a second call. Call it paranoia.

Blue jays scratched leaves on warming ground and cocked their heads to listen deep. Children ran and screamed, released from school. I smiled and waved. They smiled and waved.

There was the edge to Harry's voice I'd heard in Vietnam. After a successful recon he'd grin and shift his weight from foot to foot like a kid who has to go to the bathroom but is having so much fun he can't spare the time.

"—Listen, Lieut, I've got something." Harry calls me "Lieut" because it suits his fancy. He promoted me on his own without consulting the army.

"Yeah?"

"Your man needs money. He's been cozy with a lady that has it. I mean real cozy."

"What's her name?"

"Wait a minute." There was the sound of pages flipping. He mumbled something I couldn't understand.

"What? Get the pencil out of your mouth."

"Emily Craddock, a widow."

"Uh-huh," I said, and paused as if to write it down.

"That one didn't work out. Then he slipped around with Kinnerly Morris." He spelled her name for me. Every letter was like a dentist's drill punching into pulp. "She's married to the richest guy in town. I've got the address. It's 190 Country Club Road."

"Let me make a note." I counted to six. "You sure about the women?"

Harry's breathing got audible. He doesn't like his recon questioned.

"OK, you're sure. Is he still seeing Kinnerly Morris?"

"Don't know."

"Uh-huh. Is he into drugs? Any connection with rough stuff?"

"Didn't turn up. He's pretty clean. No arrest record. Doesn't drink or smoke."

"It looks to me like he's trying to marry money."

"Ain't we all?" Harry laughed.

"I owe you one, Harry. Call on me."

"I will. There's one more thing."

"Yeah?"

"This is kinda strange. Sooner or later something unpleasant happens to people who cross Ballard."

"Is that right?"

"He's lucky that way."

"What kind of unpleasantness?"

"Well, this sounds like a stretch. A farmer runs over Ballard's dog, then a scrub bull with brucellosis breaks in with the farmer's cows. Bangs out the whole herd. *So what?* I think. *Coincidence,* I think. Ballard argues with a neighbor about a land line, and the neighbor has her bank loan called. A guy who took him for five thousand in a Ponzi scheme serves a term in white-collar jail, gets out, and right away crashes a little airplane he made from a kit. Crippled the pilot, ex-Air Force, for life. The AAA found nothing wrong with the plane. Fuel failure, apparently. Some evidence that the fuel was contaminated, but nothing connected the crash to sabotage."

"Bad luck plagues his enemies."

"And the worse people piss him off, the worse luck they have. Remember the *Lil' Abner* character, the guy with the black cloud over his head?"

"Joe Btsfplk."

"That's Ballard—Joe Btsfplk!"

"Thanks for the recon. You're the best. What do I owe?" I said, and meant it, because recon is Harry's profession.

"This one wasn't business, it was pleasure. Take care, Lieut."

"You, too, Harry. And thanks."

I hung the handset in the hook and stared through the smudgy glass of the telephone booth into a spring-like day. I flipped the coin release lever where urgent thumbs had worn off the finish. Nothing came out. Nothing should have. Below the box hung an armored cord. I reached for the loop and slipped the metal coils between my fingers like a rosary, working them back and forth. Then—I don't know why—I snatched down, trying to break the metal and the telephone cord inside. It was the petulant act of a kid. I succeeded only in hurting my hand.

I left the booth, walked to the Jeep, crawled in, and drove slowly home.

A pretty college kid in a red sweater wobbled a bicycle on the wrong side of the road and waved in apology. Instead of smiling because of the unearned pleasure her beauty gave me, I scowled. She gave me the finger. I laughed, astonished. The jar of my laughter didn't help the pain working in my left eye and at the back of my neck. It felt like the beginning of a migraine.

It is before he uncases a weapon that a man must think. I stopped by a mail box, scribbled "No" on a pad I keep in the Jeep, stuck the note in an envelope I'd pre-addressed to Jeff Ballard, and dropped it in.

28.

When I got home I let Adel outside to do his business, and let him back in. Then I picked up a fifth of Dant's ten-year-old bourbon, a glass, a tray of ice, *The Pocket Book of Verse,* and *Chief Modern Poets of Britain.* I turned on Vivaldi's *L'Estro Armonico, Opus 3,* and crawled into bed.

I read awhile and drank awhile. Somehow, without my knowing it, the night slipped away.

The next morning the stereo roared air. The amplifier flashed red lights and a blur of green ones. I cracked an eye at winter seeping under the shades and inched an arm and a foot across the bed. The Dant bottle clattered down. A book of poetry tumbled from my lap. I bent very slowly for it, holding in my brains with my fingers. Adel came to the bed. "No petting," I whispered.

A childproof aspirin bottle wouldn't open to my fumble. I gulped whiskey-tasting water from a glass that had left a circle on the bedside table, and staggered around the loft, looking for my boots. Adel scrambled down the coiled stairway and walked to the door, wiggling from his neck to his tail. He stared at the door, he stared at me. Though he couldn't speak, Adel could generate waves of intense communication.

"Give me a minute, will you?" I complained. He wouldn't. Those hazel eyes burned into mine. I went down the circular metal stairway—something like a stairway in a submarine—walked delicately across cold floorboards on bare feet, and let him out. My head was swimming. I needed hard manual labor, that's what I needed. And no people around.

The place where I'd bought stumpage was in the National Forest. Pines stood tall and spindly in crowded conditions, like people in a city, dependent upon each other for the strength to stand.

The Soil Conservation Service had poisoned the native hardwoods and planted loblolly pine, promising to make unproductive land productive and to control soil erosion. When the program lost funding, most of the men in green left. Signs proclaiming REFORESTATION CAPITAL OF THE WORLD rotted. Woodpeckers and pine beetles thrived in the ecological deserts that pine forests are.

I parked at the stand I had bought, unloaded the chain saw, and walked into a thicket. When I opened the choke and tugged the starter, the McCullouch popped, blew smoke, and whirred its teeth as if it hoped to catch a sleeve or an arm unaware. I shoved the choke in half-way. The chain slowed and stilled. The hornety buzz of the motor evened to a more contented putter.

I bent my back, held the blade to a trunk, and triggered the gas. The chain chewed into yellow wood and ground out anthills of sawdust. A pine scent drifted into the air. When I shoved the little trunk, the tree trembled, swished through other trees, and thumped to earth.

I cut a circle of marked loblollies. Then I unjoined the trunks, nudging the blade tip upward to keep it clear of dirt. Sweat trickled under my arms and ran cold against my chest.

Cutting is rote work. The muscles control and the mind watches. *Cut, move, cut.*

A Forest Service truck churned by on the road, slinging gravel and dust. I didn't wave. The saw held my attention. As my buddies say, "A saw don't care what it cuts, or who."

A circle opened around me. Sunlight flowed behind the blade, reaching private places. Stumps gave off a heady aroma. Sawdust and resin stuck to my hands and face.

I thinned half an acre and bucked the trunks to length. It's cheaper to cut trees than it is to collect and reprocess paper. The saw doesn't care. I care, but I have to eat.

I set the saw down, put both hands in the middle of my back and straightened. The air stank of gasoline fumes. A desolate patch of green needles and angled limbs and unjoined trunks lay around me.

When I work physically and give my mind a rest, answers to my questions have a way of working to the surface.

I almost felt sorry for Tom Morris. The poor sonofabitch. His wife wanted him dead and found a fool to kill him. When sex wasn't working fast enough, her boyfriend upped the ante by $10,000. They didn't care about a divorce because they wanted the guy's entire estate. I was the monkey's paw to get it for them.

OK, I thought. Here's the way it will go down.

As soon as I hit her husband, Kinnerly will do me in. Probably as I remove the paintings. She will explain that she took a sleeping pill but awoke to a strange sound. She stumbled to the dining room and found her husband dead, and me with a smoking gun in one hand and a Stubbs painting in the other. *Bang!* Before she knew it, she'd fired.

If that scenario didn't work out, there was a backup. After doing the job, I'd get away. I'd wait for Kinnerly to join me. Instead, there would be a one-car accident. My car would burn so fiercely my body would be identifiable only by my metal social security card or my dog tags. There would be no reason to autopsy, no reason to explore the possibility of murder, it would all be clean.

Only one thing was wrong with their plans.

They'd picked the wrong patsy.

29.

I was shooting a crossbow when she arrived in response to my coded call. An empty milk jug and a piece of extruded polystyrene stood fifty yards away in front of a couple of hay bales. I fired a fourteen-inch bolt. It zipped through the jug and the bale of hay behind it, making a hell of a hole.

She stepped out of her car and exclaimed, "Why, it's an arbalest!"

"Crossbow," I said irritably. "People have said crossbow for two hundred years."

"May I hold it?" She was a little girl wanting to play with a boy's toy—hands out, head cocked, bright smile.

I'd made the weapon for taking deer. Polished walnut shoulder inserts contrasted with a flat aluminum barrel and handgrip.

About fourteen dollars' worth of aluminum flat stock, six dollars' worth of walnut billets, seven of assorted bolts, pins and other minor hardware, and sixty-seven of prod and Dacron cable from Barnett International had produced a tool capable of six-inch groups at fifty yards. Anyone tracking weapon sales wouldn't find it on inventory lists, or my name as a purchaser.

I clamped the stock between my thighs, gripped the neck, and cranked the 170-pound cable weight with a steel cocking rod. The bow fired a fourteen-inch Easton bolt with a 126-grain field point. The point sits on the end of the bolt like a large-diameter bullet.

Kinnerly snugged the stock to her right shoulder. Her left elbow socketed into the little hollow above her hip. Her left hand acted as fulcrum. The index and second fingers pointed under the forearm as she squeezed the trigger. The bolt hummed away and thonked into twelve inches of polystyrene before I could blink. If she had been aiming at a man, the bolt would have skewered him.

"Did I do it right?"

Oh, yeah, babe. You do everything right, I thought. I said, "You're playing Southern woman again."

"Can't fool you?"

You do it all the time, I thought. But I smiled.

Someone had taught her to use a rifle. The skill transfers. As she continued to fire I said, "Good shot," or, "A little wide," and clamped my jaws to keep from saying more.

"Are you all right?" she asked.

"Fine."

When she was through shooting we went inside and I struck a match to a laid fire.

She sat beside me, tucked herself under my arm, and started to say how much she'd missed me, and that she couldn't bear being apart a single day.

I drank a bourbon double, and then another. She chattered on, talking around the edge of something bigger.

She meant to kill me. I pulled her to me, and the Seven-Up in her glass splashed on her tan sweater. I kissed her hard and put my hand under her skirt. She closed her knees. "Stop it!" she said.

There is nothing sexy about your hand clamped between a woman's knees. I went to the kitchen and poured a double. When I got back Kinnerly stood by the fire, staring into it.

War pares away the layer of restraint and manners that makes people civilized. Mine was thin before I figured out the woman I loved planned to kill me. I wanted to kill her, too. I want to fuck her to death. I crowded her. She squeezed around, not understanding at first. "All right. Let's go upstairs."

I gripped her arms and kissed her hard, mashing her lips, forcing them open.

She twisted in my grasp. "Are you drunk?"

I didn't stop.

"I mean it, Luke!"

I shoved her hard toward the couch, but she landed on her feet. From somewhere I didn't see, her locked hands wedged up and smacked my chin . . . I hate the sound of teeth and crowns clacking. It brings back memories of the teeth the Cong broke.

I touched the floor with one hand and felt inside my mouth with the other. She weighed seventy pounds less and stood ten inches shorter. I was an ex-Ranger. She was an ex-Girl Scout.

"Oh, my God," she said tonelessly. She edged toward the door at an angle, looking back. "I came here to tell you—oh, what does it matter? I've made everything hopeless."

"I've got something to say, too." I walked to the couch and sat down.

She twisted her rings.

I pointed at the hassock. "Sit."

"I'm not your dog!"

Across the room Adel plopped his butt on the floor, but he wasn't supposed to because I hadn't said his name. Kinnerly kneed the hassock back three feet to show her independence, and sat with her knees tightly together.

"I don't know where to start," she said. "I've pre-experienced this conversation, but what I've imagined doesn't work, so I'll just begin." She took a deep breath. "Things are not what they've seemed."

"Things are not what they've *seemed?*"

She jumped up. "Don't make fun of me!"

"Say what you came to say." I wanted to hear the improbable lie she would tell, but she didn't speak.

"OK, then. Grabbing you the way I did was wrong."

"I didn't mean to hit you, either. I won't ever knock you down again." She laughed. "That didn't sound the way I meant it to."

I felt my lower jaw. She came to me and kissed it. My resistance began to melt. We went through the silly business of making up. A voice warned *she used you,* but I stifled it. The difference between Harry's report and what I wanted to believe was too great.

We sat on the couch. She tucked herself under my arm and looked up. I kissed her. I kissed her again. Her lips opened, and the suspicion that lingered in my mind didn't matter. Our bodies chose what came next.

Later, in a quiet voice she confessed all that Harry's recon had turned up.

"Before you came back to town I had an affair with another man. I was lonely and he made me feel wanted. I thought he was safe and a gentleman."

Her hand lay in mine. I looked at it as I massaged her fingers.

"I was wrong about that and a lot more. He liked me saying sexy things on the telephone. I had never done that before, and it was exciting to us both. He made tapes and mailed me a copy." She put her hand to her face. "They made me blush."

I figured she'd last blushed at fourteen or fifteen, but it was a harmless lie. "Now it's blackmail?"

"One day he wants a loan. Another, he says if something happens to Tom, then I'll have to marry him. He says the tapes make me an accomplice."

She glanced at my expression. "He doesn't want me in bed anymore."

Like hell. I pictured them together, but my expression told her nothing. My thigh pressed warm against hers, my fingers interlaced her slim ones.

Somewhere outside, that silly mockingbird that sang all winter trilled. Then a cloud passed overhead and the shades darkened. The bird broke off his song mid-note.

When I was a boy, birds were sailing through the sky anytime I looked up: sparrows, blackbirds, cedar waxwings. I wanted to think about the flight of birds, about feather structure, horn beaks, and scaled feet. I wanted to think about anything except Kinnerly on the front seat of Ballard's car with the steering wheel in the way, or in bed in an Indian-run motel, listening to the whisper of a window air conditioner.

"Who's the guy?"

"Jeff Ballard. Do you know him?"

It was an echo of what she had said about her husband.

"*Do you know him?*"

"We've met."

She pressed close, making contact. "I'm frightened, darling. I'm frightened out of my wits by Jeff Ballard and his grudges about land and his first wife and his jealousy of me. I'm frightened about us, and about what we were thinking of doing. I just want us to be happy."

"I want it, too," I said.

As we dressed she held up her face to be kissed. Her lips were yielding and sweet.

"See me soon, darling?" she said as she turned in the door.

"Of course."

She smiled and shut my door as if not to awaken a sleeper.

We didn't meet for ten days. She didn't call. I made no effort to see her. When we did meet it was at the Cherow brothers' farm, where I agreed to kill her husband.

Ballard was getting one free.

Notebook 6

30.

The Bridge County coroner-ranger, D.W. "Happy" Davis, dresses for hearings in a somber gray suit that droops on his huge frame. At six-feet-five and 280 pounds, he campaigned for office with great solemnity. His slogan was, "A BIG man for a BIG job." His opponent, an ex-bootlegger, had as his campaign manager a talking beagle named Whisky, who barked stump speeches, after which he watered stumps. The ex-bootlegger called the office the most meaningless in the state, and said he was better suited for meaningless office than his opponent, Happy Davis.

Mississippi coroner-rangers round up and impound stray livestock on public roads and determine the cause of suspicious or violent human death. To win office as a coroner-ranger, a man or woman must be a resident of Bridge County, a registered voter, and have a lot of friends who vote. No medical knowledge is required.

Happy's procedure on the rare occasions when an inquest is held is to first take the coroner's jury to view the body. He then re-assembles them in county court—a long, high-ceilinged room with the half-circle of the bar in front, and beyond that the judges' bench, and on either side of the judges' bench, dangling limply from staffs, the gold-bedecked flags of the United States of America and the sovereign state of Mississippi.

Happy huffs his way to the bench, greets any county officials present with big, soft handshakes, and seats himself with a sigh. He reshapes the loose wad of blank paper he habitually carries and places it on the judge's bench as if it carries significance. He looks up, re-greets the jury, and explains that members should listen carefully to witnesses because testimony can help them in their deliberations. He says he has asked the county attorney to be present to assist witnesses and jury in bringing out the evidence.

The courtroom was crowded. No coroner's inquest had excited so much county interest since a fourteen-year-old white boy was found hanged in a barn, the boy, or someone, having twisted baling wire into a rope and tied a perfect hangman's knot. What had drawn the audience this day was a rumor that at death Tom Morris had turned black.

I came early to the inquest, stood in back of the courtroom until I located Kinnerly on the first row, and squeezed into a seat on the fifth. The lady beside me immediately turned to talk. She was a faded blonde, still pretty, about twenty years older than I.

"Tom Morris's great-great grandfather was an overseer, you know, on the Beecham plantation?" she whispered. Her sentence ended with a rising inflection, turning a statement of fact into a question.

"I didn't know," I whispered.

"There were lots of mixed breeds on Beecham Plantation. Like they—you know, like the overseers and other young men—used the women? That's where trashy books about the South say mestizos come from, anyway." She lifted a hand to her mouth, as if to hide a giggle.

"I see."

"And after the war—after emancipation?—it was common practice for former slaves to take their owner's name or the plantation name."

"Yes, I know."

"Well, some of the light skinned ex-slave women took up with white trash in the county, and they had white-skinned, freckled children. I don't know why it was tolerated when the Klan was active, but the Klan was white trash, too. Anyway, girl babies from those families grew up and some of them set up housekeeping with low-class whites. The men couldn't intermarry, even if they wanted to. It was against the law."

"The law against miscegenation."

Her voice lowered, became more confidential. "Some Beecham women started claiming to be white Cherokees. Didn't change their names legally, mind you, just started calling themselves by the family name Drigger." She paused. "Let me tell the rest of this just as my husband told it to me . . . If the court recognized a common-law marriage existed with one of these Driggers after the father of children died, the children somehow *became* white. Sort of white. Do you understand? I don't know why it should be, but they did. My husband Hollis explained it better, maybe."

"Are you suggesting Tom Morris turned dark when he died because he had a black ancestor?"

She nodded emphatically. "It shows up somehow. And his grandmother was a Mabel Drigger."

"Oh," I said. But it was too much to hope that coroner's jury members might believe the absurd old southern legalism that "one drop of 'black' blood makes a man black" had physical reality.

The last spaces on the wooden benches filled. A scattered row of men stood in back. Down the row to my left I noticed Barbara Cumbest, a community vulture ready to feast on anyone's juicy trouble. She was knitting something long and stringy that looped out of her knitting bag like guts out of a gored horse.

The hum of noise in the courtroom died. In a high, jumpy voice, Happy Davis gave the coroner's jury its charge and introduced the county attorney. On cue Ben Lilly Kelly got to his feet. He's a small man with large eyes and wavy brown hair. In his characteristic courtroom stance, with one hand in the side pocket of his suit coat and one foot behind its opposite, he gives the impression of being an amputee.

As an undergraduate, Ben Lilly majored in drama. His part-time responsibility as county attorney is to translate law and regulation to public officials. He memorializes interesting cases from his public and private practice with titles out of *Perry Mason*. The brutal murder of a woman operating a bottle cleaner at the dairy became "The Case of the Bludgeoned Milkmaid." "The Man with the Golden Dong" was a track star who received a settlement for invasion of privacy because a Jackson newspaper published a cutline headed "Double Exposure," along with a picture revealing anatomy he intended to keep in his shorts.

"Call your first witness, Mr. Kelly," Happy Davis said.

Ben Lilly tenderly held Kinnerly's arm and led her to the stand. I tried not to stare until I noticed everyone around me was staring. In a dark dress and wearing no makeup, crumpling a handkerchief in her hand, she testified under oath that she last saw her husband at 7:00 P.M. on November the third when he left home to attend an 8:00 P.M. meeting in Pontotoc. She said her husband owned a cabin on Woodlie Road, but she did not know why he was driving there that night. No, her husband did not have any enemies.

"Everyone loved Tom," she said.

Following Kinnerly to the stand was deputy sheriff Joe Whaley, who investigated the accident when it was reported at 10:03 A.M. Wednesday. He testified that he found brake marks on Woodlie Road indicating that a car operated by the deceased was traveling at high speed. He found a dead doe in a ditch eighteen feet from the vehicle. He testified that the road bank was churned and cut as if there had been an attempt to back the vehicle from the ditch.

Ben Lilly's head came up slowly and dramatically. It was a trick of his when he wanted a jury to pay attention. His gold pen swirled in air, and he made a note.

Deputy Sheriff Whaley testified further that the grille of the Porsche was "bashed" from a collision, that the left fender was "bashed," and that deer hair and blood had been collected.

"That's what those biology folks at the university say it is. Of course, anybody knows what deer hair looks like!"

The members of the coroner's jury, who had been chosen from bystanders at the courthouse that morning, grinned and nodded.

Ben Lilly asked Whaley if he took photographs of the Porsche automobile and its tire tracks. Whaley shifted a spiral-bound notebook from one hand to the other.

"Yes, sir, I did."

Ben Lilly then led him to describe in detail the appearance of the deer's shoulder and ribs. He asked Whaley to again describe damage to the vehicle. Then he said casually, "Mr. Whaley, describe to this jury the deceased's appearance."

A hush fell upon the courtroom.

"Well, sir, on the back seat he had this long, whitish coat. London Fog was the label on it. I know that label because—"

"—Yes, sir. If you will, please, just tell us what you first observed about the *deceased* and recorded in that notebook in your hand immediately after you came upon the scene."

"The deceased was wearing a brown suit of clothes and brown shoes. Church's was the brand of the shoes. Real fancy. Harris Tweed was the label in the clothes. In his pocket he had a snakeskin wallet, a handkerchief, a pocket comb, four dimes and a nickel, and a little gold-handled knife. The seat anchor of the car was broke and he was scrunched up under the wheel." Whaley twisted his body to illustrate. "His face was black and—"

"—His face was what?"

"Black. Darkish."

A gasp went through the courtroom. Not of surprise. People looked at one another, nodded, and voices buzzed. Happy Davis tapped his gavel.

Ben Lilly said, "In your capacity as an investigating officer, not as a person with any special medical training or expertise— you're not, are you?"

"Not what, Ben?" Whaley said.

"A person with special medical training or expertise."

"No, sir."

"Would you say that the appearance of the deceased was consistent with that of victims of accidents whose necks were broken in those cases which you have previously investigated?"

"Yes, sir, I'd say that. Sure would. Sometimes the face turns darkish if the neck is broke."

"Would the face look the same if the neck of a victim was broken on purpose?"

"I never have seen one so far as I know."

"What are you basing your testimony on about the appearance of this deceased person, Tom Morris?"

"Seeing his body, and thirty years of reporting accidents."

In further testimony, Whaley said he telephoned the Sportsman's Club president and confirmed that Morris was to have made a speech there Tuesday, but didn't show up. This hearsay went unchallenged since coroner's jury proceedings are not adversarial.

Whaley said he found notes on pages of paper in the victim's pocket that appeared to be speech notes.

"Could've been," he said. "Anyway, they were about hunting." A separate sheet of paper said "sunglasses." Kelly introduced the pages into evidence and they were shown to the jury. Whaley said a key that fit the Porsche was in the ignition, and the motor had been turned off.

Kelly slowly and dramatically lifted his gaze and fixed it upon the deputy.

"Turned off? The motor key was in the off position? Are you sure?"

Whaley nodded. "Yes, sir."

"Had you touched the key?"

Whaley looked cross. "I did not."

"Do you know whether the person who discovered the accident cut the motor?"

"No, he didn't. And you've brought him here to say so." Whaley nodded at a man in the first row.

Jack Dunn, a red-faced man with a veined nose, testified that when he found the body he didn't cut the ignition. He didn't reach across the body or get inside the car because he was "scared of the dead."

Ben Lilly then introduced the deposition of Dr. D.W. Joiner, emergency-room physician at City Hospital. It said he examined the body of Tom Morris and found that Morris had suffered a broken neck. Superficial abrasions appeared on the neck, and a simple puncture appeared in the thigh. The puncture had bled slightly.

Ben Lilly said that in the light of the information revealed in the deposition he thought it essential that Dr. Joiner be compelled to testify in person.

The coroner shook his head. His fat lips twisted. "Now, Ben, you know we can't call doctors away from their job of saving lives. We got everything Dr. Joiner's got to say right there in black and white."

Ben Lilly got excited. He talked about the road being cut from tires spinning backward. He talked about the key being in the ignition, but turned off. He said the victim had suffered a broken neck but the Porsche was only slightly damaged. He called attention to a note in the victim's pocket that said "sunglasses," and made much of it. There was an unexplained puncture in the thigh. He summed by saying it was inescapably clear that Tom Morris was the victim of homicide by a person or persons unknown.

Happy waited patiently, and when Ben Lilly indicated he was through Happy addressed the jury. He said they were to rule on the cause of Tom Morris's death according to their examination of the body and the evidence before them. If they found Tom Morris died by accident, well and good. If the evidence showed he did not die by accident, but by the actions or at the hands of a person or persons unknown, they should say that. They didn't have to produce a suspect, or accuse anyone of a crime.

After receiving the coroner's instruction, the jury filed out of the courtroom. After five or ten minutes—which seemed like thirty to me—the men filed back and took seats in the box. The verdict was passed up on what looked to be a page of unbleached paper, the kind in a cheap school tablet.

Happy Davis read it silently, then aloud: "We find that the deceased, Tom Morris, died accidentally of a broken neck when his car ran into a deer."

Ben Lilly opened his small hands and lifted his shoulders in a gesture of resignation. Barbara Cumbest glared left and right and turned to the people behind us. *It was murder!* her expression declared. She lowered her face over the skein of her knitting, and the needles clicked.

Happy Davis thanked the jury for their service at the inquest, tapped his gavel, and announced, "This hearing is dismissed!" Kinnerly made a quick escape through a side door that led down a staircase to the chancery clerk's office. The audience stood in the spaces between benches, smiling and talking.

Most of them must have known there was more to come. A coroner's jury verdict couldn't prevent the district attorney from asking a grand jury to indict if he found evidence to believe a crime had been committed. We had a brainy sheriff, and Ben Lilly's interest was aroused. The next day at the coffee shop I overheard some businessmen laughing over the soubriquet Ben Lilly had given Tom Morris's death. It was already a "case"—"The Case of the Black-Faced White Man."

31.

I flopped on the bed. The bedspread was a brown-and-white oat-meal color that harmonized with a chocolate rug. A blue pottery lamp stood on the bedside table. Two pictures of horse paintings, reproductions of reproductions, hung on off-white walls.

We were in Tennessee in an out-of-the-way motel where I'd paid cash for a double and given a false name and the wrong car license number. Still, our meeting wasn't smart. Never mind that. We had a lot to settle.

Kinnerly was sitting on a stool looking critically at herself in the dresser mirror. I reminded her I'd forgotten to remove her note from Tom's pocket.

"It doesn't matter," she said.

It did matter. "What did you tell the boy about today?"

"I said I had to come to Memphis and then might go to

Dyersburg, that I was making arrangements about continuing his daddy's businesses."

"And?"

She made an airy gesture. "Nothing. He smiled and said good-bye, and gave me a kiss on the cheek."

"That was it?"

"Don't worry about Tommy. I can wrap him around my little finger. His kiss wasn't two inches from my lips."

"He's got a crush on you. He'll watch every move you make."

"All right, Luke." Her voice sounded tired. "My mind doesn't work like that."

"It better."

"Don't enforce on me."

We stared at each other. Then I looked at the ceiling, biting off words. Somebody would likely be charged with murder. The characters in the domestic triangle the D.A. would spin out would be "the beautiful-but-spoiled wife," "the decorated-but-regrettably-murderous veteran," and "the rich-unresponsive husband." Sex, money, and greed.

"Dead men don't try to back up after a collision and then turn off the ignition key," I told Kinnerly. "That coroner's verdict wasn't worth a dime to us. We're lucky they didn't dust that sheet of paper and find your prints. They would have, if the deputies hadn't passed it around and contaminated the evidence."

Kinnerly looked at me from the mirror. "What was it like? I don't want the details, but what did it feel like? Were you excited?"

"I was scared."

"No, really. Tell me." She came to the bed and lay down.

"At first I felt like a man going on a mission."

She stroked her hair. "You don't love me, not really. I've gotten into murder, and you don't truly love me."

"I love you."

"No, I'm just another woman to you. It scares me a little. You scare me. You're a dangerous man." She turned onto her back, drunk with images she was pulling from dark places.

"Not now, Kinnerly. Fix us a drink."

She slid across the bed, mouth in a pout, and flounced across the room. I could see one of her in the flesh, and another reflected in the mirror—curves, flatness, sulky expression and pooky lips. I felt an itch for her that had been missing since we had done murder.

"Come here."

She leaned across the bed and handed me a plastic glass of whisky and ice. "I'm going out."

I caught her arm lightly. "Bad timing."

She averted her gaze. "I may be gone an hour, or I may go home." She paused, then enunciated very clearly, "—you son of a bitch!"

I lifted my glass. She jammed her arms into her coat sleeves, stalked out, and banged the door.

I got the bottle and drank a third of it. Then I went to the john. When she returned I came into the bedroom, walking lightly. She looked at me and her eyes widened. "Who are you, Luke?"

"What does that mean?"

"I mean, who *are* you? Where have you been? Where are you going?"

I poured three fingers of whisky and grinned.

"I looked up a story about you on microfilm. About the prison camp and the torture. And how you escaped. And the North Vietnamese after you. Everyone else who ran away was caught. But not you."

"No."

"And when you told military intelligence what you'd done,

they didn't believe you because escape wasn't possible. They thought you might have become a double agent."

I laughed.

She lifted her right hand to the V of her blouse. "You *did* it, didn't you Luke?" The subject had changed. She didn't mean escape. She meant Tom. She slid the blouse off and unhooked the center of the bra.

She wiggled the skirt down, and the half-slip. Her breasts shook independently.

"Don't do that."

She hooked her fingers in the panties and inched them over the round of belly. "Come here, Luke."

There were long, swelling legs with a slender hollow between the thighs. White panties looped around her feet. She stepped out of them. "I'm wet."

She sank onto the striped couch. Her thighs separated. She ran her fingers over her breasts, and her nipples hardened. "Take off your pants, Luke."

"No." I didn't know where I would stop with her, or if I could.

"Take them off, Luke." She lifted her arms.

I took them off, and the shirt, too. The trousers with the .38 in the pocket holster thumped on the carpet. I was as hard and ready as that gun.

I crossed to the couch, and she sat up and took me between her lips.

"You won't like it tonight."

After awhile she reached for a pillow to tuck under her ass. "Yes, I will."

That night she danced on Tom's grave.

32.

I drove to Bridgeport the next day and checked my mail at the post office. One letter was in the slot. The message was short: "You think you got away with it. You won't. Believe me, you won't."

Angus? It didn't seem his style.

When I returned to my cabin the phone was ringing.

"Good buddy, this is Angus here," he said. "Where you been?"

"Cutting pulp."

"I reckon you know the town is buzzing. Don't nobody believe Tom's death was a acci-dent. It's all folks talk about."

"Is that right?"

"Miz Morris is gonna get her life insurance check, though, on account of that coroner's jury report. It don't amount to much.

Ten thousand is all the old boy had." He chuckled. "I thought you might want to give it to me."

"I don't know what you're talking about."

"Them legal ads have already been run in the paper. Folks are filing their claims against the estate. I thought I'd do you the favor of filing mine private-like."

I tried to churn up anger. "Listen, fuckhead—"

He chuckled. "Oh, I know you got to talk it over with her. It's her money. I can wait a day or two."

I hung up and dialed the *Sentinel* to put in an advertisement activating the contact-me signal Kinnerly and I had agreed upon. "Tools for sale," I told the clerk, and gave her my telephone number. "Don't put my name in the ad. I'm just giving you this for billing purposes. It's Luke Carr. That's right. Luke Carr. General delivery . . . "

The next morning at 10:05 I drove to the county library, where the clock above the door is forever fixed at 9:02. Our library is a bad architect's version of Greek Revival. Four vertical marble stripes on its red-brick face suggest white columns. The yellow walls inside display paintings of the sentimental William Aiken Walker school of art: happy colored folk picking cotton, driving mules, or bending over wash pots. The shelves downstairs hold magazines, current periodicals, records, and nonfiction. Fiction is upstairs.

Ugly, orange carpet absorbs all the sound it can, but noise bounces off the walls and vibrates the framed canvases. A fat black employee and a skinny white one yell to each other over the voices of the children left at the library for babysitting.

I looked though a *National Geographic* magazine dated 1972 and read "What is Tundra?" and "The Asmat of New Guinea." I read the New Albany *Gazette*, folded it, and put it in the rack. Then I climbed to the fiction section.

Ten minutes later Kinnerly's voice called from below, "Hello, girls! I'm looking for John O'Hara and Mr. Updike. Upstairs? Mary, would you be a dear and call my son Tommy and tell him I'm on the way? Say I stopped in for some books?"

It sounded too bright, too cheerful for a new widow. I stared at the pages of *Justine,* open in my hand, and listened for a creak of the stairs.

Unexpectedly, she rounded the aisle. We were four feet apart. I saw that not-quite-perfect face—thick brows, small, firm nose. Her eye-whites were so clear they looked bluish. She wore one strand of pearls and carried a camel coat. We touched hands, smiled. Her eyes searched my face. I took a step closer and said, "What if these people don't know Mr. Updike?"

"Shame on them!"

"Listen, Angus telephoned. He wants the insurance money, all of it."

The second floor was empty. I'd walked the aisles to be certain, but I whispered.

"How *dare* he?"

"Take it easy."

"Tom took him away from that piddling forestry job, made him a manager, and paid him a good wage." Her eyes were deep-down hard.

"It's pay him off, or—"

"This wouldn't be the end. He'd want more. The insurance money is *mine.* I'm the beneficiary, it doesn't go through the estate."

"You're right. He will want more."

The stairs creaked. I moved to the aisle where the light was better. No one was in sight. She composed her face, took a deep breath, and made a decision. "Let's pay."

"Yeah, what's $10,000?"

"Be sure Angus doesn't have someone photograph you when

you pay him." She fumbled in her purse. "Where are my keys? I've got to go."

"Remember, this won't be the end of it."

There was a sound. I distinctly heard a sound . . . upstairs. My forefinger went to my lips. Kinnerly's eyes widened. We were quiet except for our breathing. Someone was one section over, close enough to have heard us.

I went there and found him.

He was a tousle-haired kid dressed in a red sweatshirt and tiny Levis, about five. A little drool hung from his lip. He rocked in a red chair and held a picture book.

"Hi. I didn't see you when I came up. Where's mommy?" I said.

He looked at his book and rocked.

"Aren't you going to say, hi?"

"Hi."

"Where's mommy?"

A wet finger slid out of his mouth and pointed to the stairs.

"That's nice. You're reading, too."

He looked at me as if I were demented. "I can't read."

"You will be able to soon. See you later." I waved as I walked away. He didn't wave back.

"Darling," Kinnerly whispered, when I returned to her. "I've got to go." The end of a key pointed between the fingers she curled around my neck as she kissed my cheek. She whispered in my ear, "I want you."

I handed her three books. "O'Hara and Updike. I added *Far from the Madding Crowd*."

"I remember . . . your favorite."

The stairs creaked.

"Baby's mother, probably," I whispered. "Stay until she's past." I hugged her, careful not to muss her hair. "I miss you, too. I want you every night."

It was a lie. I felt no body hunger.

33.

Southern Assurance, the company that carried a ten-thousand-dollar whole-life policy on Tom Morris, paid off. Kinnerly cashed the check and delivered the sum to me. Angus picked the money up without incident, and Kinnerly and I rested in the eye of the whirlwind.

January blew in with hard, cold gusts. Quail and deer seasons were coming to a close. Adel stood in the yard with his head lifted, ears back, sniffing delicate mysteries. When I opened the door in the morning, he'd gambol toward the woods, looking back. I made promises I did not keep.

"We'll go, old son!" I shook his head between my hands, smelling the bacon odor of his ears. "We'll go soon."

Sleet dusted the yellow grass and glittered on tree limbs. I felt the unease of weather change. While drinking my first cup of coffee a week after the drop, I shook open the local newspaper and a headline jumped at me.

MORRIS MURDERED, D.A. CLAIMS

The Bridge County grand jury will be asked to return true bills of indictment in the death of Tom Morris, prominent city businessman, who died in what appeared to be a one-car accident Nov. 3. District Attorney Clark Ransome will present evidence to the grand jury that Morris was murdered, and did not die of injuries suffered when his car struck a deer on Woodlie Road after 7:00 P.M. as he was on his way to give a talk at a sportsman's club in Pontotoc.

Informed sources say the district attorney expects to call Jeff Ballard, forest supervisor; Dr. D.W. Joiner, emergency room physician at City Hospital; Angus McKay, former farm manager for the deceased; and Dr. Andrew Miller, forensic pathologist, Chester Bowles Hospital, Chicago, Illinois.

I read the story three times, looked at the editorial page to see if there was a comment, and put the newspaper on the table. One thing was sure. I was going to hear from Angus again.

It was time to arrange a new identity.

After a thirty-minute drive to Oxford, I entered the university law center. The girl behind the desk in the law library propped her chin in her hands, munched an apple, and read *Prossor on Torts*. Astonishing breasts ballooned her sweater. I gazed at her round blue eyes.

"*Mississippi Code?*"

She flipped a yellow pencil from behind her ear and pointed. "That way. Second aisle, center."

"Thanks."

The room's ceiling vaulted two stories high. Four long rows of shelves stood in the center of the first floor. The *Mississippi Code* was shelved in a four-sided desk. I pulled out an index and ran down the headings under Birth Certificates. . . . amending a name upon affidavit (41-27-21) . . . correcting a name by Chancery Court Decree (41-57-23) . . . legitimation (93-17-1) . . . filiation (93-9-29). I closed the green-bound book and strolled to the main desk.

"Miss, do you have Board of Health rules, or anything like that?"

She took a bite of apple and ran her tongue into her cheek.

"You could check the card file."

Her voice was about an octave lower than I expected from the pink wisp of a mouth. Something flickered from deep in the baby-blues—a Kewpie Doll tiger shark was what she was.

The card file directed me to chipped metal files in the basement. In one there was a worn folder labeled *Board of Health Rules*. I flipped the pages. The words I was looking for were there.

DELAYED CERTIFICATE OF BIRTH

Where a person was born in the State of Mississippi, but his birth was not registered with the State Board of Health, a delayed birth certificate may be obtained . . .

I read on. A state can make the procedure easy or hard. Mississippi made it easy. The fee was ten dollars, the form need be sworn to by only one person having personal knowledge of the facts, and only two pieces of documentary evidence were called for. For three dollars the Health Department would do a search to determine that the name chosen was not already on file.

I couldn't ask for anything better than an identity certified by the state. With it I could get a driver's license, credit card, leave a paper trail of charges, apply for a Social Security card, get onto an insurance company computer with a manufactured health record, and obtain a passport.

I could create a new citizen, innocent of wrongdoing.

I photocopied the page and winked at the blonde as I went out. She pretended not to see, but the corners of her lips tucked.

The Ole Miss campus unreeled before me. It is a lovely place, anchored by a grove of fine, tall trees and a pre–Civil War Lyceum. Women beautiful enough to be on movie screens or magazine covers still strolled the grove and sidewalks. But the classical buildings which had once dominated the campus were now sandwiched between newer buildings, some of which looked like shirt factories.

Sure, the campus had changed in the thirteen years since I had come here with clay under my fingernails, calluses on my hands, an accent as deep as the Mississippi, and a burning ambition for education. But in significant ways the place had not changed at all.

Behind the Lyceum stands the university library. A librarian directed me to the basement, where newspapers are stored.

I sneezed my way through bound volumes and dusty bundles of yellow newspapers, tied with string. I was looking for early-forties accidents in which two married adults of child-rearing age had been killed. The *Commercial Appeal*, The *State Times*, and the *Clarion Ledger* were my sources.

The April 14, 1942, *Clarion Ledger* reported an accident I could use. There were other possibilities, but for getting rid of both parents this one was best.

Edinburgh. Gerome Laudner, 23, and wife, Lovie Burkhalter Laudner, 23, of Mt. Olive were D.O.A. Monday at

Mississippi Baptist Hospital, Jackson, following an auto-mobile accident. Services are at 11:00 A.M. today, Pleasant Grove Methodist Church, Mt. Olive, Rev. Charles Davis officiating. Burial will be in the church cemetery. Mr. Laudner had been a lifelong farmer. He was the son of the late Mr. and Mrs. Ulysses Laudner of Edinburgh. Mrs. Laudner was a graduate of Blue Mountain College. She was the only daughter of the late Mr. Duncan Burkhalter and the late Mrs. Lovie Woodward Burkhalter of Mt. Olive.

No survivors by now, probably . . . I copied the details into a notebook, then went to a payphone and called Harry.

"BASO!" he yelled into the receiver, which is Harry's anagram for son-of-a-bitch. "What's going on? I'm at work," he hissed. "These mothers count every minute." By 'these mothers' he meant Universal Credit. "Get on with it. Speak up."

"I'm going to brighten your life."

He groaned. "I knew it." A little wire edge came into his voice. "What's wrong?"

"Got a pencil?"

"Does the Pope chant in the woods?"

I told him I wanted a leather-bound family Bible, printed before 1900. In it I wanted recorded the birth of Ulysses Laudner in 1896. The handwriting should be old-fashioned, feminine, and the ink black from a real ink pen.

"Show the marriage of Ulysses and Mary Povall in 1918," I said. "On the next line show the birth of Gerome in 1919. Got that?" I spelled "Gerome."

"Have an entry show Gerome's marriage to Lovie Burkhalter in 1940. In another entry, show that a son, Ulysses Burkhalter Laudner, was born to them March 3, 1942. Remember to use different inks for these entries."

"You think you're talking to a dummy? Who is Ulysses B.?"

"Me."

"Hmm. Sure the name's not spelled Useless? You weren't born in 1942."

"Negative Useless. Positive 1942. I was born in '40, but use '42."

"Anything else?"

"Yeah. I need a letter in a different hand, also feminine. Use rag paper or part-rag, not wood-pulp stuff. You can get a sheet by buying an old journal or book, anything prior to 1941 that has a good quality blank page in front or back. This is for a letter from Lovie to Alice Bloodsoe dated March 17, 1942. It needs to say, 'Dear Alice, I know you'll be pleased to hear that—'"

"Slow up!"

"—'that Ulysses has at last arrived! I had him at home just as I planned, with old Kate as midwife. I am *mortally* afraid of hospitals since sister's death. Gerome and I are going to Jackson, where I hope to see Gladys, if she can spare me a room.'"

"How long does this go on?"

"A minute. 'It is very important that we talk. Write soon and tell me when you can visit and see my beautiful son. Love, Lovie.'"

"Good thing I speed-write."

"Good thing you do."

"Anything else?"

"Yeah. I'll send Gerome's and Lovie's exact birth dates as soon as I confirm from tombstones or local obituaries. And one thing more."

"Yes?"

"Get somebody good to do this. Somebody from our receding, sordid past."

"I gotcha."

"I'm sending money to get things rolling."

"Sure." He was impatient. A woman laughed in the background and a telephone rang.

"I owe you one."

"More like five. Bye . . ."

I drove to the cemetery and took the birth dates off the stones. In due time a woman friend of Harry's drove to Marshall County and swore that she was Mary Alice Bloodsoe, to whom the letter attached had been addressed, that she was now a resident of Memphis, Tennessee, that she had formerly lived in Mt. Olive, Mississippi, that Lovie Laudner was then her best friend, that she knew of my birth at home, had seen me as an infant, had followed my childhood and young adulthood, but was never aware until recently that my birth had gone unrecorded because of my mother's and father's early deaths.

It was that easy.

With the application for a birth certificate I included the sworn statement, a photocopy of the newspaper clipping reporting the deaths of my "parents," our Bible, the letter Harry provided, an application form, and a thirteen-dollar fee.

The Department of Health created a new person and returned his family Bible.

I sent Harry $500 for the documents and testimony. It left me broke, but I wanted Harry happy when I called.

One loose end was left—Angus.

34.

Angus stood outside the equipment shed at the Morris farm on Isaquena Road, wiping his hands on a rag. I parked the Jeep, got out, and walked toward him. Two green-painted John Deere cotton pickers loomed near us. Cows bawled from a pen. Angus's gaze shifted to see who was near enough to help, if it came to that.

Two men were moving baled hay to a pasture a couple of hundred yards away, near enough to hear gunfire. Angus hung his thumbs in his belt and shifted his weight from foot to foot. His belt creaked. His boots creaked. He could flex his muscles and everything on him would creak. He squinted his eyes. He firmed his jaw. "What 'chew want, boy?"

It seemed a bit anticlimactic.

In my tight jeans and tucked shirt, Angus could see I wasn't carrying. Adel stayed obediently in the Jeep. Still, Angus's right hand never strayed far from his hip. His house was probably so booby-trapped he wasn't sure how to get inside it. He probably drank to steady his nerves.

"Good morning," I said.

"That's close enough."

Adel whined from the Jeep. He peered though the windshield, inquiring whether he might disable this gentleman.

"Adel, stay!" I ordered, without turning my head. "What's the total bill, Angus?"

He put on a puzzled, good-old-boy look. "I don't know what 'chew talking 'bout."

"Ten thousand was enough?"

"I ain't a hog! Have I ast for more?" There was no humor in his laugh. He had a gun. Help was just across the field. He squinted into the sun and cocked his hat, exposing the white line across his forehead. "Ain't 'chew afraid to be seen talking to me, being as how I'm gonna appear before a grand jury?"

"As a voluntary witness?"

"Hell, no. I got subpoenaed. Gladys in the D.A.'s office told me they was onto it that I drove to Woodlie Road that morning, so I came forward and told Mr. Ransome I found Tom dead. Told him how it was on my conscience that I never reported the death. Told him I was drunk as Cooter Brown. Said I had a married woman in my car I'd been knocking a little off of, so I just backed up and got out'a there, and never said nothing, 'cause I couldn't do Tom no good."

"He bought it?"

"Yeah. He said, 'Who's the woman?' I hemmed and hawed and said, 'Gladys.' 'You son of a bitch!' he said. 'I had *my* eye on that.' Gladys and me are old friends. She'll say anything I want her to. We growed up together. Gladys don't give a fuck." He chuckled. "But she'll probably have to give one or two to Clevis Ransome now."

Angus edged to the right, squinting into the sun, maybe worried about the advantage I had with the sun at my back.

"Luke, you figure everybody is as greedy as you are," he said. "I needed ten thousand dollars bad or I wouldn't have troubled you. A man that kills for money don't tolerate a leech. I'd be a fool to hit you up twice."

"That's right, you would."

His face shone with sweat and sincerity. He was hiding a bear trap.

35.

The next four days drifted by, eerily silent. I cut wood and came home too tired to do more than wash.

Sometimes I didn't eat. Sometimes I found bologna, cheese, or a can of red beans and some rice. I smelled bad. Adel was my only companion. I wasn't seeing Kinnerly until the grand jury met.

Thursday, I shut off the saw, put it into the Jeep, and started for home at two. I thought of having a drink or taking in a movie. I was thinking about women . . . about that black-haired, blue-eyed accountant, Billie . . . about how she looked, big-legged but fine, in a bathing suit.

I was visualizing her little waist and strong legs as the Jeep climbed the road to my cabin. The cabin stood dark as always when I parked, but something felt wrong. I listened to the motor while I looked around. "Adel!" I yelled. He didn't bark.

The axe stood by the shed where I had left it. The lane was empty of car tracks. Sunlight fell through the pines in shifting patterns. I walked slowly, opening my eyes and ears. Something gritted under my feet near the porch. Glass. A screen hung, cut in an L-shape. One window frame didn't glitter. It was hollow. I jerked open the door. A shred of brown paper fell out of the frame six inches from the floor. Adel sprawled by the window. A hole seeped in his neck. A puddle of blood spread under him. I said his name and his eyes rolled toward me, but he didn't wag his tail stub. I told him he was a fine boy who had done just right. I said it over and over, "Good boy! You did *just right.*" He panted very fast with his ropy tongue on the floor. White stuff coated it. I felt the underside of his neck. There wasn't much of a flow. Maybe the bullet had drilled right through. . . . And maybe the bastard who shot him was sneaking up on me.

"Adel, stay. You're going to stay. Head down. Head down, sir!"

He settled himself and licked his chops to say he'd heard.

"I'll be right back. Right back."

I crawled to the cabinet and took out the things I'd prepared for an emergency. I donned the headphone of a bionic ear and buckled a Colt .38 Special around my waist.

The control unit of the bionic ear is about the size of a flashlight. Power comes from a nine-volt alkaline battery. I crawled across the floor and stuck the microphone around the corner. Nothing. I pivoted the mike.

Somewhere behind the Jeep, a crow cawed. It boomed in my ear. Pine trees in front of the house rubbed together, producing a papery whisper that would have been inaudible to my unamplified hearing. I scanned the right. About forty-five degrees away, somebody hawked and spat. The spitting sounded like an air rifle firing—*phooht!* I held the mike steady. The person sniffed, and his nose sounded like a water sucker cleaning up after an oil spill. I figured the range at eighty yards. That would put him in the brush along the woods edge. He was probably watching the house with binoculars or a rifle scope.

The plywood wall under my kitchen sink, the hatch on the roof, or the trap door under the fireplace; it had to be the latter of these since the drain pipe led to the side of the house opposite the intruder's stand.

I crawled to get the crossbow and bolts from their hiding place, slid across the floor, opened the trap door, and jumped softly into the pipe. There was just room enough to inch along. A rat scurried ahead. We couldn't have passed each other. I don't hate rats. I've eaten them, but hepatitis ain't no fun.

Webs looped my face and hands. Crawly things moved through my hair. Spiders scare the crap out of me. I wanted to slap them, and rush toward the light. Instead, I inched along, elbows up, like an alligator.

The drain exit was exposed to one angle. If two shooters lay in ambush, one on each side of the cabin, the moment of exiting the pipe would be it. I slid out in one wet motion.

When you think it's coming your muscles firm pathetically, rejecting the intrusion of a bullet. You listen acutely, though it makes no sense, because bullets are swift and voiceless. The boom of the explosion that sends them your way limps along behind.

There was no shot.

I scuttled away low, with leaves slicking under my hands, keeping a hill between me and the intruder I heard.

A creek of cold, bubbling water stopped me. Beyond it stood clumps of orange sedge grass, swaying with the wind. If the shooter waited at the hilltop I would be exposed while crawling through it.

I aimed the bionic ear. The snuffling sound it picked up was straight ahead, but weak. Probably he was over the hill.

I crawled through the water, across the low grass, into the sedge, and up the incline. Nearing the top, I took another survey. Leaves scuffled. Something creaked.

I cocked the crossbow and peeped over the crest. Twenty yards ahead Angus sprawled on his belly with binoculars to his eyes. A bush broke his outline. He had placed himself to watch the house, front and back. A bolt-action rifle lay beside his hand. He put down the glasses and picked up the rifle. He crouched, took a look through the scope, and waited.

I checked behind me instinctively. Adel was snuffling along, casting for my scent. He picked it up where I emerged from the tunnel. The old head lifted in symbolic baying. He crossed the twelve feet of yellow grass where I had escaped detection. Trotting now, more certain, rubbery nose inches off the ground, stern waving, he followed the trail of his master.

Angus took the rifle from his shoulder to watch. The dog circled the hill just as I had. He cut a sharp little arc and followed a line parallel to Angus's position. He splashed across the creek to enter the sedge.

Something worked in Angus's face. He gasped and turned, lifting the rifle.

My crossbow sight V'd on his belly. The stiff trigger jerked under my forefinger. A bolt whirred across the distance and nailed Angus to the tree behind him. His rifle flew out of his hands, flipped end over end, and hit the ground.

Angus looked down. The crossbow bolt stood in his middle. His fingers curled around it and pulled. His face reddened as if he were constipated. He said *ummm . . . ummm* in an angry buzz.

His head came up. "You shot me in the belly," he said informatively, as if I hadn't seen him get pinned like a bug.

I squatted on my heels and chewed a twig. Adel came over the hill and tottered toward us. I disciplined him a little for leaving Down-Stay. "Bad dog!" I hissed. "Bad dog!" He lifted his nose, made an "O" with his mouth, and bayed. "Hush . . . bad dog!" He hung his bloody old head. "Adel, lie down. Head down, too." He sank beside me, back end first.

All the time I was talking to the dog, Angus made that *ummm* sound, his fingers twitching on the bolt. "Something's coming out," he yelled. "You've cut a gut. Get me to a doctor."

He wiggled in panic. His hands clawed air.

I slid a fresh bolt into the nock on the crossbow and cocked it.

"You ain't going to—?"

"Why'd you lay for me?"

"'Cause, you bastard, you was going to kill me. I could see it in your mad-dog face."

I lifted the crossbow to eye level. His features momentarily firmed. "You think you've got it all. Well, there's more than one has sampled them goods. You're stupid, boy, real stupid."

"Go on. You might earn yourself a minute."

The rifle was four feet away from his hand.

"Try it."

He smiled an evil smile, all the more evil because it sat on a pale, sick face. "I've had that girl myself."

"You lie."

"Me and her was gonna git rid of old Tom before you come along. She needed me till you come along."

He saw something in my expression he didn't like, and he wiggled against the shaft. "Get me to a doctor! I'll give the ten thousand back. I'll never trouble you again, 'fore God."

"Keep talking. Maybe I'll do you the favor of killing you fast."

"I'm talked out."

I got up and kicked him in the side. He screamed. "You dumb bastard. Who'll teach you your ABC's if I'm dead?"

I said something I didn't want to say. "Have there been other men?"

"Lots. Me and Jeff Ballard for two. Jeff wanted her because Tom had *his* wife. It was a getting-even thing. Then he got hooked."

"Keep talking."

Angus sneered, an ugly thing on the sweating face of a dying man. "There wasn't any man she wouldn't have took on if there was advantage to it."

"Liar." The word was a pathetic protest rather than firm denial.

"She'd planned for a year to get rid of Tom. I was goin' to hire the hit man. Then you—you dumb bastard—you come along and do the job for nothing. She planned to get rid of the hit man. Never thought of that, did'ja?" He looked at me with hate. "When you said *you'd* hit Tom, she changed her mind about me killing the hit man, said to me, 'Get back! No! Must not,' like I was a yard dog after a chicken. It was her sent me to Woodlie Road to be sure the job was did right. It was her planned how I would go the the D.A. with a tale to clear you. You dumb bastard! I could'a cleared you, and you've killed me for nothing."

"No. You got that wrong. I killed you 'cause you shot my dog, and I was next."

He drew up his knees and squeezed his eyes tight. Blood and stuff trickled on the broken shaft. "I ain't really gonna die, am I?"

"Yeah, you are."

"OK, then. You was right to shoot me! I was gonna kill you soon's I got a bead. If I wasn't gonna have her, neither was you."

"Why didn't you just back-shoot me and clear out? Why shoot the dog?"

"I wanted to see you cry and whine. I wanted to make you

suffer, and know you wasn't gonna make it to the vet with that old hound."

I lifted the crossbow.

He pulled his nerve together and looked straight at me. "You better believe me. She'll sell you out."

The trigger squeeze is heavy, twelve or fourteen pounds.

He looked off at the trees behind my cabin. "Ain't it funny how things—"

The bolt hit him in the throat. He bucked and kicked like a pig at slaughter when you've aimed a .22 bullet to the brain, but missed the sweet spot. Air sighed from his lungs. Liquids from his veins, bowels, and bladder spread earthy odors. He got the empty stare you recognize even if you've never seen death before.

As I squatted beside the body, figuring out what to do next, only one useful idea came to mind. Serial killers don't haul meat. They bury victims under their houses, or become hunter nomads.

There wasn't a vehicle on the road. That meant Angus had hiked cross-country with his rifle.

I went back to the cabin, pressure-bandaged Adel's neck, buckled him into his trailing harness, and took him to the place where Angus must have stood when he fired through the window. Adel shook himself and looked up, ready. "Adel, *track*," I said.

He back-trailed Angus through the woods to Highway 30, three miles cross-country, where I found Angus's truck. I returned on the same trail, dusting behind me with pepper.

Back home, I cut two poles, hitched the body between them with Angus's belt and a rope, and hauled his body to my dirt-floored tool shed. I buried him six feet deep, with his rifle, then back-trailed and brushed away the lines the travois poles had cut into the soil. Neither Adel nor any varmint would dig up the body inside brick walls.

Part of one of the crossbow bolts was buried in the trunk of an oak tree. I dug it out with a knife and burned it in the fireplace, along with the one that had hit Angus's throat. The smears and clots of blood would disappear into the earth or an animal's belly.

Even a dead mule turns to clean bones in a month.

Notebook 7

36.

Adel's temperature measured 101 degrees, normal for a dog. I gave him a penicillin-streptomycin shot and trimmed flesh and hair from the wound. It was a clean hole. Hydrogen peroxide from a rubber syringe squirted in one side and bubbled out the other. After blotting the surface of the wound dry, I stuck in a drain. Mycetracin was the only antibiotic in the medicine kit. I used that, and put a standing collar on Adel's neck that rose like Queen Elizabeth's ruff. The first time his foot crept up to scratch, I said, "Adel, no scratching." He flattened his ears to say he understood, and put the foot down. I showered and dressed, jammed the .38 special with the Tyler grip inside my waistband, got a bottle of whisky and called Kinnerly.

She answered on the third ring. She always answered on the

third ring. I pictured her standing with her white hand curved above the receiver, waiting for third rings.

"Your flowers are ready, Mrs. Morris."

"Oh. I hadn't expected them so soon."

"Can you pick them up now at the usual place?"

"Now?"

"They may wilt."

"Oh, that would never do. I'll hurry as fast as I can."

I drove to the barn on Clay Road and waited for her. She drove up minutes later, parked and came to me. I slapped her hard.

She rubbed her face.

"If you're going to scream, now's your chance."

"I'm not going to scream."

I slapped her again. She went down. Her hair looped over an eye that was puffing. She looked like she liked it. She looked like a slut.

"Are you going to tell me what this is about?"

"You'd lie your way out of it."

She got up and I shoved her. She sprawled against an iron-rimmed wagon wheel. Her hair fell loose and the brave little shine of her spirit went out. She looked used and afraid.

I twisted the cap off of the Dant pint I'd brought along and took a drink.

She didn't move, sensing I wasn't going to let her stand up to me.

The anemic sun hanging in the east hadn't burned off the frost. Crystals sparkled around our footprints. I grasped Kinnerly's wrist where the little green veins crossed and dragged her into the barn.

"What are you going to do to me?"

I jerked a hemp rope off of the pulley of a hay hoist.

"If there's anything wrong, we should talk. If I've done anything to offend you—"

"*Offend* me?" I jerked the rope and it cut into the flesh of her arms. I pulled her toward me and her hair flipped with the momentum. Our faces were six inches apart. A thin cloud of frosty breath floated between us.

"You need to be beaten every day. Then you'll be a good woman."

"I'll never be a good woman. I've done things I shouldn't have." I laughed.

"But I've never hurt you, or betrayed you, or let you down."

I jerked the rope and dragged her to a stall. She stumbled after me. Her hair flew around her face.

The stall walls were slatted. There was room between the slats to push the rope through and tie her hands high. I stretched her until her forehead was squeezed between her elbows. She got a look. All of the sunlight in that barn concentrated in her eyes. "I won't scream, whatever you do," she said.

"Shut up." My hands shook and my breath whistled in my nose. I backed off, overturned a bucket and sat on it. I needed time to think, so I took out my pocket knife. Southern men will whittle, clean their nails, cut a straw.

"What are you going to do with me?"

"I don't know." I tried to hold the anger, but it was draining. Whatever I did to her, I'd have to do cold.

"You've never found a woman who matches you like I do."

A crow cawed in the distance. Two blackbirds flew a short sortie from the weedy pasture and settled in the lot. In the dark recesses of the barn a rat or a mouse scurried.

"What are you accusing me of? At least tell me that."

"Angus and Ballard."

"That happened before I met you. They have nothing to do with us. I've never been with anyone else since you."

I stabbed the knife into the ground. "You were going to kill Tom all along."

"I'd thought about it."

I stabbed the knife into the ground again. "You sent Angus to Woodlie Road."

"I sent him to help you. I made him check the scene, and go to the D.A. for you with a story that would clear you. And I'm sending him to the grand jury to protect you. And—"

"And you planned to kill me."

"That's a lie! Who said that? Angus? You must have tortured him to make him tell such a lie. No, he's *jealous*. He can't stand it that we have each other. He lied to make you hate me."

It was her best performance, or it was the truth.

She jerked her wrists against the rope. "Turn me loose."

I flopped the knife into the ground. The anger I had built up was turning to cold, sour ashes of indecision. There were two certainties. I couldn't trust her, but I couldn't hurt her, either. I untied the rope.

She paced in the barn alleyway, rubbing her wrists. "He deserves to die for what he's done to us."

"He got what he deserved, then."

It didn't shock her. She said, "He ruined everything between us. It will never be the same. You'll always doubt me. Quicksand runs between us now. Luke—" She dropped to her knees. "Don't you see? If you don't trust me, there's nothing left. We'll turn on one another. Kill me. I'll make it easy." She looked around wildly. "I'll tell you how I made love to Angus."

I hit her before I knew it. She sprawled on the dried manure and dust of the alleyway.

Her voice whispered on, telling a story that twisted my guts.

"Angus?"

"He was safe. He worked for Tom, and wouldn't talk. Tom was a sexual cripple. I'd meet Angus in the woods. I'd—"

I was on my knees beside her, covering her mouth with my hand. "Shut up!"

She pulled my hand away. "Hate me."

I wished I could.

37.

Dogs that smile overdo it. Adel's smile was a curled-lip grimace that bared his teeth and wrinkled his nose. He tilted his head to the side to be ingratiating and charming. He looked like a rattle-snake with a bandage around its neck, aiming a bite.

The large, neatly-dressed man who got out of the police car in my driveway kept his hands away from his pistol. He moved crab-wise across the yard. His body language said *Don't notice how big I am. You don't need to be afraid.*

I was afraid. It had to do with having a guilty conscience.

Grady Prather was back.

Grady's lips jerked up at the corners, making what he must have thought was a smile. He set a dusty, booted foot on my bottom step.

"Howdy, Luke," he said.

"Howdy, Grady."

"You staying out of trouble?"

"I'm trying."

I'd known Grady since high school. He was the gun-crazy, car-crazy kid teachers expected to enlist in the Marines or go to prison. Here he was in a law officer's uniform, a .357 Ruger in a Bianci holster on his hip, two citations for bravery in his file.

"That's a nice pooch," Grady said. "What's he wearing around his neck?"

"A bandage."

"He don't bite *people*, does he? He looks like he might bite people."

Adel smiled fiercely.

"Just other dogs. This time he took a whipping."

"Why's he drawed his lips back at me?"

"He likes you, Grady. He means to be friendly. That's a smile."

"I ain't so sure." Grady's hand fitted to his crotch, cradled his balls to adjust things. He nodded as if to say, *Here it comes; this is what I came for . . .*

"Luke, the sheriff wants you to come in for a talk."

"Why?"

"I ain't privy to the sheriff's deep thoughts. He bid me say would you be so kind as to pay him a visit."

"When?"

Grady looked toward the woods where wind stirred the few remaining leaves. His voice was a soft blur. "Now would be fine."

"Now suits me."

I put Adel in the house. Grady and I went outside to the brown car with the yellow shield, and I got in and sat on the vinyl-covered bench seat.

Grady is like a shirt starched from a spray can. His finish isn't deep. It doesn't take much of a temperature rise to rumple him.

I let him do the talking on the way to town. He told me not one damn thing I wanted to know.

Grady parked in a space marked "Reserved," we got out, and I walked ahead of him up the green-painted steps of the courthouse. I led the way between Corinthian columns and through a heavy door with a sign that said "Push In." In a hallway darkened by oiled wood floors and tan walls, we passed public bathrooms, the chancery clerk's office, the circuit clerk's office, the tax assessor's office, and entered a door marked "Sheriff."

A rosy-lipped old dispatcher with pale skin and puffed hair smiled from behind a green metal desk. A skinny deputy sat in a straight chair against the opposite wall, reading *Guns and Ammo*. He'd sat in the same place so often his head had made a greasy spot.

"Go right in. The sheriff is expecting you," the woman said. Grady and I walked through the sheriff's open door.

Hovey Coonan liked things neat: plaster walls bare of citations except one from Mensa, a photo of him with two lanky bird dogs, and a splashy lithograph. Around the room I glimpsed a gun cabinet containing a parkerized Mossberg riot gun and a scoped Remington 700 sniper rifle, two green metal filing cabinets, three chairs, an oak desk, a telephone, a stapler, and a folder of papers.

One of the straight chairs cuddled at the side of his desk and one sat rigidly against the opposite wall. I suppose the psychology of the arrangement was that if you wanted to cozy up you sat close. In the far chair you would feel distant, maybe guilty.

Coonan wore a navy suit, shined boots, white shirt, and a patternless maroon tie. He wore no smile, though he waved hospitably and said, "Thank you for coming in, Luke. Have a chair."

"Thank you." I scraped a chair halfway to the wall and sat. Grady leaned against the door frame. No smile from Hovey. I bet he was the last boy to blink in grade school stare-downs. And even though he was a Coonan from Louisiana, no kid called him coon-ass but once.

On the wall behind his head hung a lithograph of a beach house, porch, and sailboat. Grainy shapes you could make out as a man's back, arms, and hands dominated the foreground. It was the kind of print an art appreciation society would sell in a signed, numbered edition for a hundred twenty-five bucks a copy to ten thousand art appreciators.

"Nice print."

"Thank you."

"There is a crazy geometry to the thing. It looks almost like a late Seurat," I said.

"That's what the literature with it said. I wouldn't know. You were an art major, weren't you?"

"English, but I've always liked Impressionists." I chuckled. "Do you know a way to make a living out of recognizing Impressionists and post-Impressionists?"

"The only other fellow around here that knew anything about art was Tom Morris. Now, there was a man you'd have had a lot in common with!" He locked his hands behind his head and leaned back. "Did you know him?"

"I met Tom, but didn't know him well."

"Tom knew good stuff. If it wasn't good, Tom wouldn't have it. He was that way about cars, furniture, clothes, women—" Coonan got up, legs apart, hands in the middle of his back. He stretched, then walked around the desk and looked out of the window beside the gun case. I saw over his shoulder a gray sky and an oak tree.

"I've admired his widow, myself," Coonan said to the tree.

"I reckon you're saying, Sheriff, that you know I'm seeing Kinnerly Morris. Did you bring me here to tell me that?"

He turned and glanced over my head. "He don't understand, Grady."

Grady laughed. "He don't understand at all."

Everything sounds worse when you're guilty. But when a Southerner with a Mensa plaque on his wall says, *He don't understand,* watch out.

"Yes, you're seeing Kinnerly Morris." The sheriff crossed the room, sat down in the far-away chair, poked out his feet, and stared at his shiny lizard boots.

I turned my chair to face him.

"Then a witness that was supposed to testify before the grand jury last week turns up missing. You got any idear what might have happened to Angus McKay?"

"I've no idea, Sheriff. Do you?"

"Yes and no." He scratched his head. "Tom Morris was murdered, no matter what the coroner says, and you were on the scene."

"Who says?"

Coonan's eyebrows lifted. "Didn't I explain?" He rubbed his chin and said to Grady, "I didn't explain that, Grady."

"You better explain that, Sheriff."

"Sorry, Luke. I meant to explain that, sure did. Didn't Angus tell you about the letter he wrote?"

"What letter?"

"Angus left a letter in his safe deposit box. The jailer told us that if Angus ever turned up missing we were to look there. I got Judge White to issue an order to open it." Coonan walked to his desk, reached across, and slid open the center drawer. It seemed to take a month. He took out a folded sheet of paper and smoothed it. That took another month. He sat against the front edge of the desk. One finger ran down the page. He made a humming sound. "It says here, 'Then I came upon Luke Carr carrying a bow and arrows. He said he'd found the body.'" Hovey looked up. "Now, Luke, everybody knows you poach on private land. But what I want to know is, who'd want to frame you for murder?"

"Good Lord!"

"I've taken you by surprise, have I?"

"You have."

Coonan scratched his head. "My theory is you were stalking deer and spooked 'um. They ran across the road. Tom hit one with his car. Somebody was in the car with Tom. That fellow took this chance and broke Tom's neck before you got to the scene. You found the body, *then* Angus came along and saw you there."

"Why would anybody kill Tom?"

"I've thought about that considerable, Luke . . . considerable." He tapped the page. "First off, I thought about your motives: Tom's wife and her money." He looked shrewd. "But Tom Morris's lawyer is an old friend of mine. He got to talking around the edge of lawyer-client privilege and disabused me of the notion that anybody would kill Tom to get at money through her."

I nodded, pretending I understood what he was talking about. I didn't.

"So, this other idear came to me. Tom's bank accounts are—let's say, sizeable. He was into some big-money deals, not easy to trace. I got to wondering about criminal activity."

"Drugs?"

"Money-laundering, drugs, gambling, prostitution, pornography. Some kind of criminal activity. We have an investigation going on."

I shook my head. "I can't believe it."

"Now, hear me out. Did the man go out of town all the time, or didn't he?"

"How would I know?"

"Sure you know. That's when you and she got together. I've got a list of Tom's airline tickets out of Memphis and Little Rock. We know some of the folks he met when those airplanes touched down." He scratched his white-thatched hair and gave me a straight, hard look. "Don't waste my time with lies. Now I'm gonna run my theory by you one more time. You were illegally hunting. You scared a deer and it jumped in front of Tom's car. He hit the deer and ran off the road. Someone else was in the car with him. This person saw a chance to kill Tom and make it look like an accident. He broke Tom's neck, and left. You came out of the woods, then Angus drove up and saw you. You couldn't turn yourself in and tell me you were at the scene because you had to have a reason to be there. The only one I'd believe, or a jury might believe, was that you were breaking game laws or trespassing." Hovey smiled, pleased with himself.

"If your theory has any truth in it, and I'm not saying it does"—I drew a deep breath before going on—"I'm a more logical suspect than some hypothetical gangster."

"You *were*, boy. You were *numero uno* until I found out you got nothing to gain by Tom Morris's death. That prenuptial agreement Mrs. Morris signed cuts her off. She gets a monthly allowance and that's it."

I said to myself, *Pre-nup?* To Coonan I said, "How does your hypothetical killer get away?"

"Cross-country."

"Here's another problem for you. Tom wouldn't have been an easy man to kill, hand to hand."

Coonan sat back and locked his hands behind his head. Hair poked between his fingers. "Beg to differ. Using a stranglehold to pop the neck of a man who isn't expecting it is easy as pie. Now I want you to consider this. Maybe you saw something important to this investigation that didn't seem significant at the time. "

He was pushing me to admit I was present at the scene of a murder. I didn't trust him. "Can't help you, Sheriff."

"'Didn't expect you to!" Coonan said expansively. "You didn't know what you were looking for. Now you do. It's some little detail the killer overlooked and you didn't. Something that will identify him, and clear you." His chair banged down from its back legs. He stood. "Grady, drive this man home. He's wore out. Us having a sworn statement he was at the scene of a murder caught him by bad surprise."

"It sure did, Sheriff. He's all shook up."

I got to the door before Coonan stopped me. The small sound of my name spoken had never sounded so compelling.

"Luke?"

I turned.

The sheriff stretched his back, showing his hip bones and privates. "I got a theory about what happened to Angus, too."

I waited.

Coonan nodded solemnly. "Ben Lilly will call this one 'The Case of the Man Who Knew Too Much.'"

Oh, hell. Here it comes. You thought you were so smart. You thought you had Coonan fooled.

I said, "Why so?"

The room was plenty quiet. I told myself to move, say something, do anything but stand frozen.

The sheriff crooned in a wily Irish voice: "What did Angus know that was so dangerous that he left a sworn statement to protect himself? Was it about Tom's money-laundering and taste for porn? The sexual activities of Tom's wife? Or was it the identity of Tom's killer?"

The sheriff's black eyes didn't have any light in them. They didn't look human.

I went into my bubble. It's a relaxation response to crisis.

When it works, I center myself. Outside disturbances lose their power. I chuckled and said, "Damned if I know, Hovey! I do know Ben Lilly is nothing of the actor you are."

Coonan sighed. "Grady, take the man home. He's tired. His mind is tired. He needs a rest."

I laughed, trying to make it the puzzled laugh of an innocent man.

38.

Sheriff Coonan was said to be so smart he did crossword puzzles in his head. I couldn't figure the act he'd put on in his office.

"What do you make of what the sheriff said, Grady?" I asked on the way home. "Anything to it?"

Grady's eyes shifted. "That man knows which way is up. You can count on it." He nodded twice.

I telephoned Kinnerly after Grady let me out and talked casually, without giving her a chance to reply, about the prenuptial agreement she'd signed. She caught on that I was signaling her that our telephones could be bugged, and said little.

After I finished my monologue there was a long silence. I broke it by talking agreeably about other things. She had misled me, sure, but what did a prenup matter? I wouldn't have killed

Tom Morris for money. That would have tainted everything between us. *Stealing* his money was another matter.

That night I lay in bed remembering Vietnam.

Sergeant Baker would say when he sent me on patrol, "Carr, your nation calls." He had a lot of sayings. When we ran out of supplies he'd mutter, "The richest company in the world!" When he opened his C-Rats box he'd say, "The grateful republic rewards me." When the gooks yelled in high, accented voices, *Fuck LBJ! Today you die, Marine!* it was kind of funny. We weren't Marines, and we couldn't imagine a starving whore fucking LBJ for a fifty-dollar bill, but he was the president of the by-God USA. The sergeant took it ill for an enemy to insult him.

Baker would call in an air strike, or artillery. He'd burn three one-oh-five shells to get one gook who insulted the president. Then Sarge would mutter, "Did I get your attention, son?"

Sergeant Baker was team leader on a bad mission that stays in my mind. After insertion, we monitored trails and found a whole network under double canopy. The prints were mostly cleat marks of NVA canvas combat boots. Our commo wasn't dependable and there wasn't much hope of backup.

We set six Claymores in a daisy-chain on the side of the most-used trail, running the wires perpendicular to the Claymores a few meters before turning them toward the position where we would lay dog. I cleared my area of rocks and sticks in case I shifted. There would be no smoking. We even worried about pissing because Mr. Charlie knew our ammonia smell just as we knew the rotten-fish stench of his shit.

We laid dog about three hours over this little two-foot ridge. I had penflares, compass, poncho liner, D-ring and rope. I had a K-Bar, M16, albumin, medical supplies, signal panels, and mirror.

Also two canteens of water with cherry Kool Aid, grenades, Claymores, det cord, hell box, and about 400 rounds. I had to take a head call something awful but was afraid the NVA would smell it, even buried, so I racked out with my clothes on and my gear close at hand.

In the bottom of my pack was a paper picture of Kinnerly I had cut out of a yearbook and sealed in plastic. It was a yellow square about the size of a four-bit piece. Sometimes in base camp I went to sleep with it between my fingers, treating it as a talisman that would bring me back to the world. I was obsessing. She was only a college girl. She didn't have any power. But a man without someone to come home to is a weaker man. Getting a Dear John letter drops you 50 percent. Men die after getting Dear Johns. You try to bring down the odds against you, and controlling emotions is one way, so I made up stories about Kinnerly and me. Facts didn't matter. She was my girl. She was waiting faithfully, seeing no one else, refusing to go out with Jody. What did it matter if I lied? I never lied to anyone but myself and Mr. Charlie.

I lied to Mr. Charlie every way I could. I dug up his ammo caches and reburied them with booby traps. I speculated where he would dive for cover, and left him a surprise there. I put black boxes out to pick up sweat and sound in his "safe" high-speed trails. The black boxes sent a signal back to firebase, where each box was gridded. He drew saturation artillery fire.

Trail-watching is damn tedious. The NVA move like the deer do back home, at sunrise and late evening. I think I dozed on this ambush. About daylight, Craig reached back and touched my shoulder. A zipperhead came loping along the trail in that Vietnamese shuffle, carrying a big NVA pack on his back. I watched through the ferns, leaning over the clacker of the Claymore. Two more NVA came into the kill zone. Seconds ticked off, and no more gooks came. I squeezed the handle clips and the Claymores fired together, blowing vines and dust and blood. Each one threw six or seven hundred steel balls. Then M16s chattered and the pump guns opened up, blamming out 16 BB-shot to the shell. When I lifted my head from the jungle floor, Harry and Craig and Billyrag were in the path, emptying magazines into bodies. The recoil is so heavy on a full-auto M16 that the barrel climbs toward the canopy. A magazine empties before the first casings touch down. I pulled my K-Bar and jumped into the trail to take the .45 and holster off the officer. Unaccountably, another body staggered up and ran toward me. *How in hell? I'm looking at a miracle,* I thought. The click of magazines jamming into M16s sounded behind me.

The gook held his hands out to the sides. His fingers turned up and his knees turned in. The K-Bar in my hand was swinging up to get wet until I got a look at his face. He wasn't a *he*. Her eyes flashed toward mine and she whimpered. A splotch of blood showed on her forehead and her left breast. She kept running in that female way, kicking her calves and feet to the sides.

"Kill her!" Harry yelled, but I watched as she ran past my knife. He shoved me aside and fired, ringing my ears. Bullets dusted her jacket. Her back bowed and her hands flew out. I hated the air I had to breathe, rich and thick with the smell of blood. The flies come fast in Vietnam, incredibly fast. They buzz every inch of raw flesh and skin in seconds.

Harry's gun barrel scorched my hand, so I let go. "You should have taken her prisoner," I said. He looked at me like I was a dope, and I was. Harry protected my back. There is nothing better in life than a friend you can depend upon. I turned away from the useless dead.

We cleared the site, stripped the bodies, and slung them on poles like shot tigers. It had been a nice, clean ambush. We carried the dead and the ponchos containing their gear two hundred meters. The packs held medical supplies, pitiful stuff really. Harry and Billyrag squabbled over the .45.

Leeches sucked on my mouth from my having put my face on the ground. I burned them out with a cigarette, then opened the C-rats, but I didn't have any appetite at all.

Killing women, that got to me. I drank a canteen of water I'd put Kool Aid powder in, then gagged on the sweet, hot stuff. Harry broke out the commo and called for extraction. I found a place and took a crap. The sound of the extraction chopper was the sweetest sound I'd heard in a long, long time.

The next morning I sat up confused—uncertain where I was. The sun was high and a helicopter was *whackety-whacking,* but I was in my own bed. There were my boots on the floor. My plaid shirt and blue jeans from yesterday draped across the chairback where I'd thrown them.

The sound of this helicopter was anything but sweet.

39.

I pulled on my robe and ran outside into whipping dirt and leaves and stinging sand. The state police markings on the chopper were unmistakable. A man in uniform looked down from the glass dome. The pilot slanted the bird and it swept away, making a familiar racket.

I went inside, started coffee and oatmeal, switched on the radio and sat at the kitchen table. At the *swish* my hand made in brushing the tablecloth, Adel's ears pricked. He soft-footed across the room, intending to lick crumbs.

We disagree about this.

"Stop it," I said. He looked up. "It isn't becoming. Go to your place."

———

The thirty-minute early morning show, popular with locals driving to work at the shirt factory, contains ads for lost dogs, items for sale by individuals, and notices about community events. In between ads and announcements, girl singers wail about loves that got up and went, and male quartets harmonize on standards like "The Old Rugged Cross," and "What a Friend We Have in Jesus."

The station has no reporters. News is limited to a feature-of-the-day and items called in by listeners: usually revival dates, the appearance of guest preachers, school closings because of bad weather, and charitable events such as Brunswick stew cookings or cookie bakings to raise money for county volunteer fire departments or unfortunate people in need of surgery.

The radio's hum and the syrupy voice of the announcer were background noises for my thoughts until I heard the word "bloodhounds."

After that I hardly breathed.

Billy and Bob, star trackers of the Parchman Prison Recovery team, arrive today to assist in the search for Angus McKay. McKay, who was to have testified before the grand jury this week about the death of businessman Tom Morris, was considered a key witness. McKay's abandoned truck was found near the city limits. He was last seen two days ago.

"The reason we're beginning a search so early," Sheriff Hovey Coonan said, "is because of Mr. McKay's importance in a murder investigation. We are asking anyone knowing his whereabouts, or anyone who may have seen him, or who may have knowledge about his disappearance, to contact the sheriff's office immediately."

I poured my coffee, spooned the oatmeal into a yellow bowl, stirred in butter and brown sugar, cut down the radio, and sat again.

I didn't think bloodhounds could pick up the trails to and from Angus's truck with all the pepper I'd spread, but I wasn't sure. I hadn't been composed enough to use the bottle of fox urine I keep to cover my scent.

Coffee cooled in my cup and oatmeal congealed in my bowl. I thought, *What are my chances?* I wished the trail was washed, but there had been no rain. *A dog can't follow a three-day-old trail,* I told myself. *No way! Not even a bloodhound.*

Still, I went to the bookshelf. *The Complete Dog Book* said, "The famous bloodhound Nick Carter picked up a trail 105 hours old, and followed it to a subsequent conviction. Several specimens have followed human quarry for more than fifty miles, and one led the detectives 138 miles."

It was three miles to where Angus had left his truck.

I dialed Kinnerly's number. The boy answered. "Hello," he said. "Hello." His voice chilled me it was so much like his old man's.

I hung up. She would have gone out of town if my slap had made a mark she couldn't hide with makeup. I tried not to think about hitting her. There was an immediate problem.

I drove to the store, bought four yellow boxes of Arm and Hammer baking soda for $1.40 plus tax, and went home.

Soon, my rubber boots soaked in it. Coveralls and underwear and socks soaked in gray, sudsless, baking soda water. While I let the washing soak, I sharpened an axe with a bastard file. Usually it's relaxing to see metal coil from a shining edge as you set a blade angle. Not this time. I pinched wet clothing out of the chipped enamel tub and hung it to dry.

Then I took a baking soda shower, hair and all, and brushed my teeth, tongue, and gums with the stuff.

My TINK's Red Fox P Cover Scent is kept in the storehouse in case of spills. You don't want to spill fox urine in a house where a dog lives. I went to the storehouse and found a roll of cotton and the bottle. The label on the bottle said: "100% Natural Red Fox Urine from 100% Meat-Fed Red Foxes. Real high-quality Red Fox urine will cover the hunter's tracks and help cover human scent."

I turned my head, stopped breathing, and daubed the scent on the soles of my boots with a wad of cotton. Four drops went across the knees of the coveralls and four across the backs. Very lightly, I touched the cotton wad under my arms, to my neck, to the backs of my hands.

Then I went to watch the bloodhounds work.

A truck from the state prison and a metallic-brown police car sat where Angus's truck had sat the day I killed him. After parking, I walked across a field and up a hill, following the baying of hounds.

Officer Tolliver Pegues stood in the trail just over the hill. Tolliver has a high-set butt and big legs that anchor a lot of strength. His "move-it" gestures snap from the elbow, saying he has MP experience. He'd rather deal with a suspect physically than pull a weapon.

I edged a few steps downwind. "Where are the bloodhounds, Tolliver?"

"You got to move on, Luke. The dogs, they got they job to do. Can't have you stumbling 'round the trail."

"I'd sure like to see the Parchman man-trailers work."

Tolliver eyed me a long time. Then he said in a soft, high voice, "Wasn't you at the walker hound trial last spring? Didn't I see you there?"

I nodded.

"You just a fool about dogs, ain't you?" His tone was mock-scolding.

"I am that."

"You see whose treeing walker took second, and should've took first?"

"I did. Why don't you have Hobo out here today?"

"Hobo don't dirty his nose with trash. But lay down a coon trail and watch that dog travel!"

"I hear he's the best tree dog in the state."

Tolliver grinned and waved me on.

Over the hill, in a sunny valley, two big red dogs circled. Every few steps one dipped his head and sneezed, making his long ears jiggle.

Their handler looked to see if I was a plainclothes officer in need of an ass kissing. He was a sharp-faced little man with rolled sleeves. Blue tattoos ran up both forearms, and his billed cap pointed forty-five degrees away from his nose.

"You're not a plain-clothesman, are you?" the trusty asked.

I let him wonder. The big dogs lifted their heads to wind me. Since I smelled like a red fox with a bladder problem, they waved their sterns and grunted profoundly but didn't show special interest.

If I had to I'd use their faithfulness to a trail to attack their credibility. I'd ask a jury how they could believe a pair of bloodhounds had trailed me three miles when they were incapable of identifying me from thirty yards?

"I've got a man-trailer at home," I said. "Wondered if we could be of some help." It was a safe offer. This guy wouldn't want another dog on the job.

"If these dogs can't trail a man, he can't be trailed."

The larger dog sneezed, and turned unhappy, red-hawed eyes toward us.

"Track!" the little man ordered.

"They don't look very interested. I like to see them lean into the harness and nearly yank my arms out of the sockets. Did somebody foul the trail?"

The trusty scowled. "It looks like the trick of some bozo with pen time."

"How's that?"

The dogs jerked the lines, interrupting the little man. "Cook, he orders pepper. The guy working in the kitchen steals the pepper and makes his run. He pokes a hole in the pepper sack and ties the sack to his ankle. Pepper drips on his trail. The hound that tries to track him gets a snout full."

"Does it work?"

"Naw, the good dogs run pepper. We give 'um more meat when they trail pepper."

It was slow work. The dogs jerked and hauled the little man, bayed a track, and lost it. Their wrinkled faces looked puzzled, and their red eyes grieved.

"They don't seem to like trailing pepper."

"They don't like it but they'll get the man. You wait and see."

"Bet you a dollar."

"Make it a beer, ice cold." His eyes looked dreamy at the thought.

"You're on."

When I stepped out of the woods another police car was parked beside the road.

Antennas sprouted on front and rear fenders. A black grille separated the seats. A riot gun was racked over the driver. When I approached the window, I saw a pressed blue uniform, white thatched hair, and a profile I knew. Not a speck of dandruff or lint dusted the uniform. Hovey Coonan is a hard, keen man, as the Irish say.

He set aside a clipboard holding a sheaf of papers, capped his pen, and looked up. "So, you're visiting the scene of your crime, are you, Luke?"

It took me three seconds to draw my lips into a smile. It was a poor thing at that.

"Don't you know criminals visit the scenes of their crimes?"

"You mean murderers, Sheriff, but did you ever hear of a guilty man with an IQ of 145 doing anything that stupid?"

Coonan's eyes skimmed me as if I were a first-grade book containing large pictures and one-syllable words. "Hell, boy! I never met a murderer with an IQ more than 80. That's what makes this case interesting."

He picked up the clipboard again and uncapped the pen. He was a man of unceremonious departures, un-Southern in that way. His eyes moved down a *New York Times* crossword puzzle attached to the clipboard. Every word but one was filled in.

"See you later, Sheriff."

"Luke, you take care, ya' hear?" Coonan said without lifting his gaze.

He wore the smile of a man enjoying himself.

Notebook 8

40.

The dog pound sat in a circle of thin gravel on the east edge
of town.

Five baggy chain-link pens with rusting poles faced me.
Behind the pens stood a gray concrete-block building. Two broken windowpanes were covered with cardboard. Somewhere
inside, a dog yapped without ceasing. Water trickled from a rup-
tured pipe. The stench of the place could choke a possum.

A young woman in green rubber boots stood toe-deep in a
foamy yellow wash of dog feces and disinfectant. She wore a
denim shirt, yellow plastic gloves, and designer jeans. The brown
scarf covering her hair was patterned like a Hermès scarf of Kinnerly's, but maybe it was a cheap knock-off.

Two black pups with big bellies padded through the water in

a puzzled way, lifting their paws. Other dogs hid in boxes to avoid the spray.

I walked inside the kennel, hooked the gate, and glanced at pointy-faced curs with cycle tails, an old gray lab with a wet stick in his mouth, mangy puppies slinking in corners, and a cocker with crazy eyes who barked incessantly. They weren't the dogs I wanted.

The woman looked up and I got a nice smile.

"May I help you? I'm Mary Jane Pelegrin. I volunteer here." She swung a yellow-gloved hand in a sweeping gesture.

"How do you do. I'm Luke Carr. Are there other dogs for adoption, Ms. Pelegrin?"

She followed me inside the building, and pointed to wire cages against two walls. "You can have any of those."

A friendly collie, a part-beagle, two or three fice mixtures and a forlorn shepherd puppy peered at me. In the farthest cage to my right a black and tan male hound humped the air in a lonely sexual dance. In the cage next to his, a fox terrier lifted a leg and peed on the wall. The fat bassett in the third cage was the focus of their attention. She lifted a deep-brown, feminine gaze. I opened the door, stroked her long ears, and turned her around.

"This is the one. I'll take her."

"Molly *is* sweet, but she's in season." Mrs. Pelegrin shook her head. "We won't release her for adoption until she's spayed."

"I've got a tight fence, and I'll pay to have her spayed."

"Oh, that's good of you. Let me fill out the adoption papers."

She couldn't find her purse. When I located it on a white enameled cabinet, she took off her gloves and searched for a pen. The diamond in her ring was impressive, but the Mont Blanc she took out of the purse wouldn't print through to the pink copy of the form. "This *pen*," she grumbled.

I handed her a Bic. "Want to swap?"

"I would, but my daddy gave me this old thing."

———

For an eighteen-dollar adoption fee and a promise to spay her, Molly was mine.

I held her at arm's length on the way to the Jeep, placed her on the floorboard, stroked her shoulders and ears, tied my belt to her collar, and pulled the strap up under my shoe. She bucked at the restraint and walled her eyes. "Good girl," I said. "G-o-o-d girl. You're OK."

I drove one-handed to Highway 30 where Angus's truck had been parked, waited until traffic cleared, jumped out of the Jeep, and started with Molly to the woods. She sat. My belt, pulling her collar, flapped her ears forward and wrinkled her skull. I loosened the tension, ordered *Heel* and stepped out.

She walled her eyes and backed up. "Good girl, Molly," I wheedled. "Here, Molly. H-e-e-re, Mol-ly. Come."

This was the stubbornest bitch alive.

I straightened her body, stood beside her, patted my leg, and walked away. "Walk-ies," I cooed like that English dog trainer on television.

Molly didn't walkie. This was sixty pounds of dignified bassett who didn't know me and wasn't going anywhere with a stranger.

In the distance sounded the roar of a car. I awkwardly picked Molly up and ran for the woods. She flopped, threw her head, and pawed. Scratches burned my side. When we reached cover I put her down, leaned against a tree, and panted.

Molly was my only hope to foul the trail the hounds followed. If a bitch in heat crossing their noses didn't turn two males off a pepper trail, nothing would.

I gave Molly a brief lesson in heeling, but a belt is not a check cord and the limp strap she wore was not a training collar. The lesson did not take. She rolled onto her back and stuck her feet up. She was too big to carry far. I plodded on, certain that her head, at least, would follow.

When gagging piteously didn't work, Molly scrambled up and waddled behind as I cut through the woods to intercept Angus's trail. The hounds were still two hills away.

We returned to the Jeep, without being observed, so far as I could tell, and went home.

As I turned into my driveway Molly pushed her head under a seat. I dragged her out, lifted her, and staggered toward the house. Water dripped from her tongue. Sweat fell from my face. I put her down and sat on the ground with my arm around her neck.

I didn't have a chain. She couldn't go into the house, dripping as much as she was. That left the tool shed. But the tool shed had a dirt floor. She might dig out.

Adel bounced toward us wearing a silly grin . . . ears perked and tail wagging.

"Get out of here!" I growled.

He wiggled all over and crouched in front, dog language for *Let's play.*

I dragged Molly toward the shed. The pull against my arm and shoulder grew heavier. Looking back, I saw Adel riding her, pumping vigorously.

I kicked empty air and yelled, "Adel, *back*. Get back."

He backed away, dancing and whining. I jerked open the shed door, shoved Molly inside, latched the door with a padlock, and leaned against it.

Could she dig six feet to Angus's body? Sure, she could. Would she? She'd more likely dig under the shed's brick footing to join Adel. Or she would sit on her fat butt and do nothing.

I went away and returned with a bucket of water and pan of feed. Adel scratched the door while I was inside with Molly.

I came out, pointed to the house, and commanded, "*Adel, in!*" A certain imperative note rang in my voice. He trotted to the door and sat.

As I sank into my easy chair with a drink in my hand, Adel made nose prints on the window glass and looked repeatedly at me.

"Forget it!"

I took a gulp of bourbon, imagining the prison trusty's expression when his bloodhounds turned toward the highway.

I visualized him hallooing the deputies, and pointing out the direction when it turned ninety degrees. I imagined the wail of highway patrol sirens as cars surrounded the area. I could see everyone's disappointment when the hot trail turned cold at the blacktopped edge of Highway 30, where Molly and I had reentered the Jeep.

I went to bed and slept. It seemed only moments later when I awakened to Adel's full-throated warning, jumped to my feet, and ran to the window.

It was a sound—not a sight—that ran a cool feather up my spine. Bloodhounds bayed fast on a hot trail. Their voices chorused *He's here! He's here!*

They'd trailed pepper. They hadn't turned aside for a bitch in season. Truer dogs never lived.

I told Adel *hush,* and went back to bed.

Five minutes later he rumbled at the back wall, then at another wall, then he went down the stairs and barked at the door.

Bloodhounds yowled outside. The meaty bottom of a fist pounded wood. "Open up! Police!" a man yelled.

I ordered Adel to *sit-stay.* Then I went downstairs, walked to the door, and turned the key.

Grady Prather's large frame blocked most of the entrance. Behind him, a trusty held back the bloodhounds, and a highway patrol car sat on the road with its top lights whirling. Deputies stood at each visible corner of my house.

"'Morning, Luke," Prather said. "Keep your hands in sight and don't do nothing foolish."

"You got a warrant?"

"It's on the way. We radioed for it. I'm just asking. We want to look in that shed."

"Nothing in there but my dog."

He shifted his weight from one cowboy boot to the other. "Then you won't mind if we look. We ain't asking to search your house. Fact is, you can put on some clothes and come with us." His gaze flicked down.

I was barefooted, wearing a T-shirt and cotton drawers. Everything I wore smelled of TINK.

"What'ja do, pee yourself when you heard us?"

"Suppose you wait outside."

"I'll come in if you don't mind." He followed me inside and lumbered up to the loft, where I dressed. Adel followed us. He seemed especially interested in the big man's hands. He licked his chops as he watched.

"Why's that dog got'a eye on me? Don't make me shoot him." Grady said. "I'm scared of dogs."

"Grady, he's not going to hurt you and don't you hurt him. I never meant advice more kindly, and never gave it more sincerely."

I pulled on jeans, combed my hair, and jammed my feet into brown loafers. The jeans were ripe with Molly's scent. The fox-urine odor had faded, but I couldn't re-perfume myself.

We went outside. Two deputies eased around my house. One was tall and thin, a stranger. The other was Jack Dean. Deputy Jack Dean wore a rumpled uniform and had a mouth shaped for dirty laughter. He was too dumb to wave the Stars and Bars and whistle Dixie at the same time, but Jack Dean was dead-game and earned respect. We nodded to one another.

The trusty bared greenish teeth as we walked to the shed. "You owe me a cold beer."

"How do you figure?"

"You bet me these dogs wouldn't follow pepper. You lose."

The hounds extended their noses to sniff my trousers. The male wanted to lift his leg on me.

"What'cha call that? What'cha call that?" The trusty pointed to the dogs' investigation of Molly's scent.

I ignored him, and called to the deputies, "There's nothing in my shed but my bassett hound, like I told you. She's in season."

The bloodhounds extended their necks longingly as I walked away.

I threw the shed door open, and caught Molly by the collar. The bloodhounds curled their tails and yowled. The bassett twisted my fingers in her collar, turned her body, and lifted her tail.

Grady walked into the shed. "We got one aluminum water bucket and one pie pan." His voice had deepened. It sounded as if he were dictating. "That's the inventory. The ground ain't broke up much. Looks like the bitch might've dug her a bed. Somebody hand the probe here."

The thin deputy brought him a three-foot steel probe with a circle welded to one end. Grady held the circle in his hands, and leaned his weight on the probe. He pushed it down in a dozen places. There was no abnormal resistance. He picked up the soil sampler, stepped on the blade flange and worked the cylinder nine inches into the soil. When he withdrew it, the sample of earth in the cylinder showed normal layering—loam on top, sandy-loam underneath, and yellow clay on bottom.

The law enforcement officers looked disappointed.

The highway patrolman was a six-foot blond. The blue uniform fitted his chest and waist in a way that said custom fit, ladies' man. He lifted the grommeted cap straight up so as not to muss his hair. "How long have you had the dog penned, Mr. Carr?"

"Bitch. She's a bitch. I ran her yesterday afternoon, but got worried we might meet a male dog, some stray, so I came home and put her in here for the night."

"When was that?"

"Just before dark."

"What direction did you hunt in?"

I pointed south, the direction the bloodhounds had come in trailing Angus.

"Shit!" the dog trainer yelped. He spread his arms and whined, "Yawl don't believe that, do you? These dogs don't lie. They trailed the man we set them on—McKay."

His appeal didn't matter. Fine lines in the deputies' faces eased. Their shoulders and arms relaxed.

"I been working hounds for twenty years," Jack Dean said. "What them two bloodhounds cold-nosed here was a bitch in heat."

The highway patrolman set his cap squarely on his head and adjusted the brim. "I've got to get on the road."

Grady waved his thanks. "We've got everything taken care of here, Bill."

The patrolman walked to his unit. The three deputies drifted toward the brown county car with the mustard stripes and shield. The trusty stood by the shed, glowering. The dogs sniffed the ground, collecting unimportant information. They were happy. They'd done their job.

Grady opened the door of the county Dodge. "Load the dogs, Charlie. You don't get no steak tonight." Then he said to me, "Luke, sorry for your trouble."

"Can I put the bitch back in her shed?"

"Sure."

"You tell Coonan I resent this intrusion."

"I will. It'll make him smile."

Jack Dean and the other deputy squeezed onto the front seat with Grady. The dogs and handler hopped into the back, behind the grille. The vehicle backed, turned and left.

It was 8:00 A.M. I already needed a drink but there wasn't time. I had to misdirect Coonan. Coonan was a thinker. He'd laugh about the trusty and the misguided bloodhounds. Then he'd look at the record.

The record would show that the Parchman bloodhounds were credited with twenty-two apprehensions and three failures. They'd located four lost children. They'd trailed a felon down the main street of Greenville without being diverted. They were truer to the joy of work than any man. Why would they turn aside for a bitch in heat?

Coonan knew what a man might do to possess a woman. But would a sheep dog abandon sheep to follow a bitch? A bird dog turn away from game? A bloodhound betray a trail?

No way. Or, not often.

I could visualize Coonan sitting in his office alone, brooding, shaking his head.

41.

That night, I delivered a bassett, a collar, a leash, a sack of Purina, a portable kennel, and a book titled *No Bad Dogs* to Billie.

Molly dangled her ears and looked appealing. I waved aside Billie's gratitude, said the gift was nothing, nothing at all, and made my way home.

The street I followed wound through gloomy warehouses and shuttered office buildings. Most of the streetlights had been knocked out by vandals. When I reached Jefferson Davis Avenue and Fifth, I saw a guy in jeans and biker jacket and another in a gray suit dragging a small woman toward an old Lincoln.

She was a wiry Latina with extravagant hair who turned an angular face from man to man. Her slender legs in toreador pants did a jerky dance step. The toes of her ballerina slippers scarcely touched pavement.

"Keep moving," I said to myself. "It's none of your business."

She looked at me and yelled, "Help me!" The Jeep's brakes screeched without command. Before my brain got involved I was gripping an axe handle I kept under the seat, and walking toward trouble.

"Hey!" I yelled. "What's going on here? Are you all right, miss?"

The men stared. The girl stared. If I hadn't been riled by seeing a woman abused I'd have noticed the men held her lightly . . . that when I yelled "Hey!" the three of them relaxed like actors when a director yells "Cut!"

It was a set-up, but I got wise too late.

A third man stepped out of the alley behind me. My peripheral vision registered white running shoes, blue track pants, a stocking mask, black jersey, and a whole lot of danger. A galvanized pipe, drawn back above the top knot in his stocking mask, was about to descend upon my head.

No time to turn . . .

I shoved my axe handle backward into his belly. He folded over it, leaking air. The piece of pipe fell from his hands and clanked on the macadam.

The three-person frieze in front of me dissolved.

The Latina with bushy hair and dancer's legs ran to the street and looked both ways.

The big guy in the gray suit hobbled toward me as if his feet hurt.

The slender guy in the biker jacket pulled out a nunchuka about a foot long.

The woman returned and circled me. The men were closer now, separating. The big guy rocked from side to side. The biker whipped the nunchuka in the air. I held them off with the axe handle, and backed toward the brick wall behind me. Then a weight landed on my back, scissors locked around my waist, an arm twisted my head, and nails peeled the skin of my face. The raw tracks across my cheeks and nose burned and stung. I felt body heat, and weight, and hot breath, and the tickle of long hair, and smelled lilac perfume.

She wears perfume to an ambush? I wondered.

My bucking bronco act dislodged the woman. Then I felt a numbing blow to my side and heard a sweet little sound like Rice Krispies encountering milk.

"You made . . . the wrong man . . . mad, boy!" a voice said.

I screamed "No!" to my popping ribs. My hands opened and closed spasmodically on the axe handle. I swung it blindly, wincing at the pain in my side. Instead of hitting the man, it grazed the girl. She yelped and grabbed the biker. I bayoneted his balls while she held him. He collapsed, screaming one pure, sustained note.

My left toe hooked the heel of the guy wearing the knuckle duster and my right leg drove a boot into his knee. It cracked loudly and he passed out.

As I rolled under the Jeep the woman scrambled inside and turned the key. She meant to drag me. I slid out from under and went after her. She threw up her hands and cringed as I tangled my hands in her hair.

The guy with the injured cods sat on the pavement vomiting. The guy with the crushed knee swooned. I muscled the girl into the air by her neck and left thigh and slammed her against the passenger door.

The guy with the soft white shoes circled me. The loose sweats he wore hid his body shape. A stocking mask blurred his features. The galvanized pipe he'd blindsided me with waved like a baseball bat in the hands of a lead off hitter.

"Come on," I said. "I've got something for you."

He didn't want any. He went to the Lincoln, and left.

I hobbled to the Jeep. The girl cowed inside, whimpering. "Please, mister," she said.

I dragged her out by her elbows. "Please," she cried, "no, mister!" but I kicked her muscular butt and watched her sprawl. Then I eased my broken body into the Jeep and cranked it. After a block her curses faded into the night.

The gray-curtained cubicle in the emergency room of City Hospital brought back mournful memories: gunshot holes, splintered bones, and heavy bleeding. I lay supine on a bright metal table under a wrinkled sheet, and counted thirty-two vertical tiles, and thirty-four horizontal. I read warnings posted on the walls. I studied the buildup of dirt and wax in the corners of the room, and eased chemical-smelling air in and out of the shallows of my lungs.

The middle-aged nurse who came in and bent over me wore no makeup and possessed no glamour. Her uniform was dingy polyester and her sponge-soled shoes had been made for comfort. The liver-speckled hands she checked me with were quick, sure, and strong. Hands no better than hers were worth a million a year to baseball players.

"Hello again, Marge," I said.

Marge is fifty-something, or sixty-something, trim and sinewy. Her eyes are cynical brown, her hair long-gone blonde.

"Three unknowns bashed me," I said.

"Which guy clawed?"

"I wasn't counting the girl." I moved to sit up, and winced.

"Lie still. You could puncture a lung."

A woman in a brown skirt and orange blouse waddled in, filling the doorframe. Her thighs were the size of old oaks and her bosom could have smothered a bear. She sucked an ice cream bar, and scolded. "Marge, you know everyone has to be logged in before receiving attention!"

Marge reached across me for scissors, and her breasts softened against my arm.

The woman with the clipboard wore purple lipstick, and her skin was white and clear. "Name?"

"You know me, Bertha."

"You can't be treated until you are logged in, Luke."

Marge ripped my shirt without asking.

"Hey! That was my good one."

"Not any more."

Blue showed along my ribs. My left hand looked like a chopped beef patty. Blood was in plenty.

Marge filled a syringe and eyed it against the light of a neon bar. "Would you fill out the form for radiology, Bertha? Dr. Bass will want skull and chest X-rays."

"The attending physician has to issue that order."

"Then get Mr. Carr's medical record. His is the thick one under 'C.' I'll bring the insurance information you need when I'm through here."

When Bertha had gone Marge said, "Is this a police matter?"

"Paid guys. I'll never see them again."

"Were you drinking?" Marge holds up my vices before my eyes like little trapped mice.

"Yes."

She pushed the needle into my arm with more force than necessary. I winced.

"Can't stand the needle, tough guy?"

"No, and I don't have any insurance, either, so the joke's on you."

"Why do you think I got Bertha out of here?"

Dr. Bass pushed aside the curtain. He was thick-bodied, round-eyed, sallow-skinned, and tired. His white coat hung like the automobile dusters you see in old movies. "What's the matter with *you?*" he growled.

"He took a beating. Possible skull fracture," Marge answered.

Dr. Bass put a soft hand under my chin and stared fixedly at my pupils. His half-glasses enlarged his eyes until they looked like something in a fish tank. "Blood pressure and pulse all right?"

"Yes, Doctor."

"What's this?" He picked up the empty syringe. "What'n hell is this!"

"I gave him a sedative."

Dr. Bass breathed deeply. "You nuts? Why did you do that, Marge? What if the man has a concussion? You want to get us sued?"

"I'm very sorry, doctor."

She wasn't sorry at all. They went through this routine all the time.

"You aren't a bit sorry." He touched my lower jaw. "Can you talk?"

I nodded.

"Do so."

"Hello, Dr. Bass."

"Hello to you. This hurt?" He gently felt my side.

"Yes."

"I thought it might. Get him to X-ray." He scribbled on the chart. "Skull, ribs, left tibia." He scowled at Marge. "If I didn't need you so much—"

"I know, doctor. You'd run me out of medicine."

Ribs aren't set, they're taped. Dr. Bass wrapped my chest, rigged my left arm in an aluminum brace, and slung a strap over my neck. Then Marge put me to bed in a semi-private room that happened to be empty.

"Cough every fifteen minutes unless you want pneumonia," Marge said cheerfully. Then she poured a cup of water, held it to my cracked lips while I drank, and left.

The beating wasn't meant to kill. It was meant to hurt so bad I would come down with a case of rabbit blood. It was a warning to leave town. I very much wanted to, except that there was somebody behind the goons who deserved cracked rib for cracked rib.

Lying in the dark, I went over the candidates.

Ballard was number one for all of the good reasons. He'd nursed a grudge for twenty years, his rival was dead, yet I had the prize. What's more, I knew him for the shoddy bastard he was.

Kinnerly was number two. I didn't believe it emotionally, but logic said so. The lady had used two men unto death. It's a hard habit to break.

Tom's son, Tommy, was number three. He was a weak kid who would hate me for having rescued him. I was a suspect in his father's death. He was jealous about me and Kinnerly.

Mr. X was number four. In life as in algebra you solve for the unknown. There is always an unknown. Someone hates you or wants what you have. Someone from your regrettable past. Or the friend or relative you least suspect.

42.

The day they released me the wind blew sharp little ice chisels that rattled on the windshield and piled around the Jeep in glittering mounds. As the Jeep crunched its way out of the parking lot, cutting black tracks through an expanse of white, I snuggled into the collar of my thin jacket. The heater huffed volumes of cool air from its defective innards.

On the drive to Ballard's house, gusts slipped the vehicle sideways. I wrenched the wheel, and wrenching the wheel hurt my ribs.

Ballard's house was burnt brick, and rambling. Three square columns supported three concrete arches that curved over the entrance to the dark front porch. In a glassed-in breezeway at the left side of the house I saw ferns and green spears, looking exotic in winter weather.

It was a spacious, Depression-era house. Ten thousand would have paid for it back then. It was worth eight or ten times that now.

Wind swept across the yard, lifting ice crystals into a spume. Limbs in the big pecan trees swayed, breaking the crystal bands that circled them, and dropping them to tinkle on the hard white surface of the yard. I was feeling sore and fragile. The house was a cold, long distance from the road.

When I touched the bell button, a gong sounded inside, and the white paneled door opened immediately. A tall woman stood behind a screen door, hugging herself. Thick white hair piled on her head. A pince-nez, attached to a silver chain, sat upon her nose. Her smile lay in a net of wrinkles.

"May I help you?" She glanced over my shoulder at the sky as she spoke.

"How do you do? My name is Luke Carr. I'm looking for Mr. Ballard."

She opened the screen and extended a soft hand. "How do you do? Come in, won't you? I'm Jeff's mother. We are getting ready to attend the Jesse Hill Ford lecture tonight, but I'm sure he can see you for a few minutes. The library is this way." She led me down a dark hall, into a small library, and offered a seat. "I'll tell Jeff you're here."

I looked around at a leather sofa and chair, Oriental carpets, Steiff brass lamps, and antique candle stands. The books in the glass-fronted bookcases—the kind you usually see in lawyers' offices—seemed to be leather-bound classics. I slid up the protective glass on one shelf and looked at the titles—*The Mayor of Casterbridge, The Return of the Native, Far from the Madding Crowd, Jude the Obscure.* I pulled *Far from the Madding Crowd* from the shelf, gently opened the pages, saw the date—1874—and smelled again the rich odor of old leather and book dust.

A sense of being watched caused me to turn. "I was admiring your collection of Hardy," I said, as I closed the volume and placed it on a table. "This one is a favorite of mine."

Ballard wore a navy suit, white shirt, subdued tie, and black, cap-toed shoes. His green eyes bored right into me.

"Mr. Carr," he said, "I thought you said we had nothing to discuss."

"We have plenty to discuss. Somebody sent tough guys to see me and work me over. I thought we should talk about it and see if it is likely to happen again."

He laughed, and it was not a nervous laugh. This was a different guy from the one who had come to my place.

He glanced at his wristwatch. "I don't want to be inhospitable, but we're attending a lecture. Mother doesn't like being late."

"Sure. But if the guys that busted me up were thinking of doing it again, maybe you could get word to them."

"I don't know what you're talking about."

"I understand that. If I'd tried to arrange a hit with someone, and he came to my place, maybe wired, I wouldn't know anything about anything, either. You don't have to know what I'm talking about. You just have to be in a position to pass the word."

His pupils were shot through with bright splinters, like fractured ice. "I repeat. I don't know what you are talking about. You'll have to excuse us. We're late."

"The sheriff thinks somebody wants to set me up for murder. He thinks somebody wants a fall guy. I said I don't have an enemy in the world. But then, guys with pipes and fighting sticks and brass knuckles—guys that do this for a living—make me think I've got it wrong. They make me think I'd better make a sworn statement and put it in a safe deposit box. Which I did."

His eyes held mine.

"If I don't get beat up again, that sworn statement will stay there because it isn't anything I want made public. If it is made public, it will be as hard on me as it will be on other people. All of us that got involved in a certain matter will go down."

"This is the most peculiar conversation of my life. If you don't leave I'll call the police."

"Yeah, I can see now, after looking at your house and your furniture and your books and your mother, you're not a man who would know about a thing like this." I started for the door. "I'll leave now."

He followed. I opened the door. He made an impatient gesture. I hobbled across the yard with my coat whipping against my legs as he shut the door behind me.

One thing was clear. I had badly underestimated Mr. Jeff Ballard.

43.

When Kinnerly came to me, there was no hiding the bruises or the scraped hand. She saw all of me.

"Why didn't you call?" she said. "You should have called. I'd have taken care of you."

"I go into a hole when I'm hurt."

"We can't wait any longer, darling."

"You're right."

I took her arm and we went to her car to talk in case my cabin was wired.

She reached across the seat and held my tenderized hand. "Let's get the money and go before Jeff Ballard does something even crazier."

I nodded.

"What's the plan?" She watched my mouth, waiting for words that would solve our problems.

"It's as simple as can be. We switch the art before delivery to the museum for appraisal. We sell the good stuff and deposit the money in a Swiss account. I know how to do that. Or, in a Caribbean bank. We go to Brazil, pay off the right officials, and stay there."

"There has to be more to it."

"There is. The key is no one knows, maybe for years, that we've looted the estate. That keeps the insurance detectives off our necks. Those guys are relentless."

I strung the plan out, making it sound more nailed down than it was.

"We'll start with the prints in the art collection. We sell the original engravings through a dealer in New Orleans and substitute restrikes. They look the same—hand-colored, and all—except the underlying lines are not as sharp on restrikes. Then we'll do the same with the original bronzes. Substitute third-generation copies for originals."

"I'm not sure I understand."

"OK. In nineteenth-century England the best sporting engravers—Brown, Pollard, Roviskere, Stubbs, Ward—guys like that—they engraved on copper. The copper plates were inked and prints were pulled. Women and street kids, working in garrets, painted the prints. Usually one color was laid down by each child."

"Street waifs, you mean."

"Yeah, child labor. They did piece work, like in Dickens. The engraved copper plates were used to pull prints as long as people would buy. When the market ran out, the old plates were stuck away and forgotten."

She nodded.

"Now the old plates have been brought out of vaults. Prints

are being pulled from them again. But the engravings are worn, so the bite of the lines into paper is less sharp."

"But the new prints are not colored, are they?"

"People still color them by hand. Amateurs, art students, and dealers do it."

"Can't people tell new prints from old? I think I could."

"Sure, if they lay them out side by side. Sure, if they're experts who have compared originals with restrikes, or if they know enough about paper to tell old hundred-percent rag from bleached woodpulp."

I explained that dealers in sporting prints advertise in *Antiques* and in *Sporting Art*. Since prints were issued in multiple copies, our advertising a good collection of original prints wouldn't attract as much attention as our advertising one-of-a-kind oil paintings.

"So what you're going to do is sell originals and substitute restrikes?"

"Yes. Then we leave here separately, rendezvous in New Orleans, fly to Mexico, and get you new identity papers. Then on to Brazil."

"But how will we get the money to Brazil?"

"You're going to courier it."

Her eyes filled. "You'd trust me that much?"

"Of course."

That afternoon I spent a couple of hours in the library looking through Nevill's *Old Sporting Prints*. I didn't check out the book because I didn't want that record established. The illustrations and print lists reminded me of which originals I had seen in the show Tom had at the library.

After I had made a list, I checked the *London Catalog* to get the names and telephone numbers of print dealers.

In *Antiques* I found the names of legitimate American dealers who might buy originals. One was the Sporting Gallery in Middleburg, Virginia. That looked promising, as did Taylor Clark in Baton Rouge. A small boxed ad named a dealer who especially interested me—a specialist in nineteenth-century sporting prints. Rene Sousa in Charleston, South Carolina.

I made calls to London from a payphone. At Fores a young man with a languid accent sold me a restrike of Flying Childers for seven pounds. The other prints I needed cost from three pounds to eighteen. I reached Henry Southern and bought four Wards and Pollards for thirty-eight pounds. In the print department of Foyles there were five more on my list, and at Weinreb and Donwma, I bought restrikes of Alken's series on partridge shooting.

After that, I called the American dealer, Rene Sousa. A man answered. I asked for Rene. He said *he* was Rene. I told Rene I was interested in selling my collection of first-edition sporting prints for cash. He said that might be difficult. I said I had anticipated that, and gave him enough detail about artists, engravers, and publishers so he knew I knew what I was talking about. We agreed that I would send the prints insured. He would pay by cashier's check if they passed examination.

After the calls were made, and money was sent to England by air to pay for restrikes, there was nothing to do but wait a few days.

We decided to make the exchange in the old cotton warehouse Tom and his father and grandfather had operated.

44.

She turned the brass key and swung the door open on a vast, low-ceilinged room that had once been a feed store. It was private enough, with dim, high windows and paint-puckered walls. Its scent was dampness, sour grain, rat crap, and something else . . . maybe fear.

In here generations of tenant farmers had accounted to generations of Morris men for their furnish—had struck deals at usurious rates for a few dollars cash for Christmas—had bargained to hold over for another year. The odor of nervous sweat permeated the place.

I had already cut Japanese paper into hinges and brewed rice paste. On a long store counter Kinnerly removed dust sealers from the backs of picture frames. Then she slipped out original prints and detached the rice paper hinges connecting the prints to their mats.

I placed new hinges on the restrike prints. Then I glued the other half of the hinges to the old mats the original prints had been displayed in. Over and over I did that. Carefully, delicately.

It was sixty degrees in there. Even so, a bandanna circled my brow to keep sweat from dripping onto the work. I was doing in fifteen or twenty minutes what a professional framer would have spent an hour doing.

Each hinge had to be placed in the exact spot that had been occupied by the one it replaced. The work was as delicate as painting dials of a watch with a one-hair brush.

After an hour of it, Kinnerly pressed her hands to the middle of her back, shook her hair, and flashed a smile. The old prints were neatly stacked. Their mats were prepared for restrikes.

I guided her through a mat replacement with her fingers following mine.

The first print was an Alken. It showed a pink-coated rider's top hat falling as he jumped a bay gelding over a rail fence. The hat jiggled on a cord. A foxhound scurried under the fence and another scrambled over it.

The door handle rattled. Kinnerly and I looked at each other, then stared at the door. Someone outside bumped it. I tiptoed to a window and saw a grizzled man in khaki pants and a thin jacket careen away. He looked like a drunk.

Kinnerly was shaking. She forced a laugh. "I'm ready to get out of here."

"We can do four to six an hour. We'll give the paste just an hour to set."

We finished at 4:18 P.M. Kinnerly loaded her car, drove to the museum, and delivered the substitute prints to the curator. She had the curator sign a receipt, and returned home.

My new friend Rene was delighted with the originals he received in the mail. For forty-two choice, nineteenth-century sporting prints he sent two cashier's checks, one for $2,400 and one for $9,000, to my new identity, Ulysses Laudner. I cashed the checks in Memphis at different banks, using my new driver's license and social security card. That was it.

Kinnerly wasn't pleased. "*Eleven* thousand? That's what we get for all that work and risk?"

I explained that it was dealer price, and low at that. The bronzes would bring more. "We ought to net a hundred grand," I told her. But I was talking to a woman who had been married to a millionaire.

When I cataloged the bronzes I found an equestrian figure by Earl Haig, signed and dated 1911; a group of stallions and wolfhound, inscribed E. Canana; a sheep inscribed *Brebis née à la Douarriere;* a setter dog signed T. Cartier; a stag signed C. Va; a bull by Rosa Bonheur; a long-haired retriever with a pheasant in his mouth standing beside a tree stump, signed Fratin; a setter and a pointer surprising a hidden partridge, signed P. J. Mene; a pointer, a pheasant, a rabbit, and sporting equipment, signed P. J. Mene; and a pointer by Dubucand, Mene's son-in-law.

Kinnerly sold two furs in Memphis, some small antiques from her attic, and took out a loan on her convertible to raise cash for us to begin the scam.

From a "picker" in Coral Gables, who bought from estates and sold to hunters through *The American Field,* I bought second- and third- and fourth-generation impressions of eleven of the originals. I paid $800 for a copy of the Mene pointer and setter, and $250 for the little Mene setter.

I sold the Mene original through the Southby Park Bernet auction house in New York for $5,000, and the other pieces proportionately. The total for the eleven came to $31,000 after commissions and shipping fees. We kept the little Dubucand pointer because something about him reminded me of Adel.

"So we have forty-two thousand dollars," Kinnerly said. "We're rich." She had her hands on her hips, a sarcastic look in her eyes.

"We've got forty-two thousand dollars and nobody suspects a thing. That's a beginning."

I told Kinnerly to have Mrs. Tate at the museum complete an inventory of the art estate as fast as possible, then Dr. Billingsley from ⁺he university art department could appraise the restrike prints and second-generation bronzes.

"He'll *know*," Kinnerly said.

"All the better," I said. "Billingsley will provide proof that Tom was 'taken' on some of his purchases."

Billingsley, Kinnerly later told me, sucked spittle in his pipe and looked owlishly at the too-perfect patina of three bronzes. He used a wet pipe stem to point to the lack of detail in the musculature of dogs. He suggested that Mr. Morris had been cheated. Kinnerly was indignant. Later, over a brandy, she and Billingsley commiserated about how dealers take advantage of purchasers.

Kinnerly told Dr. Billingsley she so much wished her husband had asked his advice before buying.

45.

The next day Adel awakened me by bowing and stretching beside the bed.

In the kitchen I drank orange juice while coffee brewed in a pot plugged into a wall timer. Standing on one bare foot and then the other on the cold floor, wearing my underwear and a terry robe, I soon had bacon popping in the black iron skillet, two eggs sliding in grease, and four pieces of wheat toast tanning. I wolfed down the food and drank the juice and three mugs of coffee while sitting in the living room, looking out over the tricky, false light. Our Southern weather, which can leap seasons overnight, had changed. It wanted me to think it was summer. It wanted me to trust it.

Not me. In the woods you're on your own. You'd better have everything you need for survival if the unexpected happens.

THE HIT

The dog wanted to go for a walk. I didn't. He begged.

I went to the bathroom, picked up a razor, and looked at my bearded face. Thirty-two, and already gray at the temples. Sinewy muscles ran across my shoulders and knotted my arms . . . endurance muscles, not showy, not the weight-lifting kind. I ached from the beating I had taken.

When I stopped smiling the light went out of my eyes. They looked like black holes that had taken in too much.

I shaved, showered, and pulled on fresh underwear.

I did all the things to begin a day right. Yet something was wrong.

The dog scratched the door and pushed in. He looked at me and wiggled. "All right—a walk!" I said.

The woolens I pulled on felt hot and hairy. All the gear I packed—rain slicker, compass, fire-starter, knife, .38 Detective Special, bionic ear, stocking cap, and emergency blanket—felt heavy and useless. I packed it anyway and went to the woods.

I'd killed my first noncombatants. There were three easy explanations. I was a dumb, simple tool anyone could trigger; I was a mix of bad genes and rotten experience and couldn't help it; or I was a free-willed human being who liked violence and chose situations that led to it.

I sat under a huge pine and sweated and scratched, and kept my mind on one meaningless phrase, hoping for wisdom to sift in, Zen-style.

I looked a little to one side of—not directly at—unformed ideas that floated through my mind, because that's how you best see things in the dark.

The dog walked in a circle and settled head to tail so he could watch me. The sun warmed my eyelids with a red glow. My thoughts drifted.

There was that Greek frieze again, the one I'd dreamed about. I saw a runner with indistinct features and a band around his hair. Kinnerly was running ahead of that guy, looking over her shoulder. Her mouth twisted in a grimace of fear, and one of her hands extended pleadingly. A tall, mean-looking kid ran ahead of her, carrying a dagger. And coming around the curve of the urn on everybody's blind side was Jeff Ballard. Jeff's head was thrown back and his chest bulged. He ran like a winner.

Adel whined and pawed me. I awoke with a start and the edgy feeling that I had missed something important.

I dug the headphones out, cut on the microphone, and scanned the area. Nothing much. A breeze quickened against my damp face. Clouds rolled in, darkening the sky in the east. Trees creaked and thunder rumbled. Birds fell silent.

I shouldered the pack. Adel and I trotted toward the house. I kept the bionic earphones set on low. When we neared the cabin we went to our bellies. Rain spattered on dry leaves. Then it pelted us. I lay with the mike extended, surveying the perimeter. The dog stood and shook. I ordered him down, and when he half-squatted, cuffed him. We endured it for ten minutes, then went in.

Something was missing in my Zen vision. I had awakened before I'd seen the whole frieze. So I put in a call to my special friend.

In the first moment when I'd think of Harry I'd remember being very alone, with VC gunfire plucking up mud beside me.

I was a blood striper with a short life expectancy. The men didn't trust me. I had led them into an ambush, doing things by the book. Looking around from my position, I saw they were gone.

I dived into a hole. A grenade arced toward me and landed

five or six feet away. The explosion and concussion shook me senseless. Then, from my left flank, Harry opened up *wham! wham! wham!* with a shotgun. He could have slid back with the rest of the patrol, but he'd stayed.

If there was anyone I could trust it was Harry.

46.

Harry popped the cap on a Miller and gave me a slate-eyed stare. The gangling length of him stretched from my big chair to the middle of the floor. An olive T-shirt hung loosely from his sloped shoulders. He yawned and exposed a mouthful of yellow teeth. You could count on an apologetic grin after each wide-mouthed yawn.

"OK, Lieut. You got me here. Where's the action?"

When I'd telephoned him, Harry had just enough money in his wallet for food, but he didn't stop for more. He pounded on my door at 8:00 P.M., carrying a satchel that looked like business, and wearing fatigues and one of those photographer's jackets, handy for concealing big pistols. He promptly put away six fried eggs, a half-pound of bacon, a saucepan of grits, five slices of wheat toast, a half-cup of sorghum, and a quart of coffee.

He had a disarming grin and hard eyes. The eyes searched my face.

At six-foot-four and 250 pounds, Harry was a big enough man to go into the tough parts of Memphis on insurance investigations. He wore a cheap suit and spoke politely. He stared at people with unafraid eyes. In the city he looked like a cop. This night he looked like a patrol leader, ready for a fire fight.

"Hope I didn't get you down here for nothing," I said.

It was hard for me to ask Harry the questions I needed to have answered. I got up and paced the room. I told myself *Stop bleeding, Luke. This is the guy you trust most.*

I told him that I liked . . . *no, loved!* . . . the woman he'd told me had been sleeping with Ballard. She'd lied to me about that and more at first, but she'd been straight with me since, so far as I knew. Now we were in a scam that could turn sour, and I felt uneasy.

He held up a hand with palm spread, signaling halt. "Does this have an insurance angle?"

"Not that I know of."

"Go on."

"I know in my military mind, as we used to say, something's wrong. She may be setting me up. There's a chill up my back. If I were in country instead of here, I'd be busting bush."

"So?" His eyes were the flat gray of gravel. He told it like it was, how it had to be. "Do what we did in country. Set a trap. If she sticks to the straight and narrow, well and good. If she goes off-trail—*bang!*"

"That's hard."

"Life is hard. Surviving it is harder."

"I don't want to get her hurt."

"Even if her and the other guy intend to plant you? Then lead with your neck, turkey. Gobble, gobble, season's open."

"She could make an honest mistake."

"There ain't no such thing as 'honest mistake' if you set it up right." He gave me a long look. "You're not pussy-whipped, are you, Lieut?"

"Shut your mouth."

He gazed at the dog to give me time to cool off, so I took it. Truth be told, the idea he was pushing had crossed my mind. Ballard was seriously interested in *taking* my Scotch-Irish ass. She could be urging him on. I was the only living connection between Kinnerly and Tom's murder.

"The only way," I began, "the only way would be to warn her she was being tested, and rig a trap that couldn't harm her accidentally."

"You sure are particular these days!" He rubbed his whiskery jaw. "But no sweat. Flag a minefield."

In World War II and Korea, we marked our minefields. Their purpose was to slow the enemy. We couldn't leave them unmarked because we might have to retreat over that same ground.

I walked to the window, stared out at blackness, and turned. "Am I paranoid?"

He was getting a faraway voice and his little eyes looked bored.

"You've got the guts of a fighting cock, Lieut. Not much sense about women, but the guts of a Toleman roundhead."

"I asked if you think I'm paranoid."

"You could have been a soldier of fortune with Mad Mike and got rich, but did you? You fought for your country." Harry shook his head. "Nuts, yes; paranoid, no."

"I've got to prove her," I said.

"Damn straight! Prove her." Harry got up and stretched. Adel limped between us, wagging his tail.

Harry reached down to tickle an ear. "This is one fine dog."

"The best. Want to see what he can do?"

"Not on your life. Nice doggie."

"In case I should have to pull out of here fast, how'd you like to take care of him?"

"Are you kidding?"

"He's no trouble, and better than most men in a fight. The reason he's limping, he didn't get whipped. He got ambushed."

Harry's whistle was long and low. "Things *have* been rough here. What can I help you with?"

"The guy I mentioned, Jeff Ballard. He's the fuzzy-edged piece in my puzzle. I know he wanted Morris dead. I know he and Kinnerly had an affair. I'm not sure where he stands with her now. I got beat up by professionals, and that makes me mighty suspicious. Put a *make* on him for me. Isn't that what detectives say?"

"I didn't bring my cheap suit and narrow-eyed stare, but I'll mosey around and see what I can learn."

Notebook 9

47.

The money from the sale of the prints and bronzes would get us to a safe country, but there wouldn't be enough for bribes and maintenance. I'd have to rip off the paintings.

We could decrease the risk by lifting them before inventory. The safest ones to take were those no one liked, but Kinnerly wasn't sure which were Tommy's favorites.

"The little stallion is one," she said, making a small rectangle with her hands.

"The Troy."

"And the long-legged rocking horses racing at Epsom Downs?"

"The Sartorius. What about the big oil of brood mares, the Stubbs?"

"I don't remember Tommy paying any attention to that one."

"Or the Pollard? It shows a coach-and-four."

She shook her head. "You know the paintings better than I do, and you've only seen them once. He's crazy about the Pollard, adores it. Has it in his room."

"That one's out."

"The Wootton is a good one for us. It has a Turk holding a stallion. The horse's ears are cut like a doberman's."

"He doesn't like *that?*"

"It wasn't a favorite of Tom's, either. He couldn't understand palm trees and a Turk being in an English countryside."

If a museum curator had displayed the Wootton, she'd remember it. She'd have it in a catalog, too. Let something be missing and curators raise a stink.

When I asked about paintings not on display, Kinnerly said, "We've got an *enormous* painting in the attic of two bird dogs, an Osthaus, I think." She stretched her arms as far as they would go. "It nearly covers a wall."

"We can't take that. There are probably not three bird dog paintings in the world as good. We need out-of-style Victorians. I should take a look."

"Tommy's always about."

"Then take him to lunch. Make it a long lunch, and leave the door unlocked."

A rusty green Chevrolet passed me as I walked the last block to her house. Its bumper hung. One light was dead in its socket. The other fingered the pavement with wobbly stealth. The guy behind the wheel, sitting very erect, waved a Budweiser can. His wipers dry-swished across a bug-spotted windshield. It wasn't dark and it wasn't raining.

Wearing a service uniform and belt of tools, I looked innocuous. You'd have let me into your house to check for a gas leak, or to make a telephone switch-over.

That's how the Boston Strangler worked.

Kinnerly's house sprawled on top of a hill, screened from other houses by skillfully arranged plantings of African love grass and Lombardy poplars. I knew the downstairs layout from a map she'd drawn for me.

Inside the hallway, I paused. The living room and the gun room beyond it were empty of people, but overstuffed with things. Rose-carpeted stairs stood at my right. The grandfather clock on the landing bonged the half-hour as I went up the stairs two at a time. The boy's bedroom faced the stairs on the second floor. There was a huge aquarium in there. A pump fluttered. Beta fish fanned bright challenges as bubbles cascaded up through trembling plants.

I climbed the stairs to the attic and fumbled for a key, then remembered I didn't need one. The door opened as if the hinges had been oiled just for me.

Light from my flashlight brushed chests of drawers, built-in wardrobes, cases of books, boxes of toys—the accumulation of generations. Something rectangular, covered by a sheet, leaned against the wall by a gable window. It was a painting frame. There were others.

I moved frames to the center of the floor and stripped the dust covers.

The paintings were of a different style from those I'd seen in the library show. Tom's grandfather had probably collected them.

A watercolor with pigment laid down solidly held my attention. In it, two horses with rat tails and Roman noses were led by a hunchbacked boy before a sharp-faced buyer. The signature was

Robert Bevan. Next to the Bevan was an economical sketch of Lady Mary Heyrik, by Landseer. Eight or ten cunning lines had formed it.

Faced against the wall was an Alfred Munnings of two strong cobs, hair bristled against the cold, carrying red-faced fox hunters.

A brown gouache by someone I didn't know showed a brood mare under an oak tree, nuzzled by a flat-eared, spraddle-legged foal. The mare lifted one leg and turned her head to nip.

I scribbled notes in a pocket pad. There were ten paintings we should take. Should I get a truck and come back for them, or ask Kinnerly to move them? Both were risky.

An hour later I backed a rented panel truck up the driveway. A ming aurelia in a pot big enough to boil clothes in partially blocked the back entrance to the house. Somebody had dragged it there for the light. Somebody strong . . . not Kinnerly.

I carried down the paintings two at a time, stacked them in the van, and closed its door. After the third trip a telephone rang deep in the house. It stopped mid-ring. I wiped my face, making a dusty smear, and climbed the stairs again.

That was when he came in.

From the top of the stairs I looked down at the clipped hair and dark, intelligent face of the houseboy.

"Mrs. Morris!" he called. "It's *me*. Anybody home?"

I tried to make myself part of the wall. In Vietnam I had become part of the jungle, the rot, and the stench. Vanished into it. But the Bevan under my left arm and the Palmer under my right wouldn't blend into this background.

His heels clicked on polished floors. "Mrs. Morris?"

He was going to see me.

The house boy's expectations had to control what he saw. I had to become a delivery man. "Jack," I said in a nasal twang. I hitched a painting higher on my hip. "Give me a hand here, will you?"

He jumped. A hard, black face aimed at me. The guy wasn't buying. "I don't know you. How did you get in here?" he said.

"By the door, just like you." I went down the stairs. "Mrs. Morris said for me to deliver these to the museum. Here, take one. I gotta open the door."

I handed him a painting and walked to the back door.

"Isn't the museum closed? I think it's closed."

"One hour more," I said. "I got to hurry and get the receipts signed. Else, I got to bring this stuff back."

He followed me. I edged around the iron pot. "This fugging plant is in the way. Why don't you move it?"

He edged around the plant.

"Be careful! Don't jam that pitcher on anything. It'll be my ass!"

Hostile and distrusting, he went to the back door of the van.

"In the front!" I grumbled. "I can't put no art pitchers in back. In the front!"

I opened the passenger side door, blocking his view, and slid in the painting I had carried. I took the other from him and put it inside, too. He watched as I picked up a yellow pad and wrote a receipt for two animal paintings. I signed it Palmer; City Delivery; Destination, City Museum, and closed the van door. "You give this to Miz Morris."

"Do I know you?"

"You ever go to the Hot Sauce Bar?"

"That's not my scene."

"Maybe you saw me on television in the gay rights march." I walked around the vehicle, opened the driver's side door, got in, started the engine, and called back, "Tell Miz Morris I took care of her pitchers."

Then I pulled out.

———

Six or eight men lounged outside the hiring hall, two of them wearing tight pants, big combs in their hair, hostility in their eyes.

I stopped and cranked down the glass. "Hey! One of you want to make ten bucks in ten minutes?"

A tall man jive-stepped to the van. "What you got in mind?"

"Deliver a package. I got a bum knee. Can't get in and out."

Jive Step slapped his own knee. "Man can't make his delivery! Man wants a nigger to make his delivery!"

I drove further down the line.

A shorter man in overalls and a ragged jacket gave me a tired look out of bloodshot eyes. "This on the up?"

"All you got to do is carry two pitchers twenty yards." I shrugged. "You don't wanna carry two pitchers for ten bucks, I'll get one of these other guys." The motor raced.

He put a hand on the door. "I'll do it." He walked around to the other side, opened the door, and slid in. He spread his knees to avoid the paintings.

We left. At the museum, I parked and told him to carry in the pictures from the front of the van. Say Mrs. Morris sent them and ask that a receipt be signed. I prepared the receipt and handed it to him. "Take 'um in one at a time. Don't bang 'um against any-thing. Got it?"

He made two trips, then opened the side door and got back in.

"Everything OK?"

He handed me the receipt.

"They say anything?"

"Naw."

"Nothing?"

He poked a finger in his ear, dug, and examined what he'd

excavated. "Woman said a man called from the house. Asked had you got here." He studied his fingernail and flicked out the debris under it.

"Yeah?"

At Jefferson Avenue I handed him two fives and put him out.

"You got any more little jobs, remember me," he said.

"I will," I said. "You did good."

So I pulled it off. Right?

The houseboy saw the delivery man he expected. He saw two paintings removed, not twelve. The museum person signed a receipt for two, not twelve. Nobody but Kinnerly knew we got away with the paintings from the attic. Everything checked.

They were worth $250,000—$300,000 at auction. And we were in the clear.

48.

The next evening Harry sat in my living room to report. His eyes sunk into his head like the red-hawed eyes of a coonhound that's been up all night.

"I picked Ballard up at his house and followed him," Harry said. "He went to the library."

"That figures. He's on the library board."

"Then he went back to this farm. Went to a garage. I saw him go into the house. He was carrying a bunch'a books. I couldn't stick around, so I spent part of the day patrolling the highway, hoping to pick him up when he came out."

"Which farm was this?"

"Big old place. Mansion on it, like Tara in *Gone with the Wind*, except smaller."

"On Corinth Road? Lots of big trees along a lane, and the house on a hill in a grove?"

"You've got it."

"The Ballard place. That's the plantation Tom Morris took away from the Ballards about twenty years ago. What's he doing there?"

"Got no idea. The man carried a stack of books. It was like a shelf of them from a library. I didn't stick around."

"But—"

"Let me finish." Harry sat very still, hands in his lap, and spoke like a kid reciting. "At sixteen-hundred hours, when it was getting dark, a car came by the filling station where I'd stopped for a Coke. Red Ford driven by a pretty redhead. I followed on a hunch. She went to the house, parked in front, and went right in. I drove toward town, trying to figure out what to do. But the pretty lady passed me, fanning that Ford. She passed me on a curve going about fifty-five. I tailed her to a house on Morris Street. It was clear from looks and address that she was your lady. She didn't come out of the house again. Around twenty-hundred hours I went to a motel, which, incidentally, is your ticket." He handed me a yellow receipt.

"Can you stay another day?"

He shrugged.

"I want you to set up a black box so we can record the phone calls."

"I'll have to go to Memphis for that."

"I've got one." I crossed the room and got the box out of a cabinet in the kitchen.

A black box is a trade term for a voice-activated recorder that can be placed anywhere on a telephone line. It starts recording when the first voice speaks and cuts off when the last stops.

"You want it on her line, or his?"

"Put it on the bait."

While Harry was tapping a recorder onto Kinnerly's line I went through catalogs and ordered equipment I might need.

A *New Science* mail-order catalog offered light switches that activate when you walk into or out of a room, and a security door alarm that trips when a door is touched. I leafed the pages. The item I wanted was a security travel case. Security travel cases have false bottoms for important papers. The things are rigged so that if anyone attempts to open the latches without using two keys in correct sequence, an alarm is activated. The case screams. The one I found was made of black vinyl, with a leather-like look. It cost ninety-six dollars.

Out of a model-airplane catalog I ordered a compact electric starter and battery pack. The few sticks of dynamite I needed would be purchasable without a record from a building site worker.

To review how to make a bomb, I looked in a copy of Colonel Rex Applegate's *Explosives for Sabotage* I'd bought earlier at a gun show. Everything I needed to know was there. Then I burned the book, in case my place was searched.

That afternoon I drove to Tupelo to buy explosives and a half-pound of ten-penny nails.

The clerk of the construction company wore a checkered shirt, blue jeans, and a John Deere billed hat. He had a long nose, bushy mustache, and weak eyes. His gloomy little cubicle held a one-board counter littered with blueprints, coffee cups, a Mason jar of sugar, a dirty spoon, and a stack of ledgers. He blinked at me. "What can I do for you?"

"Do you sell dynamite?"

"Are you kidding?" he said. "That's against the law without a permit. How much you need?"

"Two sticks."

"What for?"

"To blow tree stumps in my pasture."

He squinted. "Do I know you?"

"No."

"Ain't you Marvin Gooch?"

"No, wrong man."

"I'm *sure* you're Marvin Gooch, the licensed dynamite man from Meridian."

"Oh. Yeah, I'm Marvin."

"Well, Marvin, you forgot to bring your license, didn't you? On account of that, this stuff will cost you fifty dollars a stick. I got a risk here, see, letting you take it without that number. I got a risk until I get it."

"OK."

He looked me over some more, chewed his mustache, and walked around me. "You're not a cop, are you, Marvin?"

I said I wasn't a cop.

"You're not bothering niggers or nigger churches, are you, Marvin? I don't want the F.B.I. knocking at my door just because I helped a fellow blaster blow stumps. You got my meaning?"

"I'm not a Klansman. I want to blow tree stumps."

"Stumps, huh." He went to the magazine marked EXPLO-SIVES, unlocked a padlock, drew a chain through a hole in a wooden door, and returned with two greasy, paper-wrapped sticks of dynamite ten inches long and as big around as sausages. He slapped them on the counter.

I paid him in twenties and tens. He put the money in his wallet. The sticks would be reported as used on the job.

"You got to be careful with this stuff, Marvin. George Allman blowed hisself up six months ago. He thought a fuse had done gone out when it slow-burned on him. Maybe you heard. Terrible thing."

THE HIT

"I don't believe I did hear."

He poised a pencil over a pad and made circles in air. "How do you spell Gooch?"

"G-o-o-c-h," I said.

He wrote it. "And you're blowing stumps?"

"That's it. Blowing stumps."

"I'm writing you a receipt for five dollars. This is what is called an accommodation sale. You got to bring your license number to make it right."

"All right." I was looking for the door.

He lit a cigarette and puffed smoke from the side of his mouth. "If the F.B.I. comes knocking, you better give your soul to God. I mean it, 'cause your ass will belong to some friends of mine."

"They won't come knocking."

"You sure you're not after a nigger?"

"I'm sure."

He rubbed his chin. "Catfish now. That's the coming thing. A man could blow him a hole in the ground, let it fill up with rain water, put in catfish fingerlings, and feed them things corn. They turn grain into meat better than pigs. Feller here has got him some. Calls 'um up like pets. Them things mill around on top of the water, saying 'Feed me, feed me.'"

I marveled at that.

"A man would need more than two sticks to get in the catfish business."

"Right," I said. "Thanks very much. This is all I need."

Harry was drinking a beer when I drove into the yard. The business parts of a bomb lay in a paper sack on the seat beside me.

Once I was inside, he waved me to a gook chair. "All done, good buddy. I attached the box to the telephone line. A drop wire runs down the pole. The box is head high."

"In plain sight?"

"That's the best way."

"How do I pick up the tapes?"

"Get yourself a lineman's uniform and a pair of blinkers. Keep your back to the house. Or stop by at night. It only takes fifteen seconds to change tapes."

"What's my bill?"

"So far? That's twenty hours of surveillance at a special price to you of twenty dollars per, and four hours of travel at ten dollars, plus mileage at \$64.80, plus motel at thirty-five dollars, and meals and incidentals at thirty-six dollars. You also owe me for two days' leave at Commercial Credit."

He got up. Adel got between us. Harry eyed the dog. "You serious about leaving him with me?"

"Yeah."

"Then make the bill \$275.80. That's mileage, out-of-pocket expense, and my leave time."

"You're not buying my dog."

"I'm not trying to."

"Thanks." I counted the money and he tucked it into his side pocket.

After a week I picked up the tape in the black box on the telephone post. I chose a rainy night. The pick-up and my return home went as smoothly as Harry had promised.

The tape player whirred to reverse. I clicked "Play." She'd called the cleaners, the Methodist Church, two women about playing bridge, and a clothing store. Ballard had called her, but never got very far. She'd hung up. All he'd do was say her name and she'd hang up. But one time she didn't.

I watched the tape unreel on my cassette player while words filled my mind.

He said, "I've got to see you. I'm going crazy."

She said nothing.

"This man is wrong for you."

She said nothing.

"Get rid of him or I'll get rid of him."

She hissed. It was very dramatic. I didn't know her voice. "Stay away from me. Don't call me again."

"I was desperate. I am desperate. Listen to me."

"No, you listen to me! Stay off of my property and out of my house. Don't come back."

"You've talked this way before. You're the one who always comes back."

"Not this time."

"Yes, this time."

I smoked my pipe, walked to the porch, and looked at the stars. Adel got in my way, wagging his stub. I kneed him and snapped, "Get out of my way." Hard talk made him happy. He adored me awhile.

I went inside to the phone and dialed her number. Someone picked up the receiver, and I knew it was she. I hung up.

Part of me wanted to take the cash and forget Kinnerly. Ninety percent of me wanted to prove her so I could trust her forever.

49.

Ten thousand is the magic number the Feds are interested in, the figure bank officials are required to report. The money for the paintings I sold came in a series of nine-thousand-dollar checks, as I'd insisted. I deposited the checks in different out-of-town accounts under my new identity. When the checks cleared, I closed the accounts and took the cash.

Then I put together the working part of the booby trap from memory of the diagram in Applegate's manual.

All it took was an electric burglar alarm, a model-airplane starter, the battery pack, a pound of nails, and two sticks of dynamite. The bomb went into the false bottom of the briefcase. It would explode if someone didn't operate two keys in the right sequence, or if someone forced the locks.

I noticed that I kept thinking *someone,* although the someone had a name, and a scent, and a familiar touch.

Kinnerly counted the bundles of currency as I stacked them inside the case. "Excuse me," I said, stepping into the space she yielded, putting my broad back in front of her as I closed the lid. First, the key marked "R" went into the left lock, then the key marked "L" went into the right lock. I turned the key in the left lock, then I turned the key in the right lock. The mechanism was set. I took a deep breath. Blocking her view had gone well, but if I had wired the bomb wrong it was going to blow. If the case had a faulty lock with one little wire sticking out, it was going to blow.

Nothing happened.

"Well?" She was impatient to leave.

"One more minute." I put the two little keys, hooked together by a beaded chain, into her hand. If it was going to be a test, it was going to be a real one.

"You're not to open this case for any reason whatsoever."

"Goodness. How many times do we have to go over it?"

"As many as it takes. This is a lot of money and it will attract hard guys. When you get off the plane go straight to the lockers. Put the briefcase in a locker and take the locker key. You do that before you go to the bathroom, check into the motel, or anything. You open this case and somebody will kill you. Got it?"

"Don't bully me."

"I've trusted you to carry the keys, but don't unlock this case. Understand?"

"For God's sake, shut up! Do you think I'd run off with my own money?"

"*Our* money. Don't think you can double-cross me. It would be the worst mistake you ever made."

"Stop it. Don't say any more. If you don't trust me to do it, you take the money to New Orleans. I'll join you later."

"This way is better."

In the last month or two she had changed and I had changed, but she showed it more physically. Her hair had turned from strawberry to metallic red. The dark lipstick she wore looked hard and predatory on a face so pale. Once she no longer loved me she no longer tried to be beautiful. Or maybe she couldn't be. That's the way I figured it.

"Why is this way better? So you can get me more involved? Remember, I'm clear of those murders. I don't have a motive. Those murders cost me a husband who was a good provider."

"It sounds as if you're practicing for a jury."

"Maybe they can prove I've slept with you, but they can't prove I knew anything. Maybe they can prove I helped you steal afterward from an insurance company, but"—she put on an innocent expression—"I'm just a poor girl in love."

I was going to tell her straight-out. I was going to flag the minefield because I loved her, and couldn't help it.

"This is a test."

Her eyes got big and she went out of the room. The bathroom door shut and water ran in the sink. When she came out her eyes were red. "Don't say any more. While we've got something left, don't keep on. We're scared, and you're turning on me, and I'm turning on you."

"I'm not turning on you," I said, and put my arm around her. She was stiff in my embrace. One hand gripped a handkerchief and she darted her gaze around the room.

After awhile we went out to the Jeep. I put her hanging bag and the briefcase on the floor.

"Don't let a Skycap carry the briefcase."

"For goodness' sake, Luke!"

"One may try to take it from you, but don't let him. Keep walking. Stay in lighted areas."

"Will you please shut up?"

"You've got to listen to me."

"No, you're confusing me."

We drove to Memphis, hardly speaking. I felt calmer behind the wheel. The wind was up and it whipped around the doors and through the loose seals where the cab sat on the body. She put her small feet under the heater, pointing her legs right at me. I wanted to reach over and take her hand, but I didn't.

When the lights of Como glowed on the horizon to the right she said, "I guess you've thought what you'd do if I took the money and ran."

I didn't answer.

"Don't lie, Luke. You've thought of everything."

Sure, I had. I'd bought the trick briefcase and made a bomb, but I believed in her more than I didn't. All of our money was in that case, and all of my hope for the future was in her.

She said, "Maybe there isn't any money in your ugly briefcase."

"You saw me pack it."

"Maybe you put in bundles of cut green paper, with hundred-dollar bills on the outside. I saw someone do that that in a movie."

"What makes you think I'd do that?"

"Because you're a planner, Luke. You're tricky. You think ahead. You're not about to let me run off with a satchel full of money."

I didn't answer.

"You ever play chess, Luke?"

"I've never played the game."

"Answer this. If you put real money in there, what are you going to do if the worst you think is true? Track me to South America and kill me?"

"I wouldn't let you get away with it. You're right about that and about me sending you ahead to see if I can trust you. But the money is real. It wouldn't be a test if it wasn't."

"We thought we were going to get through this, and still love and trust each other, too. But you're rotten, Luke."

"We're a pair. Don't tell me you haven't figured out that if we get caught I'll go to the chair."

"Yes, I thought of that." Her profile in the dash lights, with her hair blown back, looked as valiant as a ship's figurehead.

"Sure, you did."

"That was the bad part of me, the part that wished Tom was dead, the part that made me man-crazy. The ratty part of me knows I'll probably get off if they arrest us. All women are actresses, and I'm one of the best. But don't forget this. I love you. I've given up everything for you. Here I am driving through the night with less than a third of a million."

I put my hand on her knee. She pushed it away.

"I'm leaving a sixteen-year-old boy without a stepmother or father. That will do terrible things to my self-esteem." She was silent a moment, then said, "This is no time to fool ourselves. If we're not honest now we never will be. The truth is, Tommy doesn't matter."

"Not one damn bit."

I drove her to the Memphis airport, carried in her luggage, and stood back with my coat collar up while she bought a ticket.

There was just time to board. We walked down two long corridors to the Delta loading area, and found her gate.

You could see the big, dirty, four-engine Boeing through the polished terminal window. Her glance flickered over people ahead, waiting to board. She smiled the perfect smile. "Think lovely thoughts, darling. Miss me. Now, say goodbye."

She wasn't talking to me—to the two dozen others, maybe,

but not to me. She was talking to the old man with rheumy eyes and the spotted tie carrying a plastic carry-on; to the sleek brunette in the navy skirt that fitted her like underwear, and who searched her purse for a boarding pass; to the green-eyed attendant in the lime blouse who had just a touch of lipstick on her front tooth; to anyone who might be listening. . . .

I bent my head. My lips mashed hers. She came up tucking her hair. Then she walked down the chute to the plane, and I walked away, lonely and empty, without looking back.

50.

A bomb exploded in a room at the Airport Marriott in New Orleans, the *Clarion Ledger* reported. One dead. That night the Memphis television stations identified her. No terrorist organization claimed responsibility.

There is a place beyond pain, well into numbness, where I go. It's a tricky place covered by ice. Put one foot wrong and you break through.

A memorial service for her was held in the Bridgeport Episcopal Church. Her day was sunny. She would have liked that. White-painted houses stood stark in the winter light. The shadows under the eaves looked drawn by a black Magic Marker.

I squinted in the sunlight, felt it warm and promising on my skin. Sat blinking in it, lethargic and stupefied. If I were a seed, I'd have begun to split my hull.

An envelope postmarked the day Kinnerly's body was identified arrived in my mailbox. It contained a marked page torn from Hardy's novel, *Far From the Madding Crowd*. The man who sent it knows I killed her, but he is not going to the police. No, he has other plans.

A circled paragraph tells the story of a young and reckless sheepdog named George's Son. George's Son bit quickly and with little provocation. He could not be taught or controlled. One night he drove his master's sheep out of an enclosure and over a cliff to their deaths. Hardy wrote:

> George's Son had done his work so thoroughly that he was considered too good a workman to live, and was, in fact, taken and tragically shot at twelve o'clock that same day—another instance of the untoward fate which so often attends dogs and other philosophers who follow out a train of reasoning to its logical conclusion and attempt perfectly consistent conduct in a world made so largely of compromise.

I know the man who sent this. I have stood in his library and handled the volume from which the page was ripped. He is a literate man who respects books. Mailing me a page torn from a first-edition Hardy was as cold a warning as if he had sent me a severed hand.

I packed the things I needed, and the sixteen-hundred remaining, ready to get on with my life. I didn't know where I was going after Costa Rica. I didn't know what work I would do, but it would be manual labor in the open air. I liked horses. I thought I might end my days in Argentina, working with polo ponies.

I drove with Adel to Harry's house in Memphis. Harry came

outside to meet us. He'd stretched a tiny, narrow-brimmed gray hat onto his big head. He looked fat-faced and thicker-middled. His meaty breasts showed under a tight, cheap shirt. His black, size-thirteen shoes glittered. He rocked back and forth on them with his hands locked over his belly.

"How you doing, Lieut?"

"Fine. How're you, Harry?"

"Oh, I'm fine as can be."

Such shit as that is the way we talked. I've never figured it out. You can be closer than a brother with a guy in one situation, and have nothing in common with him in another.

We put Adel in the house and got into Harry's gray Monte Carlo. I said, "You didn't lock the house." He said "Let's see if Adel will get lucky." He said he wanted to take me to the Peabody Bar. I said I wanted to go to Blues Alley. All the while I was thinking about how soon I could get free of him. The look of Harry, fully civilianized, was deeply depressing.

The car following us, hanging back about half a block, was a beat-up yellow Caddy with a plastic top.

"Have you seen anything of Ballard?" I asked.

"Ballard? You're not about to start something with him, are you?"

"Did he make you when you watched him in Bridgeport?"

"No."

"Take a left here."

He took it.

"Left at the next corner."

"Why?"

"I need to see a guy who lives down here."

He took it. We made the block in silence. Then he said, "What guy?"

"The guy on your tail."

He gave me a smile. "Imagining people are following you is natural after you blow somebody up."

"Thanks so much."

Harry had never been a sensitive guy, and I wasn't sure he had a conscience, but he was hallmarked loyal. He glanced in the rearview mirror. "The yellow rattletrap? That's what you think is tailing us?"

"Yeah."

"Naah!"

"OK, let me tell you what's going to happen, wise guy." I leaned close. "Sometime you're gonna get where you're going, and pull to the curb. Or sometime down here in black man's land you're gonna come to a red light. Either way, that rattletrap will slide up beside you. The window will be down on the right side. A guy with dreadlocks will yell, "Hey, man!" He'll do that to get you to turn. The barrel will be sliding out—Model 12 Winchester pump with a sawed-off barrel—something like that. It'll be loaded all the way down the tube with number-four buck. And when you turn you get it in the face. Then a guy jumps out of the rattletrap. He sticks the barrel into our window and gives you another. He gives me the rest, down where I'm trying to dig a hole in the floorboard. He gives them to me in my back because I damn well ain't going to watch them coming."

"Shit!" Harry gripped the wheel. "You ought to be committed. Taking that woman out addled your mind."

"You may be right."

He watched the mirror. "What makes you think they're after us, Esso?"

I didn't answer.

"Exactly what did you see? Did they follow you from Bridgeport?" He pounded the wheel with his hand. "'Cause if you don't tell me—"

He really looked silly: a one-time soldier in a cheap shirt, his belly pooking over his belt and a tiny hat on his big head. I didn't say anything.

"Answer me."

"I feel it in my gut."

"That's different!"

We were nearing a road sign that said "Airways." The light was green. He made another left, and tires screeched. The yellow rattletrap made the corner, too.

"Coincidence," Harry barked.

"That's not such a rattletrap."

"No," he said.

"That's four coincidences."

"Maybe it's whores," he said hopefully. "One time I stopped for gas and nodded to a girl I thought I recognized. Four whores chased me to Interstate 55. Pulled beside me at every red light."

"Ever hear of hit women?"

He laughed. A look came into his eyes that was excited and happy. The Monte Carlo lurched ahead in passing gear. It wound up to fifty before downshifting. The rattletrap sped to catch us.

Harry wheeled between and around cars, jerking me in my seatbelt. My hands spread on the dash. "For Christ's sake, there's a police car ahead."

"Flag him down!"

"Flag him down?"

"Wave," Harry said. "Wave your arm while I blow the horn."

He slammed the horn button with the heel of his hand. "Arrest me, arrest me!"

I waved. "Maybe he's made his quota."

The bumper and trunk and license of the cruiser closed fast. The cop's head turned left, then right. His blinker flicked on.

"Watch out! You maniac, you're gonna hit him," I yelled and threw up my hands.

A bang and the grind of twisting metal sounded. Rivets popped. The cruiser's rear fender ripped off, caught between our bumper and the pavement, making a horrible screech, throwing sparks. In the second it took us to yaw past the police unit and stop, I saw the cop's beady eyes and bristly blond hair, and saw his mouth stretch to shriek, "You son of a bitch."

He spun into the curb, jumped it, then flung back the door of the unit and hopped out with his right hand above his piece. Harry got out and put his silly little hands on top of his silly little hat.

The yellow Cadillac cruised by with the faces of the driver and the other guy turned away. Here was an automobile crash in front of their noses and they wouldn't look. Likely, huh? I scribbled the license number, but it wasn't going to do any good. These were street men, too far down the scale even to know who they were working for.

We went to jail, and that's how I lost the use of Harry.

You see, Harry thought we'd be safe there until we could talk to somebody and find out who had hired the hit men. He had no idea the cops would release me and keep him in jail. He hadn't thought about much of anything except stopping that cop.

So he was inside the cell and I was outside.

Harry's hands gripped bars worn white from other desperate grippings. There was loud talk and crazy laughter. In one corner a black man who could have wrenched your arms out of their sockets cried.

I stood too long at Harry's cell, thinking of things we should have talked about. This was not going to end well. No gunship was coming to the rescue.

"I've got to go," I said.

"For a minute or two it was like old times."

"Yeah."

He laughed a wild, silly laugh. "Watch out for yellow Cadillacs."

I stuck my hand between the bars and we shook. We had not done that since the day he routed four Cong with a shotgun, and saved my life.

I started walking away. He called, "Luke!"

"Yeah?"

The cell guard strolled toward us, thumbs in his belt, looking bored. "Come on, come on. You guys going to chat all day?"

On each side of the aisle prisoners watched—some middle-aged drunks, some strung out youngsters, a dozen prostitutes. A girl with purple lipstick and silver hotpants batted her mascara-clotted lashes. "See you later, honey," she said.

"You too, sweetness," I said.

Harry yelled again. "Luke! When you get a pup by Adel, call him Harry!"

"I can't stand but one Harry in my life," I said over my shoulder.

I took a cab back to Harry's house, went to my Jeep, and took out a manila envelope. Inside the envelope was a pre-written note and two lemon-scented leashes.

I think things out, as Kinnerly said.

The note told the hundred or so words Adel understands. It referred Harry to a dog-handling book written by Adel's trainer. It told Harry that he was to let Adel smell one of the scented leashes, attach it to his collar, and command, "Come, Adel. Heel!"

I explained that the scented leash was a way to transfer the dog, and that Harry was always to keep two leashes, one scented overnight from a spray can and closed in a plastic bag while the other was in use. I told him that if he tried to touch Adel in the next week without the leash, he'd lose an arm. I also said if I could ever manage it, I wanted him back.

I went inside the house to say goodbye to Adel. He knew. He crept to me as if the solid pine floor had turned treacherously thin. His ears were flat, his head half-cocked, and his eyes were profoundly sad. He acted as if he understood, but of course he didn't, because he licked my hand in apology for something he might have done wrong. When I walked to the door he offered his paw. My throat thickened so that I couldn't swallow.

"Adel, lie down. Stay," I commanded, and left him. I couldn't look back to see the head flat between the paws, the dark eyes following me.

51.

There was no pursuit.

I sold the Jeep in Nashville and bought a second-hand suit, shirt, and tie. In a sixteen-dollar motel room with a splintered door and a bed imprinted by too many bodies, I called on my makeup skills from college acting days.

I added more gray to my hair, a mustache, and drugstore glasses. In an hour I looked ten years older. The seedy, middle-aged man I saw in the mirror was a glimpse of my future.

As my old identification papers burned in the bathroom trash can, a coil of acrid smoke spiraled up and flattened along the ceiling. No alarm rang. There wasn't one, or the battery was dead. I threw my clothes into a dumpster.

The satchel I carried to the airport was light. It contained one thousand five hundred and forty-two dollars, supporting documents for my new identity, four paperback books, and the small bronze casting that reminded me of Adel. In my pocket was the little plastic-covered picture of Kinnerly I had carried through Vietnam.

In Nashville, I boarded the Delta flight as Ulysses Laudner. The flight was uneventful. In New Orleans I walked quickly to the Pan American desk.

The man behind the computer looked up. "May I help you?"

"Do you have a tourist-class seat to San Jose, Costa Rica?"

He worked the terminal keyboard. "Sure do. We leave at 8:05 from Gate 26."

"I'll take it." I put the satchel close to my foot and handed over the passport of Ulysses Laudner.

"Round trip?"

"One way."

He looked at the passport and wrote the ticket. I paid him $240.64 in cash.

"Is this all of your luggage?" He glanced at my satchel.

"That's it. Just my carry-on."

As I took my ticket from the desk clerk, two guys detached themselves from the lines at windows on each side of me, and closed in. The smaller, dark haired, Latin one must have worked out two hours a day with weights. His partner was six foot three, blonde, and friendly looking.

"Would you come with us a moment, Mr. Laudner?" he said. "Bring your luggage, too."

"Why should I?"

The weight lifter bent close, smiling. He whispered, "Because it would be best if you do."

We went to a little soundproof room with a glass door. They showed their badges and told me I was under arrest for interstate flight to avoid prosecution. They told me additional counts would be forthcoming—murder, burglary, and grand larceny. They read me my Miranda rights.

The short one asked if I minded if he looked through my satchel.

"Yes," I said.

"Too bad. I've got to see if there is a weapon here." He opened it. The small bronze dog by Dubucand I took from Tom Morris's house was of great interest to him. He held it up to show his partner.

The big guy shook his head. He wore a pitying smile. "Stupid, stupid," he said, and reached for a pair of cuffs.

I wasn't going to get to be Ulysses Laudner much longer. They'd find Laudner's bank accounts, and the transactions he'd made, and the art trades he had been involved in. I held out my wrists for the cuffs. "How'd you guys get onto me so quickly?"

The little guy looked at the big one. The little one's neck was so thick it turned only a quarter of the 180 degrees it should. The big one nodded. The little one reached into his suit coat and took out a folded sheet of paper. "The Bridgeport sheriff got a court order so he could watch your mail." He unfolded a photocopy of a letter and held it for me to read.

Hello Darling,

There is just time to say I love you. I'm looking forward to spending my life with you. And I'm so glad you trust me again, that the cloud that has been between us has blown away. I don't think I could have stood it if you hadn't trusted me now.

Your sending me on this 'mission' has made me very happy. Did I seem cool when we parted? It was because my heart was pounding so with pride and love that I didn't trust myself to let go. I had to pretend I was in a box within a box within a box to keep from bursting loose and clutching your neck and bawling.

Everything is going according to plan. There's just one tiny thing wrong. The briefcase you bought is hideous black plastic.

It says very clearly it doesn't belong to me. It says, "I belong to a man who is smuggling diamonds, or something, and the sweet girl carrying me is a courier." So I bought a lovely leather case in the airport shop, and I'm going to our hotel room to make the change. Don't be angry. Don't let's ever be angry again. Yes, I know you told me to keep the ugly thing with me, and locked at all times, and under no circumstances open it. But don't worry. No one will rob us. I'll bolt and chain the door and look under the beds. I promise.

All my love,
Kinnerly

Epilogue

My psychiatrist has grizzled hair, and wears the puzzled expression of an intelligent dog. Cheap drugstore glasses ride his nose. He sits on a shiny metal stool in the corner of my room. Rusty spots stain his jacket. He knows my name because I'm his favorite patient.

"Luke," he says, "what's been happening since we talked last. How are your notebooks coming along?"

Doc wants my story.

He says writing it is therapy. He says facing what I have done is a huge step toward recovery. My notebooks are privileged information and can never be used against me, he assures me. He says there is no reason why I can not be released one day because I was in a state of diminished capacity when I committed three murders.

I say that's a *crock*. I am not crazy. Hasn't he heard of the M'Naghten Rule?

He says realizing you are disturbed is necessary to recovery.

We stare at each other.

He hands me a last notebook. The covers are mottled gray and white, splotchy-looking. The inside pages are white, with a vertical margin and firm blue horizontal lines that keep my writing from sliding down. I wrote my first notebooks in a small, cramped hand that no longer is mine. The sentences started neatly and the letters marched away as erectly as soldiers, but by the ends of the lines they jumbled out of step.

Now I write in a brown scrawl like the handwriting of a mass-murderer who leaves messages on bathroom mirrors . . . STOP ME BEFORE I KILL MORE!

I think Doc means to try to get my notebooks published. He wants to be a celebrity. He thinks my story is like *The Three Faces of Eve*. A guy he knows, who knows an editor, says we can make some money.

I ask Doc, does he think I'm stupid? Does he not know that anything I tell the public loses privilege and is admissible as evidence, whereas anything I tell him in confidence can't be used against me?

He smiles. "Trust me. We'll call it fiction."

So what becomes of my story is one of the things I worry about. The other is a message delivered to me yesterday.

Sheriff Coonan came to see me wearing an expression of sympathy. Sympathy is as much at home on Coonan's face as vanilla frosting would be on the cutting edge of straight razor.

He said an envelope addressed to me had arrived a few weeks ago, and the D.A. had decided I should see what was inside. "Brace yourself," Coonan said, then handed me a black-and-white newspaper clipping.

The grainy photo showed well-dressed people seated in a stadium. They could have been attending a bullfight. Maybe it was the races. The man in the center, the dominant figure, was a slick-looking Spanish guy. Four men who seemed to be bodyguards watched the crowd from the rows in front of him and behind him. From the look of the situation, he was very rich or an official in a country where succession to office is achieved not by election but by Uzi.

A silver-blonde, with her legs crossed, was seated beside him. She looked up with an adoring smile.

I think I recognized those legs. I'm positive I know that face. It's very Southern in its surface prettiness and its flattering concentration on the man of the moment. Nothing has marked it in the two years I've been in here. It's still the perfect mirror for a man's fantasy and desire.

As I stared at the picture, the unanswered part of my story—especially *why* and *how* a smart guy like me wound up in here—came to me fast.

I talked too much. I talked too much about ambushes and booby traps. I talked too much about loyalty. Kinnerly knew, or guessed, she was carrying a bomb.

This is the way it went down. This is the way, or something very like this. She watched the sequence when I set the briefcase locks, memorized it, then when she was alone in New Orleans, unlocked the case and took the money. She found a redhead her size, maybe a prostitute, invited her to the hotel, and left the keys to the relocked briefcase on the dresser. She made an excuse to leave, said she was going for Cokes and ice, maybe, but instead ran to the stairwell.

I handed the clipping to Coonan. "I've never seen either of these people before."

He looked embarrassed. The embarrassment was for me.

"Don't you know the first law of survival, Luke?"

"Hard to say what's first, Sheriff. One is watch your partner's back and he will watch yours. Another is it's better to be judged by eleven than carried by ten. Another is—"

"Luke, you're a real big disappointment to me." Coonan turned and started for the metal door. "I'll be back another day."

So Kinnerly played me for a sucker from the beginning, out-figured me every step. The intimate glances, the lovemaking, the confessions and tears were all lies. I was a cat's paw to get rid of an inconvenient husband. When I laid the ace of spades on Angus, that was lagniappe.

The other way to look at our few months together is through her eyes.

I don't know that I will. It could be a big mistake.

A man might see, if he was willing, that a woman had trusted him with the gift of her dependence. He might see that while they were together she was loyal . . . that she expected him to take care of her, and instead he set a trap for her. He had been a betrayer.

If he got that far he would have to accept an awful truth.

She had loved him. They could have made it.